Sunday Brunch

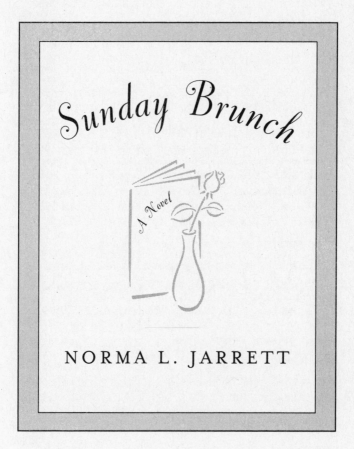

Sunday Brunch

A Novel

NORMA L. JARRETT

HARLEM MOON · BROADWAY BOOKS
NEW YORK

Published by Harlem Moon, an imprint of Broadway Books, a division of Random House, Inc.

Copyright © 1998, 2004 by Norma L. Jarrett. All rights reserved. No part of this book may be reproduced or transmitted in any form or by any means, electronic or mechanical, including photocopying, recording, or by any information storage and retrieval system, without written permission from the publisher. For information address Broadway Books, a division of Random House, Inc.

PRINTED IN THE UNITED STATES OF AMERICA

HARLEM BOOKS, BROADWAY BOOKS and the HARLEM MOON logo, depicting a moon and a woman, are trademarks of Random House, Inc. The figure in the Harlem Moon logo is inspired by a graphic design by Aaron Douglas (1899–1979).

First edition published 2004

Book design by Jennifer Ann Daddio

All quotes from Scriptures taken from the King James Version of the Bible.

ISBN 0-7394-4400-x

Dedicated to the Loving Memory
of my mother, the late Ethel Jarrett
—and—
"For those who saw a diamond in the rough . . .
For those who made the conscious choice
to magnify my strengths rather than discount my abilities . . .
and
For those who added meaning to my journey,
You know who you are. . . ."

Acknowledgments

Thank You for allowing me to discover my purpose, to uplift and inspire through writing and speaking, to help others discover their purpose and motivate individuals to be their best selves. Thanks for the journey *and* the destination. May all that I do honor You and *may I never be taken out of Your hand.*

Second, I thank my family: To my father, Norman D. Jarrett, thanks for your selflessness, your integrity, and your strength. Thank you for allowing me to explore my gifts, however crazy it seemed. Next to God, you are truly my best friend. To my sister and brother-in-law, Paulette and Al Jones—thanks for loving me *unconditionally.* My victory is your victory! I love you with all my heart! For my brother, Stephen—you will *always* bye my baby. I love you *so* much. You're always in my heart and prayers. I'm proud of you! To my nieces and nephews, Quiana, Ashley, Al (II), Ariel, and Little Stephen, I love you. You're sweet, smart, and blessed. You make me *so* proud to be an "Auntie." Also, to Arlene and the late James Jarrett, Fred Lee Jarrett, Quinne Ewing, Bessie Crutchfield, Leroy Page, Alfred and Tish Page (thanks for making me feel "mom" again), and the rest of the Page, Jarrett, and Jones families—I love you.

Thank God, I've never had to ask "Where my girls at?" 'Cause you've always *been there.* Thanks for your encouragement, prayers, love . . . and funds! To *my* girls: Denise Williams, Sherri Davidson (*still "Lynnie from the block"*—*smile*), Mildred Mareé, Kim Thomas—our bonds will never be broken (*N.C.A.&T. Vanstory Hall Forever!*); Subrina Eastland—my first "best friend" in Houston; Michele Austin, Esq. (my sister)—Where do I even begin? Thanks for your shoulder, your prayers, your listening ear, and your Big Ol' Heart. Thanks for lending me your family. Patrice Carrington, Esq.—my original "creative consultant" (while you praisin' the Lord!). Jackie Strambler—you always have a smile and positive word for me. Rachael St. Louis-Rodriquez, Esq., thanks for your prayers and loving friendship. Soror Tracey Hines, do I even need to say anything? You were the witness! Thanks for standing with me. Love ya girl! Adrienne Smith, Esq., you are a beautiful gifted angel. To Soror Alicia Lacy-Castille (and baby Castille), thanks for sowing seeds of friendship, love, and support in my vision. Love ya girl! To the great women of Alpha Kappa Alpha Sorority Inc., thanks for all the "Pink & Green" love. Special love to the Alpha Phi Chapter, Fall '86 (especially Audra Foreé, April Hinson-Mack, Michele Baker, Andrea Walbrook, and the rest of my line). Also special love to Soror Janice Taylor—you are the epitome of sisterhood and Christian love. Much love to all my other Soror authors. Also to North Carolina A & T State University—Aggie

Pride!—and Thurgood Marshall School of Law. To all the lawyers "fighting the good fight" . . . keep the faith.

To other angels who have shown up along the way, thank you for your blessings: Mary Upshaw (my spiritual *Mum*—love you); Loretta Collins, for being always ready to pray and knock some walls down! To the former 151st Civil District Court—especially Phyllis Haynes (my guardian angel) and Paul Sweeney. To all the bookstores who have supported me, especially Jokae's African-American books (Milt and Til Pettis—my family) in Dallas. To all the book clubs who have and will support my vision. To Jetola Anderson-Blair, Evangeline Mitchell, Gloria Anderson, Victoria Christopher-Murray, Parry "Ebony Satin" Brown, Tosha Terry, Consandra Jones, and others: "May you always have the pen of a ready writer." To Vivica A. Fox, thanks for the review. To Robert Rodriquez, Jr., thanks for all your help. You are an angel! To the Covingtons (Robert and Mona) for the connection. To Jerold Bryant, Pam Walker-Williams (Pageturner.net), Victor McGlothin, Patrik H. Bass, Victoria Sanders, Janet Hill, and especially Clarence Haynes (you are da' man!), and all others at Broadway/Harlem Moon.

Sunday Brunch

CHAPTER ONE

Sunday Go to Meetin'

*ord, good morning. It's me again—Lexi. I come to You this morning with humble heart and mind. I'm truly grateful for the many things You've done in my life. I'm thankful for passing the bar examination on the first try. I know it could have only been You. I'm thankful for my law practice, even though I'm not making all the money I want to make right now. I know it's coming. I'm thankful for wonderful friends, even Jewel. You've truly brought me a long way.

I know I haven't been reading my Bible like I should lately, but honestly, Lord, I've been tired. I know You've delivered me from some "stuff," but sometimes I feel like I have to fight for everything. Is this the way it's always going to be? Forgive me for questioning You. And speaking of forgiveness, please excuse my weakness (again) when I gave in to Reggie. I'll try to be stronger the next time. I know sex is a sin; I'd been doing pretty well by holding out, but some of these men are really not with the celibacy program. (Oh, why does this phone always ring *when I'm in the middle of prayer!) And Lord, please bless this day! Thanks. Amen!*

My eyes sprang open. Still kneeling, I reached over to grab the receiver from the nightstand. "Hello?"

"Hey, bud. What's up? It's Capri."

I got up and sat on the side of my bed. "Hey, girl."

"Just calling to see what time we were meeting for brunch."

"Angelica said we should aim for one, which is when I made reservations, so we should head to brunch right after church."

"Who?"

"I mean Angel."

"Since when do we call her Angelica?"

"I don't know. She's been going through this pseudo-bourgeoise phase."

"What's that all about?" Capri asked.

"She's on a 'I'm a mature business woman of the world' trip. You know Angel. She can be intense."

"I would expect that type of drama from Jewel, but not Angel."

"Anyway, girl, what are you wearing?" I asked.

"I don't know. Whatever I get up and decide to put on."

"I think I'm going to wear a dress today. I feel like being very feminine," I said.

"*Whatever*. This Sunday brunch thing is really starting to be a bore . . . all we do is gossip."

"Ummm . . . I know. But with all our schedules, it's the only way we can stay connected," I said.

"I guess you're right."

"I really look forward to our little brunch dates."

"That's because you don't have a life," Capri said.

Ouch!

I tried not to get an attitude about Capri's comment since, for the moment, it was true. Dating Reginald wasn't exactly my idea of "a life." I tried to remember the last time we'd gone out for a date instead of staying in, watching rented DVDs, and eating takeout food. It had actually been several months.

"I have to go. I have to do my usual Sunday morning makeover," I said with all seriousness in my voice.

"Alright, girl, but make sure you exfoliate those feet, because the last time I saw them, they were lookin' kinda rough. Oh yeah, and please be on time to church."

"See, why'd you have to go all there with the feet?" I said as I inspected my heels. "Some of us can't afford the weekly pedicures, OK? Some of us have to get out the old pumice stone from time to time and do it ourselves. Some of us have to slather on the petroleum jelly and use a few plastic sandwich bags. Is that OK with you?"

"Lexi! I'm just kidding, girl. I know how sensitive you are about your feet."

"And I'll be on time."

"Bye, girl," Capri said.

After I hung up, I walked to the bathroom and ran

my bathwater. I added some crystals and a little baby oil
to the water. Steam and the scent of vanilla tickled my
nose. I removed a large natural-colored towel from the
linen closet and draped it across the vanity stool. I
pulled out a mulberry-scented candle and lit it with a
match from a San Antonio souvenir matchbook. I slid
in the tub and let the clear, smooth water cover me like
a blanket. Then I tilted my head back against the in-
flatable terry cloth pillow.

I grabbed my favorite magazine, *Essence*, and perched
it on the silver bath tray in front of me. I flipped each
page, trying to find something interesting.

*Oooh, beauty secrets of Hollywood's A-list. Hmmm, let's see . . .
Oh, that's what Janet Jackson uses on her skin? Bet. I'm going to check
that out. She's still my girl! . . . Get out! Tyra Banks uses this lip gloss?
It only costs $4.99?*

I continued flipping the pages, soaking up the latest
celebrity beauty trends and outfits, enjoying a guilty
pleasure before getting ready for church. I soon
dropped the magazine on the floor and slid farther
into the warm water. My muscles welcomed the soothing liquid.

My serenity was interrupted by hunger pangs.

*I still have some fruit in the fridge. I can grab some grapes on the
way out to tide me over till brunch.*

Brunch with Jermane, Jewel, Angel, and Capri had
become our ritual ever since we graduated from Westwood's School of Law. Regardless of what's going on in
our lives (and it could be anything), we rarely failed to
meet after church every Sunday.

Although I wasn't raised in the church, I had developed a deeper connection to God since moving to Houston. In the South, church is such a normal part of life. But the longer I live, the more I realize that going to church is just the beginning. You don't experience true growth until you develop a personal relationship with God.

Back in my undergrad days, I was *way* too busy enjoying the freedom and benefits of the "Black college experience" to get deeply spiritual. Plus, some of the students who said they were saved were the most conniving, cheating folks I'd ever met. I almost resented Christians, and now here I am, going to church weekly, on my way to developing a personal connection with the Lord. God has a plan for all of us to be in certain places at certain times, to meet certain people, to grow, love, learn, share, teach, and uplift.

Despite my delayed spiritual connection, I've always had wisdom beyond my years, which has helped me to keep all of my friends connected. We're all at different places in our careers, relationships, and spiritual lives, and learn a lot from each other. Unbelievably, my friends think that I have it all together. What's even crazier is that they think I'm very spiritually grounded because I pray often and am the most expressive about my walk with God.

Still, there are times when I really struggle. My girls don't realize that sometimes, when I'm alone, I go into a hole and have my minor breakdowns.

When I go under, I go into deep thought and meditation. I may cry, shout, scream to God—apologize later—and eventually pray. Sometimes I get depressed.

What? Christians aren't supposed to get depressed? Well, it happens. What's most important is that you don't stay depressed, or claim that for your life. And I'm getting better. I don't go under as much. I'm talking to and trusting God more and more.

Still, each day is a challenge. People have a tendency to push my buttons, even more so since I've become a Christian. I guess it's all a part of my test to become more Christlike in my actions. All in all, though, my friends are right. I'm pretty together and, might I add, quite fashionable.

I cupped a handful of water and let it trickle down my chest. I looked down at my body and smiled to myself. It had taken me quite some time to appreciate it. God made every inch, including a little cellulite. I began bathing with my natural soap.

Hmmm, Reggie hasn't called.

Instead of going with me to church, as he often promised he would, Reggie usually called Sunday mornings. Reggie is my latest "S.O."—significant other—*and* my latest project.

People tell me that I set my standards too high. I disagree, but in the interest of possible self-improvement, I've decided to be a little less stringent. After a string of heartbreaks in college and law school, lately I've been meeting guys who don't fit my "ideal man" list, but have potential. Hence, Reginald, a plant supervisor, was able to get through the door.

I met him one night while I was at happy hour with the girls at The Sky Bar, a local hot spot for professionals. I've never been too into clubs, and since I've given my life to the Lord, my club days have been fewer and farther between. Nonetheless, when I first moved to Houston, I went out occasionally.

When I met Reggie, he was dressed in a black suit, French blue shirt, and dark grey tie. He looked masculine, sexy. I could tell he was staring at me, but I pretended not to notice. Finally, he eased over, introduced himself, and asked me to dance. I said "Yes."

While we were dancing, I managed to take in as much of him as possible. I inspected the areas I usually notice on a man. Hands: not extremely smooth, but clean. Shirt: ironed, crisp, fresh. Hair: cut low with short, faded sideburns.

Then I took in his face . . . smooth, milk chocolate skin, thick eyebrows, and deep-set eyes . . . *potential*.

I could tell he was surveying me as well. I had on a fitted burgundy suit, the one I wear when I want my waist to look smaller. My pencil skirt, strategically resting right above my knee, hugged my form. A hint of cleavage peeked from underneath my jacket. Plus, I wore my "killer" burgundy ankle-strapped Via Spiga (the only pair I possessed in my closet) leather pumps.

My hair was flatironed to perfection with a side bang gracing the tip of my arched eyebrows. My nutmeg skin glowed with a hint of bronzer, and my sheer lip gloss played up my natural features. Of course, I smelled good enough to bite . . . some new fragrance the saleswoman at Victoria's Secret had talked me into.

The DJ put on a slow jam—"Anytime," by Brian McKnight. I signaled to Reggie that I wanted to stop dancing, since Brian McKnight is sacred and reserved only for that special someone. After easing off the floor, I positioned myself next to him, but not too close.

"This is a nice crowd," he said, attempting to inch closer to me, trying not to invade my comfort zone.

"Yes. I haven't been here in a while. This is my night to hang out with the girls, so I decided to come out for a minute," I said, trying to sound relaxed.

"Are you from here?"

"No. I'm originally from Virginia," I said.

"Oh," he said, almost with a look of relief.

"Are you?" I said, bracing myself.

"Uh, yeah."

A native . . . hmmm.

Maybe it was my imagination, but so far, the native Texan men I'd met seemed a bit spoiled. It didn't help matters that some of the women seemed so aggressive, fighting over brothers and even setting traps to keep them. I wasn't about to do all that to get a man, so I figured I'd definitely have to wait on Jesus to guide me to my special someone. There had to be men out there who knew what they wanted and how to treat a woman. Maybe Reggie was one of them.

"Would you like a drink?" he asked.

"Just club soda and lime," I replied.

He signaled the waitress, adorned in tight black low-rise capri pants and a halfway-believable weave, to come over and take our order. She looked a little tired, but she was still polite.

"Can I get you something?" she said, not even acknowledging my presence.

"Yes," he said, trying not to look at how half her breasts were showing out of her white satin shirt.

"I'd like a cognac and Coke . . . club soda and lime for the lady," he said, trying to sound smooth.

She acknowledged the request and swished off into the sea of people.

"So, are you single?" he asked.

"Depends. What do you mean by single?"

"Unattached, not married, no one special; I can't imagine *you* not having anyone special."

Please, a little more originality. "What if I told you I had someone?" I said.

"You can have friends, can't you?"

Oh brother, so predictable. Can we just bypass all the preliminary mumbo jumbo?

"Well, I don't have anyone special, but I do have friends."

"Well, that's good enough for me. So, how can I get in touch with you?"

"Do you mean may you have my number?" I said.

"Yes, that's what I meant."

"Uh . . . OK. Do you have a pen?" I said with hesitancy.

"No, but our waitress is on the way back. I'll ask her."

When she came over, she handed him her pen and gave us our drinks. We exchanged numbers and small talk. He was articulate and seemed like a professional. I didn't ask what he did. I always thought that was a tacky question to ask when you first meet someone, although my friends begged to differ.

He called after the typical two-day waiting period, and we ended up talking for hours about our likes, dislikes, movies, sports, and relationships. The conversation just flowed. It turned out he'd been in the service and traveled extensively. Reggie was intelligent and funny. He made me laugh aloud throughout our conversation. I didn't see any immediate signs of sexual orientation issues or abusive tendencies, so even though I wasn't thrilled when I found out his line of work, I agreed to go out with him.

Our first date was simple but fun. We rode out to the boardwalk in Kemah and had lunch one Saturday afternoon. It seemed like we were off to a good start, though in retrospect I realize we never talked about spiritual issues. Then, after several pleasant outings (including a few trips together to church!), I became his "after he got in from the club" date. I allowed myself to fall into that zone because I was just happy to have the company. He was so comfortable to be around, like an old pillow. His chest was solid and broad and great to lean against. He was affectionate and loved to call me "baby girl."

Reggie was nice, but he still turned me off because I was last on his list of priorities. It seemed he had more time for everything else, including his obnoxious, unattached friends, over me.

I didn't want this kind of man, one with 10,000 male friends who liked to party. Being a homebody, I fell into the trap of sitting at home, waiting for him to call.

I wanted us to go to movies, museums, and con-

certs, and drink cappuccino at cafés, and walk through
parks on gorgeous days. I was tired of doing these
things alone or with one of my friends.

And then there was the issue of, well, s-e-x. Reggie
talked about it just a little too much. We held off for six
months. Yet in the back of my mind, I knew he had to
be sleeping with someone else.

I was trying to wait until marriage and had really
been praying in that area. But my hormones were flying all over the place.

One night, Reggie came over, in the evening as
usual, and we played chess. We ordered Chinese food
and ate on the floor. We started talking about relationships and marriage and got into a minor argument. He
made some sort of statement about how he "could see
how a man could cheat on his wife," and then proceeded to give his rationale. He had such a cavalier attitude, as if it was so acceptable. I was furious, and we
started arguing.

"I'm going to leave if you keep on acting like a
child," he said.

"If you're going to be with me, you're just going to
like it or leave it," I yelled as I pointed in his face.

Big mistake! He immediately went out the door.
Oh, boy.

In a panic, I picked up the phone and called Capri.
Her answering machine! Where is she when I need her?

Half an hour went by. I began to realize how much I
actually liked that fool. *How could I let my heart get in it—again?*

Then I heard a knock at the door. I stood on my
toes to look through the peephole.

Like a naughty kid, I slowly opened the door. Reggie just stood in the doorway with this sexy glare in his eyes and a crooked smile.

This is the night.

I took a deep breath and put my hand to my chest. I whispered a silent, "Lord forgive me."

He grabbed me, turned my back toward him, and backed up against the front door. The only light in the room was from the television. Everything seemed to fast-forward. He lightly kissed my neck, and my body shivered. I opened my mouth to speak, but nothing came out. I turned around and kissed him.

Instead of pleading for the blood of Jesus, all I could think of was how happy I was not to be wearing cotton underwear. Before I knew it, clothes were flying everywhere and I was on the couch.

I heard myself mumbling, "Maybe we should stop." But I didn't. And he didn't.

God, are you sure this is a sin?

*T*he phone interrupted my daydream. I jumped out of the tub, dripping, and wrapped myself in my robe. I knew who it was.

"Hello?"

"Hey, baby girl."

"Hi, Reggie."

"I was just lying in bed thinking about you."

Figures. He calls when he's in the mood.

"What are you doing?"

"Just got out the tub," I said.

"Why didn't you call me to join you?"

"Because it's Sunday. You know, the 'Day of the Lord.' You could show a little restraint."

"Lexi, you've really been tripping lately about sex. It's too late, baby girl. We already dipped in the well."

"Reggie, let's not get into it. When's the last time you went to church anyway?"

"You know I work the late shift. I'm dead tired. I promise I'll go with you to Bible study this week on my day off."

"I've heard *that* before. I don't know, Reggie. We went to church a few times when we first met and we've never been back. It was really nice. I don't know what happened. I know your hours aren't the best, but if you really wanted to go, you would. There are Saturday and Wednesday night services. You seem to find time to do everything else."

"Baby girl, I don't need a lecture this early. I said I'd go with you to Bible study this week. I just can't stand this nagging." His voice got louder with frustration.

"*Look*, Reginald, if it has to be like that, don't worry about it. I'd rather you want to go on your own. This just doesn't feel right. Maybe I need some time to myself."

"What?" He paused for a few seconds. "You're really trippin'."

"I don't think so. It seems like I'm moving forward on a spiritual level and you're not. Maybe this was nice for a season, but I feel us growing apart. I think you're a good person, but maybe you're not the person for me at this time in my life."

"Lexi, I don't understand what's going on with you. What do you want from me? I'm a decent brother. I've never cheated on you. Don't I bring you wings from Frenchy's and rent you *Love Jones* and *Mahogany* whenever you want on our movie nights? I'm here for you. Just because I don't want to go to church today doesn't mean the relationship needs to end."

"I didn't say I was ending it. I only said I need some time to myself. I'm confused. Maybe we're meant to be together. I just know that right now, something doesn't feel right. Besides, it's more than about church. I guess I'm starting to figure out the things I want and don't want in a man."

I paused. He was silent.

"Sure, we have great intimacy," I continued, "but sex is not the only thing that makes a relationship good. I don't want to try to change you. I just have to believe that there's a person for me who has the most important qualities that I desire. We can talk later, but I really need to go now because I'm running late for church."

"We can talk later? You're talking about ending our relationship and you just want to jump off the phone? This is important," he said.

"So is God!"

"If He was so important, you wouldn't have been having sex with me all this time."

"That's it! I'll talk to you later, Reggie." I slammed the phone down.

I looked at the clock. *I'm running late messin' around with that fool.* I ran into the vanity area. I rubbed my body with baby oil and massaged petroleum jelly on my shoulders, knees, heels, and elbows. Without enough time to flatiron the do, I pinned it up. I put on my pink lace bra, matching panties, and stockings and then searched frantically in my closet for the perfect Sunday brunch outfit.

Oh, I can't believe that man! Let it go, Lexi, let it go. OK, let's see, no, I wore that two weeks ago. No, wore that suit to work Thursday. Yes, my fuchsia knit dress—perfect! Fits my shape perfectly, and Jewel said simplicity is in. Wow, that's pretty scary. I'm actually starting to listen to her advice.

I snatched the dress off the hanger. I looked through my jewelry and put on my three-tiered matching stone necklace. Seconds later, I put on my makeup and finished everything off with matte powder. I grabbed my purse, keys, and Bible and sprinted out the door.

Lexi," someone said in a loud whisper, "over here." It was a bit too loud because people in the immediate area looked up. I smiled politely as I made my way to my seat.

Capri and Jewel were in our usual area and moved down so I could sit in the seat closer to the aisle. "Lexi, I love that dress, and the necklace complements it perfectly," Jewel said in a low whisper.

If only she knew how much I paid for my outfit. I was a "black belt" shopper, able to conquer any outlet center in a single bound, smell any secret sale a mile away, and uncover all half-price designer items.

Jewel waited for me to comment on her outfit. She had on a tailored slate-gray suit with a large cream silk flower accenting her jacket. She looked stunning, but if I knew Jewel, she'd probably used money due to Reliant Energy light company to buy her new look.

"Thanks, girl. I love your suit," I said. Capri gave us a look out of the corner of her eye, the kind of look that your mother gives you when you're acting up in church, soon to be followed by a discreet threat or smack on the leg. Jewel and I immediately started paying attention to Carla, Pastor Graves's wife, who was speaking at the pulpit.

During the welcoming of guests, I noticed two handsome men seated directly in front of us. They turned around to shake my hand during the greeting.

Woo! Thank you, Lord, for the scenery.

Despite my man-watching and occasional tardiness, I really am serious about church. I tend to focus on the sermon because I love my pastor's preaching style. Pastor Graves is young, contemporary, and a great teacher, different from any other pastor I've heard before. My uncle back home knows Pastor Graves's father and told me about his congregation at Living Truth Ministries.

I think most young men and women trying to do the right thing can relate to him. Living Truth's membership has increased to more than 3,000 parishioners and is growing each Sunday.

Once, Pastor Graves did a whole sermon using the lyrics of Al Green's old school song, "Love and Happiness" and "Fallin'," by Alicia Keys. I've been attending Living Truth for three years and I've never felt more comfortable in a church.

But every now and then, I do get slightly distracted. There was one particular incident when I had to laugh at myself. There was this guy sitting down a few seats to the right of me. He was p-h-i-n-e . . . a tall, brown-sugared, polished brother. I was just sittin' there, minding my own business, when his woodsy-scented cologne enticed me from a few seats away.

I was so busy looking at him, I completely missed the collection plate being passed my way, and my offering envelope fell on the floor. He looked at me and smiled, trying not to laugh. I was *totally* embarrassed.

"Will you please stand for the reading of the Word?" a woman said.

The congregation stood. As usual, Jewel didn't have a Bible. *All that time she spends in the mall, she could at least stop for a minute and spend $10 on a Bible. She's such a moocher!*

"Please turn to First Corinthians 13, verses 1 through 7," the woman standing up front in winter white and a feathered hat said eloquently. She read the scriptures on many Sundays. I admired her fashion sense and ability to speak with such authority and poise. She enunciated like a poetry reader. She carried herself in such a regal way, as if she knew without a doubt that she was someone special—God's child. It was as if she knew something about God that I hadn't learned yet.

After she read the scripture, we bowed our heads for prayer. Although she was leading, I couldn't resist sneaking in a request of my own.

Lord, please grant me the same peace and confidence this mighty woman of God has.

That was a wonderful sermon, Pastor Graves." I shook his hand. He'd moved everyone else along quickly, but made sure I stopped. His milk chocolate skin and endearing smile made everyone feel welcome. He peered over his wire-frame glasses and lifted his eyebrows, having an appearance that was much more mature than his thirty-two years.

"Thank you, Lexi, for your kind words. But I didn't see your girls today. Y'all were so faithful during law school. Remember, we've always got to put God first. I hope they don't forget about Him after the blessings."

I quickly looked around, then back at him. "Oh Pastor Graves, Jewel and Capri are around here somewhere. We sat together during service. We've been faithful. There's no way we can forget how we made it through law school."

"Ah, yes. I know *you* haven't forgotten, but Ms. Jewel, we had to do some extra praying to get her through the bar. She *knows* she needs to be up here at least twice a week. And don't forget to remind her we have that financial planning class."

He shook his head and smiled. "I'm just kidding . . . sort of. You girls have really made me proud, especially starting the legal ministry and—"

"You mean young ladies," said Carla, who had just finished chatting with one of the ushers.

He looked at her and smiled. "Yes, of course. Young ladies. I stand corrected."

"Lexi, how are you?" she said as she reached her hands out for mine.

"I'm blessed, Ms. Graves." We held hands, then hugged. I couldn't help but notice how together she always looked, with her feathered pixie hairdo, perfectly manicured nails, and natural makeup.

"Girl, you know I told you to call me Carla. You make me sound like an old woman. How's the law practice?"

"Sorry, Carla. The practice is doing well."

"Well, you know we're prayin' for you. God is a God of abundance and I know you are doing *His* work. I pray that he gives you favor with every case."

"Thank you."

"You know your uncle would not forgive us if we didn't look out for you. We're your family, so if you need to talk to us about anything, I mean, anything, let us know." She smiled and searched my eyes.

Do I look stressed . . . like I need to talk about something? I'm fine. Work is fine . . . well, the social life is another story. Is that even a legitimate issue? Could I possibly bother her with something so trivial? They probably counsel people on more serious stuff.

"I'll keep that in mind. Everything's going well. I, uh, really can't complain. I appreciate your prayers though."

"OK. You take care now, Lexi. You make sure you tell the other young ladies that I said just because they're big-time attorneys doesn't mean they can't come to fellowship after service." She winked at me and touched my shoulder.

"I will."

I moved out of the way so others could talk to the head couple of the church. I couldn't help but watch them, especially Carla.

She can't be more than 30. She seems so mature for her age.

She stood by the pastor's side, smiling as people walked up to greet him, laughing at the right times, and shaking hands. Everyone could feel their positive energy.

I turned to walk toward the exit door of the sanctuary, or what was set up to be a sanctuary. It was actually a gigantic, carpeted, all-purpose room with theatre-style seating. Several small clusters of people were still hanging around after service.

"That's a sharp haircut on the pastor's wife. I think she gets her hair done at Ladies and Gents salon."

"Girl, you scared me," I said as I quickly turned around. I looked at Jewel, amazed she knew where everyone got their hair done or shopped, but could never remember exactly what the sermon was about.

"Capri's in the rest room and told me to come get you." She pulled out a sterling silver compact mirror and tilted her head to check her makeup.

"Jewel."

"Uh-huh?" she said, fluffing her hair in the mirror. She pulled out her lipstick and began tracing her lips with intense concentration.

"Do you remember what the sermon was about to-day?"

"Uh-huh," she said, still looking in the mirror. Then she closed it quickly. "Oh, do I remember the sermon? Do I remember the sermon?" she said, with her hand on her hip, eyes rising up.

"I'm waiting," I said, tapping my foot and folding my hands.

"Lexi, you always do this to me. I was paying atten-tion. The sermon was, uhm, it was about ole girl. You know the one who saved the people. God, don't tell me . . . Queen . . . Queen Esther! That's it!

"Although, who would name their child Esther?" she continued. "I guess it didn't matter, because she became the queen. I mean, she ran things up in the kingdom. She had the king wrapped around her finger and worked it out. Got her people free and all. I mean she was literally a nobody and just blew up." She began digging in her purse again.

"Jewel."

"Yes?" she sang, still not looking up.

"Never mind. Let's go eat."

CHAPTER TWO

Every Sunday at Etienne's

"Yes, we have a reservation for a party of five under the name of Parker," I said, speaking to the young Hispanic hostess.

"Ah yes, here it is. Is your entire party here?" she asked as she looked up from her clipboard.

"No, but we'll be seated now anyway," I said. The three of us walked to our usual seat beside the window. Our personal waiter, Antonio, would make his way over to our table shortly.

I don't know how we ever settled on Etienne's Café to have brunch every Sunday. But it's become a tradition since we graduated from Westwood School of Law, a predominately Black law school here in Houston.

I would have been just as happy at The Breakfast Klub. Who could be mad at their big plate of fried wings and waffles. The scenery there's just as good . . . fine brothers everywhere!

I sat down and picked up the menu, knowing I was going to have the brunch buffet, as always. "Tell me, how did we decide on Etienne's again? Was this a vote?"

"Lexi, we go through this every week. Etienne's is the place to see and be seen. Jeez, you can go to The Breakfast Klub during the week," Jewel said.

I guess she's right. I'll go along with her wannabe, platinum-digger ways for now.

I took in the room's elegance. The tables were covered with white tablecloths and the floors were stained hardwood. Chandeliers hung in each room and the buffet filled the next room, looking endless in its length.

"Well, hello!" Antonio said as he rushed over. "How are my *favorite* divas today?"

"*Hello, Antonio*," we sang.

Antonio had a fabulous British accent and a vibrant personality to match. He took good care of us and earned every bit of his tip. I know he liked working our table because we always had heated conversations at brunch. He tried to pretend not to listen, but occasionally he'd give himself away when he'd interject an unsolicited comment in the middle of our discussions.

"A round of coffee?"

"Yes, for me. Thank you," I answered.

"Umm, I'll have orange juice as well," Capri said.

"Antonio, you know my usual," Jewel said.

"Jermane and Angel are running late," Capri said, eyeing the plates on the next table.

"Jermane probably ran into traffic coming from her church," I said.

"You're probably right," Jewel said as she refreshed her lipstick.

Since Jermane's Catholic, she attends a different church from the rest of us. Angel, on the other hand, sleeps in on Sundays and has no intention of attending anybody's church service. She's the oldest among us, and decided to get a law degree after a bitter divorce. She's a very successful corporate lawyer, but truly believes God had nothing to do with any of her good fortune. Angel lives life on her own terms, never giving Him credit for anything.

"Oh, here's Jermane," I said as I looked toward the doorway.

Jermane looked like a runway model, gliding across the floor in her tailored blue-and-white houndstooth suit. The silk shell peeking from underneath her jacket was accentuated by a triple-strand illusion necklace with freshwater pearls. She looked like she could have borrowed her outfit from Jackie Onassis.

Her hair was pulled neatly off her face in a chignon with a slight wave that swept across her forehead. Her dark tresses, curly or straight at the magic of a blow dryer, were a contrast to her creamy skin. Her perfectly lined red lips accented the mole above her mouth. She always looked pulled together, even during the summer when the temperature could rise to 100 degrees or more in Houston.

I guess when you have money, you can always look good. She makes me sick.

"Hello everyone. There was an accident on Interstate 45 and I had a little delay. Please forgive me," she said.

"We'll think about it," Capri said jokingly.

Jewel stood up, gave her a slight hug, and commented on her outfit.

Jermane had seemed destined to work in her father's prestigious Houston law firm. She met her husband, Rex Richmond, at Westwood, and they fell disgustingly in love. He's the only man she's ever been with sexually.

Once Rex went to work at her father's law firm, Jermane was relieved of her duties to join the family practice. She's now working on her Master of Law so she can teach.

"Is that someone's cell phone?"

"Yes, that's mine," Jewel said as she pulled the silver mini-phone out of her Prada bag. She stood up and walked away from the table as if she was a top secret agent.

Capri and I looked at each other and rolled our eyes. Jewel wanted everyone to believe she was so important. Her phone *always* rang. I found it hard to believe she had that many calls. After all, her job at Westwood didn't seem *that* demanding. Westwood made up a position for her after she kept hanging around the law school and kissing about a year's worth of behind. She calls herself a "Special Affairs Coordinator." We call her a party planner.

Capri, on the other hand, is grounded and has business savvy. She didn't have to pay back any student loans because she invested several thousand dollars a year in the stock market, which allowed her to quickly pay off the small debt that she had after her scholarships. In contrast, Jewel and I have mega law school loans, while Angel paid with her savings and Jermane's father paid her tuition in full.

Despite Jermane's wealth, she's unpretentious and very giving. When I first got to law school, I had a problem with my paperwork, so my tuition loan was going to be delayed. Jermane barely knew me, but offered me a loan to get books and cover my first payment. "It's not like I won't be able to find you," she said, referring to our five classes together.

"Well, I don't know about ya'll, but I'm *famished*," Capri said as she slid out her chair.

"Me, too," Jewel said, returning from her phone excursion. "That was Angel. She's on her way."

At that announcement, we all got up and walked to the buffet, which Etienne's was famous for. You always ran into someone after church.

I waltzed past the silver trays, seeking my prey at the buffet. After loading my plate with mini-waffles, an omelet, cantaloupe, bacon, salmon, and mini-muffins, I headed back to our table and sat down. By the time we'd gotten our food, Angel had arrived and was seated, waiting for us.

"Hey, I had a rough time this morning," she said as she grabbed a muffin from my plate.

"Doing what? It's not like you didn't sleep in. It's way past morning, and don't get hurt messing with my food," I said as I snatched my plate away.

"Is everything OK? I'll bring some coffee for the new arrivals," Antonio said as he peeked over at our table. "Jermane, you're looking too fabulous. Is that suit Ann Taylor?"

Jermane nodded with a slight smile of humility. Antonio smiled back and walked away.

Jewel shifted in her chair. She hated not being the center of attention. "You know, I love Antonio, but I bet that British accent is fake," she said. "And do you think . . ." she looked around and lowered her voice "he is, you know, on the other side of the fence?"

"Jewel, are you asking if he's gay?" Angel asked.

"Well? He does sorta act that way. Do you think that's something people are born with or is it learned?"

"Jewel, *really*," Jermane said. "It's not like some disease you can catch. People, regardless of their sexual orientation or whatever else, are simply people. I thought you'd outgrown all those little judgmental ways you had back in law school. Didn't you just come from church?"

"I'm just being real. I mean, isn't it a sin?" Jewel said, watching the syrup she'd just poured ooze over the whipped cream on her waffles.

"Isn't shopping when you can't afford it a sin?" Capri said. She raised her hand and I slapped it. Always the voice of reason, always cool and collected, Capri was my girl. She worked for a high-power law firm in Houston making *stupid* money. A doe-eyed beauty with never-ending legs that made her tower over all of us, she was a former New York around-the-way girl turned Black sophisticate.

"Very funny."

"Jewel, I just think you're homophobic. I'm not saying being gay's right, but we all have some kind of struggle . . . some kind of lust or temptation. Whether it's sexual, financial, spiritual, we all need grace and mercy," I said.

Jewel was silent for a moment. "Well, on to something else," she said.

Please. I hope we're not going to talk about men. I just don't feel like reliving the whole Reggie incident. It's hard enough as it is facing the possibility of another failed romance.

"Do you know I had to take my lunch break on Friday to go back to the nail shop?" Jewel said, her voice more upbeat.

Phew, relief. More frivolous Jewel conversation.

"All that money I paid for those Solar Nails and one of them chipped a week later. I mean, I went from acrylic to Solar because I thought it would be better, because you know before I had my natural nails and would just get the French manicure. I went to this particular place because of the sterilization system and the massage chair. Then I decided the American manicure was nicer and, well, I just decided I didn't care about saving my own nails, because one day we would be old anyway and it wouldn't matter . . ."

We sat with our forks in midair, glaring at her as she went on and on.

"Jewel! You know, sometimes I wonder how it is you can graduate from law school, pass the bar, and have nothing deeper to talk about besides the intricacies of the manicure process?" Angel yelled as she threw down her fork.

"That's it. I'm not going to say another word." Jewel folded her arms.

"Is that a promise?" Capri said.

"Come on, ladies, ease up on Jewel," I said in her defense, trying to sound serious even though I was happy she'd decided to shut up. At that moment, I thought I saw one of our former classmates.

"Hey, is that Camille Stevenson over there?"

"You mean Camille Taylor. That microwave marriage lasted all of six months," Jewel said.

"I thought you said you weren't talking," Angel said.

"*Anyway*, I heard her husband had an affair with his paralegal. Camille and I have the same masseur, and he was filling me in," Jewel added.

"Since when did you get a masseur?" Capri asked. "That's a luxury you cannot afford."

"I've been going for a while. He is fabulous. My ex, Charles, introduced me to him. Now I'm totally spoiled."

Charles was a football player. Houston has its share of both professional athletes and gold diggers. Jewel was obviously the latter, though I have to say that at least she had some class about it. She dated Charles all of three months, but he never called her back, the poor thing. I think she believed that she was really his girlfriend. She would absolutely kill to marry an athlete.

"Isn't that Tony Stanton, the center for the Houston Meteors?" Jewel asked, trying to contain her excitement. But I knew her digger radar was on high alert.

"Yes, I think that's him," I said.

"I really don't see what ya'll are getting so excited about," Capri huffed. "He's just another cocky athlete with an ego the size of this room. I'm surprised he can fit in here with everyone else with that big head of his. It's our fault. We make these men into gods. Ladies, they are only human beings."

I formed the letter *t* with my hands. "Calm down, Capri. Time out. All we did was recognize the man. You have to admit, he is kind of 'sexy chocolate.' "

"Yeah, like Godiva," Jewel added.

"Yes, but do you even care if the man has a brain?" Capri asked.

The rest of us paused and looked at each other. "Not really!" we said in unison. Everyone laughed.

"I did hear he was very down to earth," Jermane said.

"Whatever," Capri said.

"Well, how is Rex?" I asked, changing the subject.

"Oh, you know, busier than ever," Jermane said. Her eyes quickly fell to her plate and she moved her eggs Benedict slightly with her fork. "He and Daddy are working on a big class action suit, which is good I guess. I don't know."

"You don't know what?" Angel asked.

"I, uh . . . never mind. I hope this case pans out. They're putting a lot of resources into it. I really would like Rex and me to get away," Jermane said as she looked at her plate.

Rex did very well in law school, but worked extra hard to prove himself at her father's firm. In the beginning, Jermane tried to work with the situation. She would go to the office in the evenings, bring him dinner, and watch him work. We all thought it was so romantic and envied her.

She loved Rex so much because he was a departure from the controlling presence of her father, who did everything big. The one time she stood up to him was for her wedding. Contrary to her father's wishes, she had a small but elegant Catholic ceremony. We were all part of the bridal party.

Although the wedding was classy, Jermane cut up and enjoyed herself. She hired a zydeco band for the reception, and we had a ball. That was the happiest I've ever seen Jermane. She wasn't one to jump for joy too often, but lately she seemed particularly down and distant.

"Capri, I think someone is staring at you," Jewel said, trying to look inconspicious as she pointed in Anthony's direction.

"Jewel, you're tripping. That's your imagination. You may want to be a notch on some athlete's bed, but you know that's not me."

I could still sense a trace of New York in Capri's voice, very sharp and direct. She always seemed to be in control. When we were at Westwood, so many guys were trying to date her, but she didn't give them the time of day. She had her priorities in order.

Whenever she stood up in class to recite, you could tell that all the men were lusting after her, even though she usually wore jeans, a T-shirt, no makeup, and a ponytail. When she started interviewing for a job, we all went into shock when she wore a suit.

"What's up for next Friday?" I asked, lifting my cup of coffee, trying not to think of Reggie.

"Well, I heard these doctors who started this investment group are giving a party at the Silver Lounge," Jewel said.

"Not another one of *those* kinds of parties," Angel said.

"What type of party?" Jermane asked.

"You know, the kind of party where everyone comes to profile, no one dances, and the men spend half the night admiring themselves," Angel replied.

"Yeah, it's just one big clique," Capri said.

"What do you mean? *We're* the clique," Jewel said.

Capri struggled to suppress her laughter.

"Jewel, you're a trip. How can you be so bourgeoise driving a compact car?" I said.

"Lexi, I *know* you're not talking. You try to pretend like you're so down to earth, but you want to live a certain lifestyle, too."

"No, I just want to live an abundant life, as God has promised, *without* the drama. There's a difference."

"Whatever." Jewel waved a breadstick in the air.

"So, what should we do on Friday night? Come on, I want to hang out," Jermane said.

We all stopped and looked at her in disbelief.

"Jermane wants to hang out?!? Now, we have to find somewhere to go," Angel said.

"Well, I can hang out if I want to," Jermane said softly.

"Leave Jermane alone," Capri said.

I caught Anthony giving Capri one of those "sop you up with a biscuit" looks. The man was definitely interested.

"Hey, ladies," said a svelte young woman as she eased over to the table.

"Ramona, how are you, dear? We haven't seen you since graduation. What have you been up to?" Jermane finally said after no one else spoke.

"I've been traveling. I just got back last week. How is that fine Rex of yours?" she asked.

"Oh, he's doing very well."

"Well, here's my new address. Maybe we can go out sometime," Ramona said in her best southern belle accent as she handed Jermane her card.

"Yeah, maybe," Capri said.

"Did you hear about her?" Angel said after Ramona had walked away.

"What?" we whispered.

"I heard that she was involved in some scam. She might lose her law license."

"We don't know that for sure, now do we?" Jermane asked. "We shouldn't spread such gossip."

"Yeah, I haven't heard anything like that. And you know I would know," Jewel said.

"Jewel, you'll take up for anybody who has a Chanel bag," Capri said.

"That's not true. We don't even know if her Chanel

bag is real," Jewel said defensively. "But that is the quilted one I just saw in a magazine."

"Ding-dong, Jewel, is anybody home? If you were involved in something illegal and getting PAID, you'd have real designer bags, too," Angel said.

Capri rolled her eyes and dug a spoon in her tiramisu. "This town is so materialistic."

"It's not necessarily just Houston. Our generation is materialistic," I said. "Anyway, forget about Ramona. What are we doing Friday? I'm ready to go because y'all are starting to really get on my nerves."

"Let's go to the 'Male Revue,' " Jewel said. "It'll be fun. It's an all-Black male strip show."

"That tacky show?" Angel asked.

"Oh, brother. Who wants to do that? I can think of better things to do with $2 besides stuffing it down some man's drawers," Capri said.

"Let's just go. We'll have fun. We can go to that doctor thing afterward," Jermane said.

We looked at her in disbelief again.

"Jermane, just because you're so hyped, I'm going to go," Angel said.

"Well, let's meet Friday at seven p.m.," Jewel said.

I rubbed my temples.

I am not feeling this strip club or the party. What's going on with me? I just don't enjoy most of the things my friends like to do anymore. Am I getting too serious? Becoming a bore? Maybe I'm getting old. Maybe I know I shouldn't be going anywhere Jesus wouldn't. But God wouldn't expect me to live like a hermit, would He?

Everyone agreed with the plan. I shrugged my shoulders and said, "Fine."

Jermane will probably cancel by midweek anyway. She never goes out.

*A*fter brunch, I had to run a few errands. As I was driving, I felt a certain freedom. The highway was an open road with no traffic. I slipped in my Michelle Williams CD. I relaxed as the words of her song filled my car.

I heard a word . . . Girl, you'll be fine.

I love Sundays. It's a good time to reflect on the past and think about the future. The sun was getting ready to set and, although it was winter, there was only a hint of chill in the air. Texas had the most beautiful sunrises and sunsets I'd ever seen.

I reflected on brunch, realizing how blessed I was to have such a blend of friends, each unique. We often got on each other's nerves, but we were there for each other. Thinking of them helped me feel better about Reggie.

I decided to drive past my exit to clear my head. I navigated my car toward downtown. I was nearing the exit that used to take me to Westwood.

Westwood is one of the few predominately Black law schools in the country. A prominent Houston politician built it as an addition to Westwood University in 1952 because he had an employee whose son wanted to become a lawyer and none of the other Texas law schools would accept him.

My time there was one of the hardest experiences I'd ever faced. It was ugly, difficult, political, thought provoking, competitive, and challenging. Nonetheless, I'm proud that I'm part of the Westwood legacy.

I just wish my bank account would reflect my inheritance a little more. As an attorney, you don't really make a lot of money unless you work for a huge law firm or, if you're in private practice, get that one "I'm gettin' paid!" case.

I stopped at my favorite local grocery store to buy the Sunday paper, some bottled water, and my cherished banana pudding, the one thing that always got me through my Sunday evenings. Then I filled my tank with gas and charted my course back home. As I pulled into the garage, I remembered another one of my blessings—my loft. Lofts were very expensive in certain parts of town, but I managed to find a nice one right on the outskirts of The Heights area before they became trendy and expensive.

I walked into my apartment and dropped my bag at the door. I walked straight through the main room, with its shades of blue, walked to the bathroom, and turned on the shower, testing it for temperature. I stripped and eased in. I thought, as I stood under the water, *no time for a luxurious bath tonight*. After a few minutes, I got out and put on my cotton men's pajamas. I sat down with my pudding and picked up the phone to call Capri.

"Hello."

"Hey, girl. I'm gettin' ready to call it an early night and turn in. I'm pooped. But I had to call you cause

I'm getting a little nervous about going up in front of Judge Albright."

"Girl, underneath that bad toupee, he's a softy at heart. What kind of motion are you arguing? Are you prepared?"

"Motion to suppress evidence. Yeah, I guess."

"What do you mean 'I guess.' If I know you, you're over-prepared. OK, I'll give you a few tips. When he clears his throat after you've spoken, it means he's leaning toward your side. Look him straight in the eye and use lots of hand movements. Look really serious and raise your voice a lot. He likes to see young lawyers get excited. Plus he's hard of hearing. You'll be fine. Show 'em whatcha workin' with!"

"Thanks. You always pump me up, just like back at Westwood."

"Girl, you know I got your back. I'll be praying for you."

"Good night. Love ya, girl."

"Back atcha."

I was lucky to have Capri in my life. I smiled as I thought back to the first day of class at law school and how insecure and scared I was. At Westwood, they practice the Socratic teaching method. As far as I'm concerned, "Socratic" is another word for "teach yourself the law" or "make a fool of yourself." When a professor used this method, I often ended up more confused after class than before.

First, the professor would ask a student to recite information about the assigned reading. Just when you think you're finished, he'd fire questions at you. He'd

ask what you thought about the case, the decision, or
the opinion of the judges.

*Who really cares? Just let me sit down and dwell on my humilia-
tion*, I'd think. The first time a professor called on me
was during my second week at Westwood.

"Ms. Parker," Professor Calloway, my contracts'
professor, called out. I could have sworn I heard an
echo. I froze in my seat.

"Yes," I said, unsuccessfully trying to keep my voice
from cracking.

"Will you please enlighten us about this wonderful
case regarding 'Battle of the Forms?' "

"The battle of what?" I whispered under my breath.
My legs were shaking.

"Uh, umm . . . well, Professor Calloway, it seems
as though I read the wrong case," I said, bracing myself.
The whole class started mumbling. I felt like someone
had pulled out a King Kong–sized magnifying glass
and the focus was on me. There was nowhere to run
and nowhere to hide.

"Well, Ms. Parker, it seems you have come here to
play. How in the world do you expect to be a lawyer if
you can't even follow the simplest of directions? You
have wasted your classmates' time. Perhaps you should
reevaluate your decision to come to law school . . ."

*Just who does he think he is? I'm paying all this money for this man
to degrade me? What a jerk.*

I knew my thoughts were written on my face.

"At any rate, thank you, Ms. Parker, for your intel-
lectual contribution to this class. Would you like to select co-counsel to assist you?" he said smugly.

It was too early in the semester for anyone to have my back, and volunteering another person to recite for you was something you'd have to think twice about putting even your worst enemy through.

"I'll do it," offered a strong but nonchalant voice from the back of the room.

"Well, I'm glad to see someone is interested in being a lawyer Ms., Ms. . . ." he looked down at his roster.

"Sterling, Capricia," she said with confidence. "However, I prefer to be called Capri."

"Oh really? Well please proceed, Ms. Sterling," he said.

Capri blew us all away with her knowledge of the case. She saved the class. From that point on, Professor Calloway constantly challenged her, trying to break her down. But he usually ended up looking stupid, which frustrated him even more. For Capri, it was a game, her very own little power trip.

He stayed on me, too, because he thought I was weak. But, by the end of the semester, he was convinced I could handle myself. I was always prepared.

As I tried to doze off, I laughed at the memories. So many people are on one big power trip. Everybody wants respect. On the other hand, respect is something most don't want to give up to others easily.

I used to think like much of society, that if you didn't have good looks, super-high intelligence, or heavy connections, you couldn't win at the game. But little by little, I was realizing that when you have God, you have a secret weapon. Then again, even with God, it still doesn't hurt to watch your own back from time to time.

I decided to pray before I fell asleep.

Lord, thank You for another day. I love You. Thank You for Capri's guidance. Help me to be strong. Deliver me from anything that's not of You. I pray for Jermane to be happier. I pray for Jewel to get a grip. (You know what I mean.) I pray to get good cases. Help me to be a competent and ethical lawyer. Help me to be debt free. Help me deal with Reggie. Bless my family and friends, and forgive me if I have done anything wrong in Your sight. Speaking of which, Lord, is it wrong to go to a strip club? Lord, please keep me, for I'm unable to keep myself. Amen.

The phone's ringing startled me awake. Groggy, I let it ring a few more times. The answering machine came on.

"Baby girl, pick up. This is Reggie."

Against my better judgment, I rolled over and picked up. "Hell-o," I said in a raspy voice.

"Hey sweetie, what are you doing?" he said, obviously not realizing that everyone didn't work his same shift. It was one a.m.

"Why are you calling me?" I said, looking at the clock.

"I know it's late, but you know I usually have to stay over and do some extra paperwork. I just wanted to give you a shout. I thought that maybe we could talk about this taking space thing."

"Whatever, Reggie. Yes, I still need space. And I have to be in court *all* day tomorrow. I need as much sleep as possible. So I don't need to stay on the phone being silly with you."

"Come on, baby girl, I've heard that before. Can I come over, please?"

I knew he was in the mood.

"Reggie, please be understanding. Months ago, this wasn't an issue," I said, now more awake. "I want us to be about more than just hooking up."

"If that's the way you're going to be, fine," he said in a spoiled, childlike tone.

"I'll call you when I'm ready," I said, and hung up.

As I rolled over, the guilt I felt about my sexual relationship with Reggie came tumbling back. There was an uneasiness in my spirit and heart. I remembered Pastor Graves's "Al Green" sermon, so I slipped the cassette into my stereo. The words of "Love and Happiness" played in my ear as I faded off to sleep.

CHAPTER THREE

Business as Usual

As I rode up in the elevator, I checked my makeup in the mirrored walls. I was alone, so I touched up my lipstick, which had lost its shine from my morning cup of coffee. I paused for a minute and prayed.

Lord, I pray that You anoint this day, give me favor with Judge Albright and give me wisdom. Please don't have me lookin' stupid. You said You will not make Your people ashamed. And please forgive me for such a short prayer, but it's gonna have to do since I woke up too late to have a more intense talk with You. Amen.

I got off the elevator, hoping Terrance wouldn't be the first person I saw. I wasn't in the mood for his stop-playing-hard-to-get glances.

Terrance was an established Westwood alumnus who I temporarily shared office space with. I met him at a mixer after graduation. I knew he liked me, but I kept

things strictly business. Still, he gave me some breaks.
He not only allowed me to pay what I could afford for
my space, but gave me access to all of the office equip-
ment and use of his secretary. He even helped with my
cases when I needed it. I appreciated his help, but I was
looking forward to settling one of the big cases I'd been
working on so I could truly be on my own.

"Morning, Ms. Parker," Terrance said with his back
to me. "Ready for a big day?"

"Oh yeah, I'm ready," I said as I sprinted to my office.

I closed the door behind me. *Five messages already and it
wasn't even 8 a.m.* Two I had to return immediately. The
others could wait. As I made the calls, I pulled several
files and packed them into my briefcase. I downed another cup of coffee, reviewed several documents, took
a few more notes, and was out the door.

Lord, aerobics class will be a good relief tonight.

*H*ey, girl," Jewel said as we spotted one another in
the lobby of the gym.

"Hey. Where's everybody else?" I said.

"Capri got held over at work again. Jermane didn't
feel like coming, and Angel's working late, too."

"Oh, well. I'm gonna feel bad for them when summer comes and I have those tight abs like Janet Jackson," I said.

"Some of us already have it like that," Jewel said,
full of conceit.

She was right, but I wasn't going to give her the

satisfaction. After we changed into our workout gear, Jewel touched up her lipstick.

"We're only going to work out. We'll be getting sweaty and funky, so you don't need makeup," I said.

"You never know," she chided as we walked toward the aerobics room.

We came in and found our usual spot on the floor. "I'm beat. I had to go to court, but I won my motion," I said as I inspected my worn-out tennis shoes.

"Whose court were you in?"

"Judge Albright."

"Albright, Albright . . . bad toupee, right?"

"That's the one!"

We both laughed, then relaxed for a few more minutes, waiting for Darnell the aerobics instructor. Darnell had the nicest butt and the prettiest, smoothest legs, particularly for a man. His gams were kind of like Flip Wilson's in a dress when he was Geraldine.

"All right, you tired ladies! Summer is around the corner!" Darnell yelled in a deep, booming voice as he ran into the room, bright and full of energy. He took his place up front.

"We're going to work on the abdomen, legs, and buttocks," he said, lightly patting each area for emphasis. "We're also going to do steps tonight."

Everyone sighed.

"Remember this is Funk Aerobics, so I hope y'all are ready to get a little funky."

Darnell stepped up on the platform and turned his back. His behind looked like two large, perfectly round grapefruits stuck together in his yellow tights.

Darnell owns the fitness studio. Mostly women come here. Some come to get a good workout, while others come to get private training lessons from Darnell or one of the other male trainers.

"Pump it up!" Darnell said as he started stepping high.

The horns and lyrics from Beyonce's "Crazy in Love" blared out of the huge speakers, putting me in a trance. Before you knew it, I got into it.

We watched as Darnell glided across the stage. Then he started to do the movements from her video. This was out of our league, so we all gradually stopped as he continued to perform.

"Work it, Beyonce!" he yelled as he watched himself in the big studio mirror. Then he turned around and saw everyone had stopped following him.

"Uh, sorry, ladies, I got caught up in the moment. Let's go, no excuses. Step, step, pump it up, let's go . . ." He clapped his hands for us to start again.

Song after song, step after step, my visions of my perfect bikini body became more clear. That is until I tripped over my step. I tried to retain my composure even though Jewel was looking my way and snickering. I missed the other girls.

We used to work out often together since it was a great way to destress after classes. But now everyone had different priorities, and step aerobics wasn't high on the list.

Later on, as I pulled into my driveway, still a little moist with sweat, I thought about Reggie. It was time to let him go. I was tired of dealing with our issues, and, most of all, I was tired of him constantly putting off church. I didn't want to settle, and spirituality was on the top of my list in terms of what I was looking for in a man.

It was important for me to date a brother with a spiritual foundation because if the devil can't work on you, he'll work on those around you. I'd tried to carry the spiritual burden of a relationship by myself before, and it wore me out. I needed a man who was strong enough to submit to God and pray, and it had become painfully obvious that Reggie wasn't ready for that type of responsibility. It was time to issue him his papers.

I checked my mail—bill, bill, magazine. As I walked in the door, I saw that my answering machine light was blinking. I did a few dishes and picked up a few items off the floor. I undressed and took a quick shower. I had to do some reading, but before that, I needed to give myself a manicure and a pedicure. I read an article that had really stuck with me about taking better care of yourself as you get older. Next year, I'm going to be close to, well, I can't even say it. I never thought turning *that* age was going to be a big deal, but I am starting to get a little depressed thinking about it.

So I quickly dismissed the thought. I threw on an oversized T-shirt that I stole from Reggie and slipped on my salmon pink slippers.

I stretched out on the couch. I had waited all day to indulge in my favorite dessert—banana pudding. Its creamy texture was the temporary fix to every problem.

That's right, I can do this because I'm single.

If I were married, I'd have to feed the kids and a

husband, even though cooking is not my favorite thing to do. Every holiday, my brother-in-law would say, "Girl, you need to learn how to cook. I'm gonna get your triflin' behind a cookbook!"

Then I'd say, "I'll get a cookbook if you do something with those ashy, rusty elbows and arms of yours. Looks like you were a paratrooper who landed in the desert!"

I smiled as I pressed the answering machine to play back my messages.

"Hey, baby girl, this is Reggie. I'll stop through after I get off."

My smile faded. "Oh, brother."

"This is GMAC. Pleae give us a call back at 1-800-555-2000."

"Lexi, this is your father. Just calling to check on you."

My father's voice gave me comfort. Every since my mother died, we'd become very close. He'd become my best friend, and we talked about things I would have never imagined we could discuss, like relationships, movies, and politics. I think he won't rest easy until I get married.

Since it was late, I promised myself I'd call him tomorrow from work. Then I paged Reggie to see if I could catch him. I wanted to tell him I had too much work to do to be fooling around with him tonight. Besides, we were supposed to be on a break, though I had to admit that I wasn't looking forward to completely cutting him off.

There was a knock at the door.

"Hey," he said, walking in with brown bags that carried the smell of sweet and sour chicken.

He knows how to get to me—food.

"Reggie, you know I have a lot of work to do," I said, distracted by the smell of my favorite Chinese food.

"Yeah, I know, but I promise I won't bother you. I'll just go and play games on the computer while you read," he said.

"Reggie, you are really making this hard. You can't just show up and barge in like you still have it like that. We've had a discussion and I still feel the same. I still need some space."

Darn, he looks good. What am I supposed to do? Shut the door in his face or kick him out? I'm just not that cold. I walked to the couch and watched him unpack the food in the kitchen.

"Lex, don't you miss me? I miss you."

Please don't do this to me. I took a deep breath. "OK, I can see this is going to be difficult," I mumbled. "Reggie, come sit on the couch."

"Why don't you just relax and enjoy my company?" he said.

I was silent.

"Okay, alright. Here I come," he said. He sat next to me on the couch.

"Reggie, this is not just about you. Of course, I'm going to miss you. I have missed you. But you need to respect my feelings and what I'm trying to do." I refused to look in his eyes.

"Well, what *are* you trying to do?" he said.

"I really feel like I'm not getting through to you. I

really need space. I tell you that, and you continue acting as if things are still the same. I'm growing spiritually. You're not. And there are other things. I feel like
a convenience, like you take me for granted. You rarely
keep your commitments when we make dates to go
somewhere. How much more plain can I make it?"

He shifted on the couch.

"Lexi, I hear you. But, you know, honestly, maybe
things would be different if you wouldn't nag so much.
Maybe it's the way you say these things. It just sounds
like whining and complaining," he said as he got up.

"Reggie, that's such a cop out!"

I wanted to continue, but I was already out of energy. I let out a deep sigh.

*I'm too tired to fight. These last several nights have been lonely. I
really would like his company. Lord, it's so hard to make a clean break
when you don't have many reserves left. I've just gotten so used to him,
but I want more . . .*

Reggie ended up having his way. We ate and fell
asleep, cuddling. In the middle of the night, I woke up
because I had the weirdest dream. I looked over at Reggie's bare chest and placed my head on it.

I felt guilty for allowing him to stay the night. I was
relieved we didn't have to deal with the sex thing
tonight, but that usually meant I'd have to prepare for
battle in the morning. I don't know what makes men
want to go there as the sun's rising. Reggie just wants to
roll over, morning breath and all, and have his way.

I got up and went to the bathroom. The shower
curtain was clear and contained a translucent image of
a large white swan. The fixtures were all white and the

tub was in the middle of the floor. The brass handles seemed to glow. *God, I love this bathroom. If I don't settle a case soon, I might have to leave this place.*

Then I remembered the dream. I was a guest at a party, but I didn't know it was a party. It looked like we were in a cafeteria at a church. I didn't know any of the people, except for a girl who was with me. It seemed as if everybody else knew what was going on but us.

Then the girl gasped and grabbed and hugged a woman who seemed to be familiar, maybe a relative. I looked around the room and saw a woman whose back was to me. She turned around. I recognized her—it was my mother. She didn't say a word. She just acknowl-edged me with an almost Mona Lisa—like smile. That's when I woke up.

God knows when I need to hear from her.

A few hours later, the alarm clock went off, and just like clockwork, Reggie rolled over. When I pushed him away, he got an attitude.

"Are you messin' around on me?" he said in an ac-cusing tone.

"Negro, please. Yes, I am having an affair—with God," I quipped.

"Oh, no. Not this again," he said, rolling over.

"Yes, this again," I said, moving toward the closet.

"Everybody sins," he said.

"Reggie, I really think we need to talk." I saw his look of reservation. *Oh, no*, he must be thinking, *here we go again with the nagging*. But I didn't care. I'd had enough.

"I have to break this off for good. No more mid-night drop-ins. There is no 'maybe' or 'I think.' I have to close this door. I've prayed about it, and I know in my spirit what God is telling me I need to do."

"I don't believe this," he said as he shot up. "Who have you been talking to? Your girls? Or is it that ridiculous Pastor Graves. You just wanna be like him and his wife! Well, that's not me. I think you go way too overboard with this Jesus stuff."

I was seething, but focused.

"Be careful of what you say, Reginald. I can think for myself. You're being spiteful. You have no one to blame but yourself for what's happening now. I've told you for a while now that I was unhappy. You didn't listen. Now, I have to show you rather than tell you. If you care for me, you won't be selfish and will accept what I've decided."

"Whatever, Lex. It doesn't matter. There are too many women in Houston to go through all of this," he said as he began dressing.

"What?" I turned to look him in the face.

"You heard me. There are plenty of other women who I can get with who know how to treat a brother. I've had it."

My heart sank. He'd never talked to me like that before. "Reggie, just get out."

"You'll call me. You're looking for the perfect brother and he ain't out there. I'm the best thing you've ever had. Take a good look, Lex, 'cause once I'm finished, I'm through." He walked out of the bedroom.

I heard the door slam. I sat on the bed and the tears began to flow. I knew I'd done the right thing, but it still hurt.

A lexis, there's a Jewel Whitaker on line one for you."

"Thanks, Ms. Hobby."

"What's up? Don't you have anything else to do besides bug us folks that have real jobs?" I said.

"Just calling to see if Friday is still on for you. Jermane called last night to double confirm," Jewel said.

"I'm in, but I know I'll probably be dead tired. The past few days have been rough. I've been in and out of court all week. I'm looking for the Jefferson case to settle, and we were so close, but now there's a delay. I also had to give Reggie the boot."

"What?" Jewel said.

"Yeah, we finally broke it off."

"*You* broke it off with *him* I hope?"

"Yeah, two days ago."

"Did you catch him cheating?"

"No, just other stuff. I'll talk to you about it on Sunday at brunch."

"You know that's not right. Don't leave me hanging! I always tell you every single, solitary detail of my breakups!"

"Jewel, please don't take me through this drama now. I don't have time for it."

"Fine. Everyone says Friday is still good. We're meeting at my place at 7:45 p.m. There's an 8:30 show at Club Jontel, and then we're going to head to the party."

Jewel was always our social coordinator because she

had the least to do at work. She was usually finished with her work by mid-afternoon and then spent the rest of the day on her personal agenda.

I hung up, looked at the pile of papers and folders on my desk, and realized that organization was not a gift that the Lord had blessed me with. I made a mental note to add that to my prayer list.

There has to be a better way.

I dashed home Friday from the office to take a quick shower and dress for girls' night. We met at Jewel's so we could carpool. Angelica drove her car and Jermane drove her SUV. We all looked good, but Jermane shocked me.

She wore a strapless black dress that clung to her curves. Her hair was slicked back and her gold hoop earrings added to her sexiness. She had traded her red lipstick for a bronze hue, and she glowed. Men would be falling in line for her.

We pulled up to Club Jontel and had to wait about 15 minutes for the valet to take the keys and park the cars. We found a table and kept our jackets on since the air-conditioning made the room feel like a fridge. Jermane seemed more excited than usual, moving her head to the music and being silly. If I didn't know her, I would've thought she had had something to drink before coming out, but Jermane rarely drank. The waitress came over, made a quick inspection of the table, and asked if she could get us anything.

"Would you like to start a tab?" she said.

"Yes!" Jermane answered enthusiastically before we could all answer.

What was her problem? Lord, why am I here? I don't want a drink. I'd rather be at home relaxing, watching The Best Man *for the one hundredth time. Just for the part when Morris Chestnut comes around the corner at the beginning of the movie. This is too much madness.*

I looked around the room at the clusters of women drinking and talking loud. *This is so not me.*

The music was pumping and we strained to hear each other. Finally, we gave up talking. At that moment, the announcer—a short man in a royal blue suit—came onstage.

"Ladies, I want to take this opportunity to welcome you to Club Jontel."

"That must be Mr. Jontel," Jewel said.

"Shhh!" we said in chorus.

"All right, all right," Jewel said.

"We have for you tonight a show that will make your bodies scream, and your fantasies become reality." About one thousand women, or what seemed like one thousand women, started to scream.

I have a headache.

"This is ridiculous. It doesn't make sense to me. Are we this hard up?" I yelled.

"I feel you, Lexi. I can think of better things I can do with my dollars," Capri said.

"Could you both please just not be so sensible tonight?" Jermane said. "I just want to have a good time." Then she let out a scream, acknowledging the announcer.

We all just looked at her and then turned toward the
stage.

"Now, ladies, without further delay, Club Jontel
presents 'The Chocolate Delight Revue!!!!' "

The music changed, the lights went down, and
green, yellow, and red lights started flashing signs on
stage that read:

FEVER

THE MECHANIC

ESPRESSO

NICE AND EASY

MAGIC MAN

JERONIMO

COGNAC

My mouth dropped as oiled chests, bulging calves,
6-to-8–pack abs, and tight, bulbous onions paraded
by. As each man circled the stage and made his pose, I
fanned myself, 'cause I was getting a little hot and
bothered. Capri's mouth was hanging open. Jermane
was almost standing on her chair. We had to pull Jewel
back from rushing the stage, and Angel remained cool
and composed while she held her cigarette.

By the middle of the show, every jacket was off. Jermane was getting increasingly intoxicated and screamed
with abandon. Capri had stuck dollar after dollar after
dollar in the dancers' drawers. We were having a ball.

"Ladies, we have a surprise for you. Our last and final dancer is the winner of the National Male Dancer
competition held in Las Vegas. This is a special treat.
He is big, bronzed, and a love god. They call him . . .
The Black Zorro."

Flamenco music wafted through Club Jontel. Then Zorro made his entrance out of dry ice.

"Whoa!"

He was tall, about 6'2", wearing a black-and-red cape with tight black leather pants and a red peasant shirt, bearing part of his buffed, bronzed chest. He had on a mask, but even from a distance, you could see how intense his eyes were. His brown skin had reddish undertones, and his crown of dreadlocks were sun-kissed with a light chestnut tint.

He just stood there. That's all he had to do for me. Then the music got faster and he started moving his middle with a snakelike motion. The crowd went wild.

I couldn't believe my eyes. Jermane was standing alone, at the edge of the stage. After about five minutes of crowd-pleasing, Zorro eased over to her. I could not watch. He kneeled down, rubbed her face, and stood up slowly. He snatched off the cape and threw it at her.

She wrapped it around her. She was in a trance. She had lost her mind. Rex would kill her if he saw her right now.

Zorro pulled off his shirt to expose his perfectly de-fined chest. His stomach was so tight you could bounce a quarter off it. It was like nobody else was there, just Zorro and Jermane. He pulled her onto the stage and held her close, their bodies moving from side to side in unison.

I covered my eyes momentarily, then opened them to see their movements getting more . . . vigorous.

"That's it!" I grabbed Capri's arm, and we went to get her.

"Let her have some fun!" Angel yelled. Ignoring her, we made it to the edge of the stage.

"Jermane, get your butt down here!" I whispered loudly, clenching my teeth.

Finally, Capri went up and grabbed her arm. Jermane instantly snapped back into reality. She left the stage and bolted back to her seat.

"What in the world got into you?" I asked.

"Would you get off my back! I deserve to have some fun. You're not my mother!" she yelled.

"Thank God," I said under my breath.

"I told you," Angel said, continuing to take in Zorro's body and moving in her seat.

"Jermane, what's happening to you?" I said.

"Alright, alright. I'm sorry," she said.

"Are you OK?"

"Yes, just let me relax."

"Well, we better get going to the party," Jewel said as Mr. Jontel announced when the next show would be held.

"Jermane, you want me to drive?" I said, trying not to sound patronizing.

"Yeah, ah, you better," she said, lightly patting her face with a tissue.

I thought you'd agree. You may be trippin' tonight, but you know better. Rex would definitely whip your behind if something were to happen to his car.

I grabbed her keys.

———

We got off the elevator, and it was instant Black folks. Everyone was dressed impeccably, and I recognized many of the faces from my old club days. Some people make a career out of that life. I could write a book of experiences from partying in Houston alone. What is really sad is when the same men who tried to talk to you two years ago approach you again and don't even remember you from the first time. I just can't hang anymore.

"Hey, I see Roderick, one of my coworkers. I'll be back," Jewel said, gliding to the other side of the room.

Angel was at the bar, already being hounded by some overzealous guy. Jermane, Capri, and I headed for a table.

"My head hurts," Jermane said. She sounded more like herself.

"You know you can't hang. Zorro wore you out," I said.

She said nothing.

"I have some aspirin in my purse. Do you want one?" I said.

"Yes. I'll be back. I'm going to the ladies' room," she said.

"I'll go with you," Capri offered.

"No, no, stay. I'll be fine."

We watched her struggle through the crowd, delayed every few steps by some interested man.

"Isn't that Mr. Stanton over there surrounded by a small harem?" I said, nodding my head in his direction.

"Umm, yeah, I guess so," Capri said. Jewel came bouncing over.

"Hey, isn't that your man over there, Capri?" Jewel said.

"Jewel, chill out. I told you athletes turn me off."

"You are so dry," Jewel said as she eyed some man at the bar.

A waitress came to the table.

"The gentleman would like to run a tab for your table."

We looked at each other.

"What gentleman?" Capri asked.

We sneered.

You had to be careful. If you allowed a man to spend money on drinks, that meant he might want to hang around, which could be detrimental to the quality of your evening depending on who the man is.

"Mr. Anthony Stanton," she said in an indignant tone.

"We'll gladly accept!" Jewel chimed.

"It wasn't our imagination. He *was* looking at you, Capri," I said.

"*Jesus,*" Capri said, and rolled her eyes.

About ten minutes later, Anthony strode toward us. His legs and arms seemed to go on forever. Just as he reached our table, he flashed a smile, revealing a deep dimple on the left side of his face. His hair was cut close and he had a small hoop earring in his left ear. His skin, the color of dark molasses, was slightly covered by a trace of five o'clock shadow. His eyebrows were thick and he had very expressive eyes. His lips, juicy and full, looked soft and moist. I think we all got lost in his presence for a moment. None of us spoke.

"Hi, I'm Jewel Whitaker. Please excuse my rude friends," she said, extending her hand. "This is Alexis and Capricia."

I could see Capri fuming. Number one—she hated being called Capricia. Number two—she hated the oversized egos of professional athletes.

"Capri. My name is Capri," she said as she looked at Jewel, effectively cutting her off from any other voluntary speeches.

"I just wanted to introduce myself," he said "I'm . . ."

"Anthony Stanton!" a woman in a tight red dress and auburn weave exclaimed. She ran over and grabbed his hands. Before we knew it, there was a small circle of people around him. I kind of felt bad for him because he seemed slightly embarrassed and uncomfortable.

But this just gave Capri more ammunition. She sat there, staring at the gathering, sipping on her wine as if she was being entertained at a show.

In a few minutes, the circle vanished. Anthony turned toward us.

"I apologize. Sometimes it gets rough," he said softly.

"Oh, that's all right, Anthony," Jewel said.

"Please, call me Tony. May I join you ladies for a minute?" he said cordially.

I was tired of Jewel's mouth, so I spoke up this time.

"Sure," I said, "and thank you for the drinks."

"So, are you ladies enjoying yourselves?" he said, looking directly at Capri.

"It's cool," she said, clearly out of obligation.

"Yes, it's a very nice atmosphere," I said.

"We try to keep a certain clientele," he said.

"A certain clientele?" Capri asked. "What do you mean by that?"

"I mean, we just make sure the crowd isn't too young and there aren't any problems."

"Uh huh," Capri replied.

"I'm not sure I understand. Did you help throw the party?" I said.

"Uh, actually, I own the lounge."

Jewel's eyes instantly opened wide and beamed. Capri took another sip of her wine, remaining aloof.

At that, he eased out of his chair and cleared his throat. "If you ladies need anything else, please don't hesitate to let me know. It was a pleasure meeting you all," he said in a velvety, sexy voice.

I waited for Capri to say something. I could not believe she was about to let this man get away. *Is it a full moon tonight? All my friends are losing it.*

He looked at Capri once again before he walked away and passed Angel and Jermane, who were on their way back to our table.

"How in the world did you let *that* walk away?" Angel asked, gazing in Tony's direction.

"Capri," Jewel and I said.

"If y'all want him so bad, you can have him. And,

furthermore, I don't need any lessons from Gold Digger University," Capri said, looking at Jewel. "I do have a good job and I can take complete care of myself!"

Angel just shook her head and grabbed a cigarette.

"Well, I'm going to dance," Jermane said and got up. She'd apparently gotten over her headache and proceeded to groove to the music by herself.

I think we started something we're going to regret.

Angel soon went back to the bar and Jewel went, well, all over the place. Capri got up to dance as well, but not with Tony. He just stood at the bar, watching her.

As I sat there, wishing I'd driven my own car, I felt someone's hand touching my neck. Ugh! Someone who barely knew me felt free to put his hands on me. Then I recognized the cologne. It was Reginald.

"Hey, girl. You havin' a good time?"

Dang, he's lookin' kinda good.

"Hey, Reggie."

"You look good. How come you ain't dancing?" he said.

'Cause I'm scared I'll be a weirdo magnet. "Just tired I guess."

"Well, me and my boys just got here," he said, looking refreshed. He didn't seem to care at all about our nasty split.

"Yeah, I've been here a while," I said.

"Is that *Jermane?*" he said, looking in disbelief as she shook her behind on the floor.

"Yeah, that's our 'little Jermane.' "

"She looks good. *Real* good."

The nerve! He just broke Rule Number Four in the relationship code book. You never comment on how good your woman's friends look. If you do, you better make it sound like it's totally innocent, not like you're really checking them out. But I guess it doesn't really matter with him, at this point.

"Well, don't you have somewhere to go?" I said.

"Don't be so hard, Lexi. Ya know I didn't want us to stop being together."

Just at that moment, Tony walked by with a trail of people following him. I looked at him with a "help me" look on my face. He looked like he needed a break, too, so he sat down and joined us.

"Oh, Reggie, this is Anthony Stanton."

Reggie looked like he was staring at a ghost.

"Yeah, man, I know who you are. I've been checkin' your game out," Reggie said.

"Uh, may I please speak to Alexis alone?" Tony asked. "It's kind of important."

"Uh, sure, man. Lexi, catch up to you later," he said.

"Ex?" Tony asked after Reggie had disappeared.

"Yeah. It's that obvious, huh? You look like you were getting mobbed," I said.

"Yeah, it's frustrating at times. You don't know who is for real. I'm not really used to all this hype. When I played high school ball in Mount Vernon, back in New York, I got attention. But nothing like this."

"New York." I said. "Capri's from New York."

"Are you serious? Well, that's what I wanted to talk to you about."

"No problem. Capri's my girl. And you know, she

isn't as cold as she seems. She just tends to be cautious around men that she meets."

"Yeah, I know, I've seen her before."

"At Etienne's?"

"Yeah, and my lawyer works at her firm," he said. "I was up there a couple of weeks ago going over some business, and I asked about her. I couldn't get much information except her name and that she seemed to be single. She looks like a very sharp sister."

"Yes, she is, but she's very private."

"Well, tell me, what would be my best approach?"

"That I don't know. She's not too fond of athletes."

"*Wonderful,*" he said, throwing up his hands. "Well, I can't change who I am, but I'm not going to give up till she has a chance to get to know me. It's out of her hands now," he said as he winked.

My heart melted. I could still hear a little trace of New York in his voice. *Stuff like this never happens to me.*

"In the meantime, put in a good word for me, alright?" He squeezed my hand, got up, and then walked off quickly to dodge another female admirer coming his way. He dashed through a side exit. Capri and Jermane were still on the dance floor. Jewel and Angel were talking to a couple of guys at the bar. I danced with the next guy who asked.

CHAPTER FOUR

Special Delivery

ewel stretched out on her sofa, feeling the buttery-soft leather rub against her skin. She admired the long legs and flat stomachs of the dancers on *Soul Train*. One girl's hair danced as hard as she did, reminding Jewel that she needed to touch up her own weave.

From the couch, she surveyed a pile of letters on top of the coffee table. She strategically pulled a clothes catalog from between the unopened bills and started flipping through the pages.

She scanned the living room and began the almost daily ritual of admiring her own taste, going from the love seat made of supple Italian leather, to the buffed hardwood floors partially covered with a sheepskin rug, to the coffee table's wrought iron legs. Then she turned to her matching glass cabinets with strategically placed collectibles of porcelain African American women, a china plate hand painted with her sorority shield, and an ivory statue of a man and woman embracing.

Just as she jumped up to go to the kitchen, the doorbell rang.

"Who's that, unannounced?" she wondered.

As she rushed to the door, she remembered she had her Saturday morning no-frills look going on. Her hair was pulled back with a headband, and she wore a T-shirt, boxer shorts, and ankle socks. She peeked out the window to see who it might be.

"Package for Ms. Jewel Whitaker," a uniformed man said. He noticed the eyes peering from behind the curtains.

Jewel opened the door, feeling less worried about her appearance since it was only a deliveryman.

"Yeah, that's me," she said.

"So how are you?" he said, revealing a soft smile.

"Can't complain," she said, not looking directly at him.

As he stood there filling out the form, she slyly took in his frame. He wasn't very tall. He only looked to be around 5'6" or 5'7", but he was built. His tan skin glistened in the sun. She also noticed that his calves were built and that his shorts fit his thighs nicely. His crisp shirt was firmly tucked in his shorts and his sleeves were slightly rolled up. He had a clean-shaven face and his hair was cut so low that he was almost bald. He had long eyelashes and very friendly eyes.

"Can you please sign here, ma'am?"

"Ma'am? I'm not that old," Jewel said.

"Nothing personal. Just being polite," he said. "Well, that does it. Have a good day," he said, handing her a receipt.

"Yeah, well you have a good day, too," she said, feeling almost cheated because he didn't ask for her number.

"By the way," he announced with a slight grin as he reached the door of his truck, "you're a very attractive lady."

"Oh, thank you. You have a *real* good day," Jewel said. After she watched him drive off, she refocused on the package, trying to remember what she'd ordered.

"I see he didn't bother to ask for those digits," a familiar voice taunted.

Jewel turned to her right and noticed the tall frame of her neighbor, Toliver.

"He wasn't my type," Jewel insisted.

"Evidently, you weren't his either," he said as he bent down to pick up his Saturday paper.

"Don't worry. He wasn't yours either," she quipped.

"Let you tell it," he said, as he rolled his eyes. "Anyway, what's been going on?"

"Not much. You know, same old routine."

"It's rare to see you here on a Saturday morning. No sugar daddies lately?"

"Toliver, mind your business. I haven't seen you with any new business lately either."

"That's because I'm more private with my business."

"Right. Anyway, I don't have time for this . . . I'll talk to you later," she said, and slammed the door.

She walked in, tore open the package, and gazed upon the pink satin sheets she'd ordered. She threw the package to the side. She plopped back on the couch and watched the *Soul Train* credits roll up the screen. Her thoughts moved to the man who had just delivered her package. She flashed back to his chest and how she wanted to see more than what the top of his shirt revealed. She looked at the receipt on top of the package and noticed his signature—Kevin Eastland.

"What am I doing? He is not rich enough for me," she muttered. She grabbed the remote and flipped through the channels, wondering how she could see Kevin again. She parked the screen on the home-shopping channel. She watched as the model demonstrated how to use a small appliance. She immediately felt the urge to order a bagel slicer.

CHAPTER FIVE

Going Through Changes

ood mornin' Lord. Thanks for another day. Forgive me for my sins. Sorry about missing my tithes last week, but my ten per-cent will be in the basket tomorrow, most definitely. Bless my family and friends. Help Jermane to calm down. And please look out for my dad. Please send him a nice woman, someone sweet, kind, fun, spir-itual . . . BUT he doesn't necessarily need to marry her. (I know I'm being selfish. Please help me work on that.) In Jesus' name, Amen.

The phone rang.

It happens every time. At least I got a chance to finish my prayer.

"Hey girl . . ."

"What's up, Jewel?"

"Wanted to see if you wanted to go to the mall to-day. Nordstrom's is having a one-day sale," she said in an almost orgasmic voice.

"I can't. I have to go into the office for a little while and then I just need to relax after that." I didn't want to tell her that I was on a tight budget and would only be able to window shop.

"Oh, well, don't be mad at me if I get all the good merchandise," Jewel said.

"I won't. I'll see you tomorrow at church," I said.

What am I doing? This self-employment is starting to wear on me. I need something to motivate me. I'm falling into a slump. I'm tired of budgeting. Tired of not being able to shop. Tired, tired, tired!

I reminded myself that I'd just prayed.

The phone rang again.

Here we go again. I'm never going to be able to get out the door.

I let the answering machine get it.

"Lexi, it's me, Jermane. Pick up, *please*."

"What's up? You sound stressed."

"Yeah, I am, kind of. Lexi, Rex and I got into it last night."

"Really, what happened?"

"Well, I told you he didn't mind if I went out, but when I came in so late and had alcohol on my breath, he got really upset. I've never seen him like that before. And do you know what the wildest part is?"

"What?"

"That's the most reaction I've gotten out of him for the past year. I was almost happy that he was mad, because at least he was showing *some* emotion," Jermane said.

"He didn't try to hit you or anything, did he?"

"No, Rex would never do anything like that. He just yelled a little."

"Maybe he'll start realizing that he needs to spend more time with you."

"I hope so," she said.

"Last night was really a trip. I've never seen you act like that, Jermane."

"I know. I couldn't believe it myself. I was really out of order."

"Well, it's OK. We have to let our hair down every now and then," I said.

"Do you have time for a quick bite to eat?" she asked.

"Umm, for a friend in distress, yes," I said, remembering I'd just turned Jewel's shopping invitation down. "I was going to head into the office, but I can connect with you for a bit. Where do you want to meet?"

"The Java Stop."

"Sounds good to me. Give me about 20 minutes to get there," I said, looking at my watch.

"OK. See you in a minute, dear," Jermane said.

On the way, I felt a little guilty for accepting Jermane's invitation for lunch instead of Jewel's invite. But I just didn't have time for an all-day shopping excursion with Jewel. She lives for one-day sales. Between fighting the mall crowds and Jewel's limited conversation, I'd be worn out for sure. Besides, Jermane had some real issues. Time spent with her would be more constructive. I loved them both, but I had to be in the mood to deal with L'il Miss Shopaholic.

However, with Jewel it's been drama from day one. She and I first met in the financial aid center at Westwood. I walked in the office right behind Jewel. We both sat down.

I looked at her and thought I had her figured out before she opened her mouth. It was August, the hottest month of the year in Houston. Nonetheless, her hair, done in long sister curls, and her makeup were flawless. She had on a floral skirt, tight white tank top, and red sandals with a heel higher than I would've worn to law school. Plus her chandelier earrings were a little too much.

Oh, boy. Probably somebody's spoiled little daughter. What kind of clients is she going to represent?

Just as I was about to make conversation with her—only because I felt obligated—someone at the counter called out, "Jewel Whitaker, we're ready to see you." She got up.

About five seconds later, I saw Jewel's neck rolling and her finger pointing at the woman behind the counter.

"What do you mean my money isn't ready yet?" Jewel said. "Get me the financial aid director. I don't know what he thinks this is, but I'm paying his salary! I don't know why you people are going to make me act Black. This is stress I don't need!"

"Ms. Whitaker, calm down, please," said the lady behind the counter.

"Calm down? Calm down? I have no books, no money for rent or food, and I'm getting a migraine," she said as she dramatically placed her hand on her temples.

"Ms. Whitaker, it does say in the school financial aid packet that you should be prepared to pay for your living expenses by other means if your financial aid is delayed."

"If I could do that, I wouldn't need financial aid in the first place," Jewel said, staring the woman right in the eye and gritting her teeth.

"Okay, just please remain calm. We're doing the best we can to facilitate the process. Mr. Bronsen, the director, is taking names for appointments so you can find out the reason for the delay. The wait will be about an hour. In the meantime, we can give you credit at the bookstore to get your books. Once again, I'm sorry for the delay," she said in a less-than-sincere tone.

"Whatever. I'll wait, because *you* people *will* give me some financial aid TODAY!" Jewel said. She rolled her eyes and sat back down.

What a performance!

"Are you all right, girl?" I asked. Her eyes were watering.

"Yeah. I just don't need this extra stress."

"I know what you mean. I'm from out of town, and I wasn't prepared for this at first. Are you a second year, too?" I asked.

"Yes, one year closer to freedom. All my friends are working real jobs, having fun. I can't believe I signed up for all this stress. It is horrible for my skin," she said, pulling out her compact.

"It can get rough sometimes," I said.

She put away her compact and extended her hand. "I've seen you before. I'm Jewel Whitaker."

"I'm Lexi." I shook her hand.

We sat on that couch for about two hours waiting to speak with the financial aid director. By the time it was over, I felt like Jewel was a long-lost friend. She was entertaining. Underneath her wanna-be attitude, she had a good heart.

Even though she seemed ditzy, she was actually pretty smart. I eventually came to realize she just uses her brain a little too selectively at times. To this day, I can't figure out how she got one of the highest grades in Tax Law, one of our hardest classes, but almost failed research, which is a guaranteed *A* to most students.

My memories of Jewel faded as I pulled into the parking lot of the Java Stop and recognized Jermane's car. I walked in.

The Java Stop is a trendy coffee place where eclectic and eccentric people hang out. Mostly artists, musicians, and more mature students stop in for coffee and bagels. Jermane had already found a corner.

"Hey, bud," I said.

"Hello, dear." She greeted me with a light kiss on my cheek and a slight embrace.

Her eyes looked puffy, like she hadn't gotten enough rest the night before. Her face was bare, without her usual lipstick. Her normally relaxed look was replaced with a slightly wrinkled forehead.

Our waitress walked over and placed a basket of mini-muffins on the table. We ordered French roasted coffee.

"I'm so glad you were able to make it," Jermane said. She took a deep breath.

"No problem. So what's up?"

"Well, I think . . . Lexi, I really need to talk." She looked around as if someone might be trying to eavesdrop on our conversation.

"Lexi, I'm really starting to feel like I'm in this marriage alone. I don't want to give up on it, but I just feel like Rex has his priorities all wrong. I've never felt more alone in my life. He keeps saying that he's working so hard for us. Although I've been telling him how I feel, it just doesn't seem to register with him. It's like he's somebody else—not my husband. I know money is important to a certain degree, I mean for security and things, but I would give anything just to have my husband back."

I placed one of my hands on top of hers

"I just want us to spend time together," she continued, "to lie in the bed in the mornings and not do anything and just hold each other. My life is so routine, almost a drudgery. I'm tired of it!"

Her words were coming out fast, contrary to her usual perfectly paced diction.

She must've been holding this in for awhile.

"Have you thought about going to counseling?"

"Like a therapist? Lexi, we're not that bad off. We're not crazy. And I don't need some person I barely know in my business, trying to give me some textbook solution to my marital issues."

"I think a lot of people feel that way, especially Black people, because we're always taught to be strong and weather the storm," I said. "I don't mean to just talk to *anyone*. There are a lot of good counselors out there who have a strong spiritual foundation. Besides, they have to be confidential. It wouldn't hurt to try. I'm just sayin', it's an option."

"I guess I never thought seriously about it," Jermane said.

"Sometimes when you can't work out things within yourself or in a relationship, it may take an experienced third party to help sort things out."

"That makes sense."

The waitress brought our coffee over. I savored the morning medicine I always craved. In between sips, I caught the back of a waiter who somehow seemed familiar.

"Jermane, I think I know that guy over there. He looks familiar."

Jermane focused her attention toward a table a few feet away from us. His back was facing us. He was tall and muscular and had on jeans that were slightly worn with a white polo shirt. He wore the same multicolored apron as the rest of the employees. Almost as if on cue, he turned around and glanced at our booth.

"Oh, no! It's Black Zorro," Jermane said. "How is it possible we're running into him?!? God, I hope he doesn't recognize us."

I felt almost as flustered as Jermane. What were the odds that we'd casually run into a stripper on the day after his show?

He flashed a sly smile of recognition at us. Zorro looked like the type of man that could make a woman lose her mind. Some men just have that kind of appeal. It's like they release some kind of chemical that lets you know that they can make your body do remarkable things. It has nothing to do with merely being cute. Whatever it was, Zorro had it.

He didn't come over, sparing us further embarrassment. After we downed our coffee, we quietly slipped out of the café. I caught Zorro staring out the window at Jermane. She looked back as well.

I can't deal with any more drama. Rex is going to have to get on his job.

I thought about how sensible Jermane was and how much she loved Rex. For as long as I'd known her, I'd never seen her use terrible judgment. But I'd never seen her in a state like this before, either. I held onto my faith that she would do the right thing.

She's just going through a phase. Lord, help us all. When we're weak, you're strong.

CHAPTER SIX

A House Is Not a Home

Jermane paced back and forth as she stared out of the bay window. She turned around and cased the room as if she were a thief, trying to determine which prize to take and which to leave behind. She looked into the face of a Black woman that stood out on a painting on the wall. The woman looked as if she was one of the turn of the century's elite—regally attired in a crimson gown with a black hat and a large feather to top it off. She stood solemnly at the side of her man, who was dressed in a black pinstriped suit.

Jermane despised this picture, but never told Rex, who loved it. She decided that she would take it down, but later. She took off her shoes and fell backward on the sofa. As she sank deeper into the cushions, she realized that this was the first time she'd actually realized how comfortable the sofa was.

"Are you all right, Mrs. Richmond?"

"Yes, I'm fine," Jermane said, not looking at the face poking out of the kitchen. *When's the last time a maid wasn't around? They probably know all my business. They probably know Rex and I have no sex life, and I'm about to lose my sanity in this freakin' castle.* "Myra, you can take off early. Mr. Richmond probably won't be home anytime soon. You know his schedule these days."

"Oh, alright, Mrs. Richmond. I'll just cover up the food and leave you to relax." Jermane didn't bother to respond. She envied Myra's ability to have a life outside of the house. Jermane closed her eyes.

She went back to the night of the male strip show. She saw Black Zorro's face. Then she saw his body. A heavy presence engulfed her. She felt strong arms around her waist and gentle sweet caresses. She imagined him teasing her and blowing quick short breaths on her neck. When she woke up, she felt her forehead, then her neck. She was wet with sweat. As she got up, she felt unsettled about the images she'd dreamed about. She went to the bedroom to shower and change. With each drop of water, she tried to wash away her increasing desire for Zorro's touch. She slid between her satin sheets. The bed seemed more vast than usual as she tossed and turned with frustration. She finally fell asleep. Rex woke her several hours later.

"Hey, baby. I missed you today," he whispered as her kissed her on the neck and wrapped his arm around her waist. He pulled her toward his stomach.

Jermane knew that he was in the mood and wanted to work off his stress from the day. As fine as Rex was, she was turned off by his predictability. He'd been such a selfish lover lately, less concerned about her desires than his need. She needed tender loving care and caresses, not 15 minutes of wham-bam.

"Not tonight, Rex. I'm really tired."

"From what?" he asked in his properly educated diction.

"Never mind."

"What do you mean, 'never mind?' We haven't made love in two weeks. We used to . . ."

"I know, we used to make love every day. Yes, I know. We used to spend time together, too, before you and my father became joined at the hip," she said as she turned her back on him.

"Jermane, please don't start. You know my workload. I'm sorry I have to work weekends, but it's part of the job and . . ."

"And I hope it's worth sacrificing your marriage."

"What? What do you mean? You can't be serious! Is this what your behavior Friday night was about?"

Jermane felt tears well up in her eyes. She bit her lip, regretting what she'd said, but also glad that she'd said it.

"Forget it, Jermane. I'm tired anyway." He rolled to the other side of the bed and let out a big sigh.

Disgusted, she pulled the covers close to her chest and thought about Black Zorro until she dozed off.

CHAPTER SEVEN

Lean on Me

While driving to Etienne's with Jewel and Capri, I reflected on the sermon. I never thought that Pastor Graves and I would relate on the same subject so closely.

"Singles, it's OK to want a mate," Pastor Graves pronounced. "God will give you the desires of your heart. But you and your partner need to be equally yoked to the Lord. So if you meet the latest Ebony Man and he only goes to church on Easter and Christmas, there's a problem there. If you already have a relationship with God, you just can't marry anybody. You need someone who is going to be a blessing to your life, not someone who's gonna add strife . . ."

Easy for him to say when he's got somebody to curl up with at night. I wonder if he was celibate before he got married. Ugh. This is just

making me think about Reggie. Maybe I should've given him more of a
chance. Maybe I shouldn't have been so hard on him about church.

"Did you see the pastor in that suit?" Jewel asked,
turning up the radio.

"He's a little short for my taste, but he's a very
good-looking man. But wait a minute. We can't be
lustin' after the pastor now," I said.

"I just like the fact that he always lets people know
that his wife is the queen. I admire that," Capri said.

Jewel was bobbing her head and snapping her fingers to the music . . . *"It's gonna be a brighter day."*

"Kirk Franklin is so talented. I love this song," I
said. I began to sing the words with him. I turned up
the volume.

". . . Jesus, you're my everything . . ."

"It's so upbeat," Capri said. "Y'all, I'm so hungry."

"Me, too," Jewel said while reapplying her makeup.

"Hey, guess who Jermane and I saw at the Java
Stop?" I interjected.

"Who?"

"None other than the Black Zorro."

"You're lying!" Capri said.

"If I'm lyin', I'm flyin'."

"Ohmigod! What did Jermane do?" Jewel said. She
stopped applying her lipstick.

"Jermane tried to play it off. And girls, let me tell
you, he is even finer up close and PER-SON-AL!"

"Sop-you-up-with-a-biscuit type of fine?" Jewel
asked.

"Oh, yes," I said.

"Okay, enough lusting. It's God's day," Capri said.

"Forgive us, Mrs. Stanton," Jewel said.

"Excuse me, I told you I have no interest in any athletes. I don't care how good they look," Capri said.

"Oh, so you do admit he's fine," I said.

"Yeah, he's alright."

"Uh-huh," Jewel and I chimed together.

"So you're just going to forget about him?" Jewel asked.

"Thank God. We're at the restaurant," Capri said.

Once we made it inside, we sat down at the table and waited on Jermane and Angel. Antonio came over and gave his usual greeting. The place was extra-crowded today, mostly with folks coming from church. The room was warm, and the familiar aroma of bacon, waffles, and omelets teased my nose.

Soon Jermane walked in.

"Hello, all," Jermane said as she pulled her chair out and gracefully sat down. "Traffic was bad again today. Angel called and said she's right behind me."

"Ms. Jermane, what can I get you?" Antonio asked.

"A cup of espresso, please."

"Here comes Angel." Jewel waved to her.

As Angel walked through the door, I noticed she was dragging a bit. She usually had such a confident stride that it was easy for me to detect the small change.

Probably all the hours she's been working lately. Who am I kidding? Angel doesn't ever work too hard.

Unlike Capri, who put in overtime hours regularly, Angel put in extra time only when she needed to. As a lawyer for one of the big oil and gas companies, she was often in litigation over one environmental suit or another. She definitely handled her business, but wasn't worried about climbing the corporate ladder. She figured that as long as she was able to keep herself in designer bags, natural fabrics, and a luxury car, she was fine.

"Hey, ladies," Angel said as she sat down. "Sorry I'm late, but I didn't feel well this morning."

"You'd better take it easy," Capri said.

"Yeah, I had the worst cramps of my life. I know I'm getting older, but this is becoming unbearable. On top of that, I've been putting in extra time at work. My supervising attorney has been really on my back," she said. "Maybe I'm just stressed." She raised her hand to signal Antonio.

"Well, you'd better be careful. Bad cramps could mean several things in terms of your health. Don't just blow it off. Yes, you are a diva, but not invincible."

"Cute. Don't worry, I'm gonna get checked out. Octavio said the same thing," she said. Then she looked as if she'd just realized that she'd let the cat out of the bag.

"*Octavio?* Fine, young, Hispanic *Octavio*?" Jewel asked.

"Yes, *that* Octavio," Angel said.

"This is the first I've heard of him," Jermane said.

"He interned at my company a couple of summers ago. He works at a small firm here in town now."

"And . . ." Capri said.

We all leaned in.

"And nothing. We're good friends. He's not my

type. I only date Black men, and he's at least seven years younger than me. So that's it," she said.

"Yeah, right," Jewel said.

"Enough already. I'm gonna eat," Capri said, and then made a mad dash for the buffet line. The rest of us followed.

We cut all conversation as we moved through the line loading our plates with fresh fruit, omelets, waffles, Canadian bacon, blueberry pancakes, grits, and eggs. When we returned to our seats, after a few bites, we began conversing.

"So Jermane, heard you saw Mr. Zorro at the Java Stop," Jewel said.

I kicked Jewel under the table.

Jermane darted her eyes in my direction.

"Yes," she said. "I'd like to forget that little incident if you don't mind," Jermane said with her eyes focused on her plate.

"Alright, I'll give you a break. But it's nice to have someone else creating excitement here besides me for a change," Jewel said. "I cleaned up at the mall on Saturday. They had this 30-percent-off sale at Bebe's. Then I went to Nordstrom's and found these serious pumps," she said with pride and excitement.

"Jewel, do you know the meaning of the word 'budget?'" I said.

"You only live once, and I believe in making myself happy. I work too hard not to treat myself," Jewel remarked.

"You treat yourself every day," I said.

"Lexi, don't be mad at me because I have a steady salary."

"My day will come. I'd rather have my own business in exchange for a steady salary anytime," I said. "Besides, the way you spend, I'm surprised you have anything left out of your check by the time you've paid off all those credit card bills."

"Very funny. I manage my money very well, thank you," Jewel said

"All y'all talk about is clothes, money, and men," Capri said.

"And what else is there to talk about?" Jewel said.

"World peace, poverty, affirmative action . . ."

"*Please*, Capri you don't have to be so serious all the time," Jewel said.

"Well, you need to be a little more serious."

"What is this? Pick on Jewel day?" she asked, jumping out of her chair.

"Anyway," I said, "I was reading an article in *Essence* on celibacy . . ."

Everyone looked up. Jewel slid right back down.

"The article dealt with how women choose that route for different reasons: spirituality, cleansing and purification, preparation for a mate . . . I mean, it's an issue I've given a lot of thought about. Have ya'll?"

I waited for a reaction. Most of us were moving along our spiritual paths, but none of us has ever made a firm commitment about the issue of abstinence. Since I felt God was convicting me in this area, I was interested to see what everyone else had to say.

"Celibacy's possible," Capri said.

"Well, I think everybody needs to get some every now and then," Angel said. "It's human nature."

"It is human nature, but sex should be reserved for marriage," I said. "God originally intended it to be that way."

"OK, well, somebody needs to share that with these men out here," Angel said as she sliced her waffles with her knife.

I poured ketchup on my hash browns. "Well, ideally, if everyone was living like God wanted them to, it wouldn't be an issue," I said.

"If you find a man that will hold out before marriage, you need to bronze him," Angel added. "It's harder for men to control themselves."

"I guess if they're Christians and really rely on the power of God, it's possible," Capri said.

"A Christian? Yeah, right," Angel said. "Those are the main ones trying to get up your skirt."

"I know that one of my girls from college didn't have sex with her husband before marriage," Capri said, "and Jermane was a virgin when she married Rex. That's *really* deep to me."

"Yeah, Jermane, you definitely had a padlock on the panties," Angel said.

"Thank you for sharing my virginity with all of Etienne's."

"I guess it's better if you never had sex. If you haven't had it, you don't know what you're missing." I looked for someone to jump in to validate my feelings.

"True, true." Jewel stirred sugar in her grits.

"Jermane, what you and Rex experienced is something to be proud of," Capri said. "Think of how many women gave their stuff away for the first time to some fool they wouldn't be caught dead with today. When you wait for a spiritually grounded man who knows the purpose of intimacy, you have a great foundation. I'd love that type of spiritual relationship. That's the way it's really *supposed* to be, but unfortunately, it's the exception."

I was surprised at her comment. Capri never talked too much about relationships. As close as we were, I only knew of one man she was ever in love with, her high school boyfriend, Tyrek. They practically grew up together. He was her best friend and they were supposed to get married. But I'm not sure what happened to him or the relationship because she's always refused to talk about it. I figured she must've been hurt very badly.

"But what's the point of all this talk anyway," Jewel exclaimed. "Who's celibate?"

"Jewel, we didn't say anyone was celibate. We were just talking about the *idea* of not having sex before marriage," I said.

"Too late for all of that," Jewel said.

"It's not too late. God holds us accountable for things we learn through His Word. Once we have that knowledge, He expects us to change our behavior." I was trying not to sound too preachy.

"Girl, this is the new millennium. God understands. If we wait too long, our stuff will have dried up by then," Jewel said as she rolled her eyes. "Besides, if we don't do it, somebody else will service these men."

She does have a point. What were the chances of finding a man that strong? Besides, doesn't God forgive sin?

"Hey, ladies, are you enjoying your meal?"

I looked up and saw the now-familiar Mr. Stanton towering over our table.

"Hi, Tony! How are you? The food is simply marvelous," Jewel said. She gazed at him as if he were going to be the next item on her plate.

He did look extremely attractive in his navy blue suit and red-and-blue striped tie. Those smooth-as-butter lips were soooo distracting. *Capri, what is up with you, girl?*

"Capri, how are you?" he said.

"Fine," she said, barely glancing his way.

"Well, I guess I'll see you all again soon, if I'm lucky. By the way, here are some passes for the start of next season. I hope to see you ladies there," he said.

He handed the passes to Jewel, the most obviously eager one at the table, and walked away toward the buffet.

"Brother has it going on!" Jewel said as she stuffed the passes in her Fendi bag.

"Please, he's just a man," Capri said.

"Did you see that broad chest and the way he smiles, not to mention the fact that he looks like he can handle his business," Angel said.

"Angel! My goodness," Jermane said.

"Capri, when's the last time you had some?" Angel continued. "You better stop playing hard to get before you don't get got. Now's the perfect time. They're out of the playoffs."

Jermane let out a soft chuckle.

"Stay out of my business," Capri said.

"Angel, you're so concerned about the physical," Jewel said.

"I call them like I see them. You all are, too. You just don't have the nerve to say it," Angel said. "A man can look good all he wants to, but if he can't do anything for me in the bedroom, what's the use?" Angel said, pulling out a cigarette.

"Must you light up those death traps?" Jermane asked.

"*Excuse me*, miss. I'm going to go outside for a minute." Angel grabbed her purse and got up.

"Lexi, don't look now, but there's your partner Terrance," Jermane said discreetly.

"He is not my partner. We're just sharing office space," I said.

"Hello, how are you all?" Terrance asked. "Lexi, you need to check your messages at the office."

"I will," I said.

"Everyone at this table is looking so beautiful—I'm not surprised at the company you keep, Alexis. I guess I'll see you in the office bright and early on Monday," he said, and walked off.

"Girl, you know that man wants you. Stop trying to play hard to get," Jewel said.

I rolled my eyes. "Forget you, I'm not desperate."

"You should keep your options open. It's not like you're seeing Reggie anymore," Jewel added.

God, I'd forgotten I'd told her.

"What happened?" Capri asked with a look of concern.

"Another one bites the dust," Jewel sang.

Lord forgive me, but I'd really like to smack her.

"I'm fine, ya'll. It wasn't a big deal. I just realized we weren't on the same path spiritually, like Pastor Graves said in his sermon this morning. Plus, Reggie only wanted to hang when he wanted sex, and I wasn't trying to hear that. But I'm fine. It wasn't a big deal, so I didn't want to bother ya'll with it."

I thought I sounded convincing. They didn't seem worried.

"Like I said, that's all the more reason to look into that Terrance. You could work with him if the money is right," Jewel said. "He dresses nice and . . ."

"Let me cut you off right now, 'cause we're not even going to go there," I said.

"He would probably make a good husband. He's neat. And he seems nice," Jermane offered.

Angel returned from smoking her cigarette.

"Y'all are not hearing me. He has *no* sex appeal and *no* chemistry."

"Well, maybe you could work with him," Jewel said. "But on second thought, no sex appeal? No chemistry? Yeah, you'd better pass. If you marry a man like that, someone who has to 'grow' on you, you'll wake up one morning in bed and ask yourself 'What the heck was I thinking?' Then you'll be trying to find some chemistry somewhere else."

Jermane shifted in her seat. "Come on, leave Lexi alone."

"Yeah, let's just drop it."

"So, Jermane, are you going to have a rendezvous with old Zorro?" Jewel asked.

"What Rex doesn't know won't hurt him," Angel added.

"I would never think of cheating on Rex. Whatever problems we have can be worked out. Cheating's not the answer to *anything*," she said.

"I agree Jermane," Antonio said over our heads. "More coffee, ladies?" We nodded. He poured.

"Problems," Jewel said with a frown. "What problems could you be having? You have a fine, rich husband, a huge house, excellent credit, a housekeeper, and you take trips to exotic places. What more could you want?"

"It's the simple things in life that mean the most," Jermane said. "I don't want to get into it."

That was Jewel's cue to shut up. For once, she took it.

I looked at my watch. "Well girls, I've got work to do," I said as I took my last sip of coffee.

"Yep, time to be out," Capri said, patting her stomach.

"Capri, you eat all the time and never gain weight."

"Jewel, don't hate. It comes natural, baby."

"Okay, I'll give you that. But if you don't get with the program, someone's going to snatch up Mr. Stanton. He's one of Houston's most eligible bachelors," Jewel said.

"Well, it won't be you," Capri said. "I think he's at least intelligent enough to know a gold digger when he sees one."

Jewel shut up again.

Capri gave Tony a quick glance on the way out, but

he didn't see her. We walked outside and exchanged hugs. Jermane agreed to take Jewel home, while I would take Capri.

"Lexi, give me a call when you get home later tonight," Angel said.

When we reached my car, I noticed a note attached to the windshield.

"Capri, there's a note for you," I said.

"What? Let me see," she said.

She opened it, read it, and almost put it in her purse, but let it fall to the ground instead, where it was left floating in a shallow puddle of water.

"What was that?" I asked.

"Just a note from Mr. Stanton."

"I don't understand you Capri. He seems decent. You need to give him a chance," I said.

"Lexi, you really don't get it. Just leave it alone for now," she said.

"Alright, but you need to ease up. Life doesn't have to be so serious," I said as we got in the car.

"Yeah, yeah, yeah."

I dropped the subject, started the engine, and drove out of the parking lot.

I generally love the serenity of Sunday nights, but these past ones had been too quiet. There'd been too much time to think, too much time to worry, evaluate, and wonder. Sunday evenings were becoming a prime time for me to go under.

I was stretched out on my couch, still feeling warm and lazy from my bath. I rolled up in a fetal position and took in the silence. I tried to recall the last time I felt loved and cared for.

Mom's birthday is coming up soon. I wish I could touch her, feel her hugs, and tell her that I love her. Lord, I'm giving so much out, but nothing's coming back in. What's the use. Nothing's going to make me feel that type of love again.

I suppressed the threatening depression and stretched my legs out again. I grabbed the radio remote and turned to my favorite station. *The quiet storm . . . not tonight.*

The phone's ringing saved me from my heavy mood. I grabbed the receiver and hoped that someone was calling with a problem that would take my mind off my own.

"Lex, hey, it's Angel. What're you doing?"

"Just relaxing. What's up?" I asked.

"Umm, just needed to talk. I'm feeling a little run-down. You always have something positive to say. I guess I'm a little depressed."

Girl, me too.

"Hey, it happens to the best of us."

"I just feel kind of blah, like my emotions are getting the best of me. I'm tired of these corporate games. Then, on top of that, I haven't been feeling my best self lately."

"Have you gone to the doctor?" I asked.

"No. I'm kind of scared to go. You know they always find something wrong with you," she said. "If something's wrong, I'd rather not know. But it'll be time for my annual exam soon."

"Angel, you can't let fear rob you of your health. It's your responsibility to take care of yourself. Please don't take your health for granted. You know I'm gonna worry until I hear you went and got yourself checked out."

Angel paused for a few minutes. "So Lexi, let me ask you something. How do you do it?" Her tone sounded as if she'd been holding in the question for a while.

"Do what?"

"Stay so freakin' up all the time. I mean, I'm such a mess. We all have our problems, but you still remain up."

"Me? Up all the time?" I said. "Please girl, you should see me around here sometimes. I've just made up my mind that I'm not going to accept defeat. I want heaven right here on earth. Besides, if I didn't have God in my life, I don't know what I would do. It's a daily thing, 'cause there's always some challenge around the corner.

"Believe me, I have my days," I continued. I suddenly realized that now was my time to do some informal preaching to Angel. "I try my best just to focus on God's power because I know I can't make it by my strength alone. Sometimes I do struggle, but I try my best to put it all in God's hands. I try to confess His words. Philippians 4:13 says, 'I can do all things through Christ, who strengthens me.' It's not His will for us to live defeated and depressed. We often get that way when we put our trust in the wrong things, and those things either disappoint us or get taken away. But God relieves."

"Hmmmm. Lexi, I've never been a very spiritual person. Honestly, it's just so hard for me to believe. Religion was never a big thing in our family. I always thought that when you had money, all your problems would be solved. But there's been . . . I don't know how to put it . . . it feels like something's missing, like there's an emptiness inside of me," Angel said.

"God can fill that void," I said, surprised at how much of the Word was inside of me.

"Lexi, I've always felt so much in control of my life, like no one or nothing could control me. But lately I've been feeling like I want somebody to take care of me."

"Angel, you've been so independent since your divorce. It's OK and natural to feel vulnerable and needy every now and then. That's fine," I said.

"I guess. It's so hard for me to connect with people. Maybe that's why it's difficult for me to get back into a relationship. Trusting someone with this heart is tough."

"Girl, you know not many men deserve that type of trust. But with love, you have to take chances. You have to open yourself up to love while being wise about who you allow into your world and if they can accept your strengths and weaknesses. And remember, Angel, God loves you. You're special to Him. He loves you the way you are."

"I don't know. It seems like you have to be perfect

to be a Christian," she said. "And I ain't trying to be a hypocrite."

"God meets us at the place where we are right now. He allows us to grow in His grace and knowledge. He never expects us to be perfect. That's why we have Jesus Christ."

"Honestly, Lexi, I'm still not buying all of this. There's a lot of stuff I don't understand."

"Then come to church with me," I blurted.

"Well . . . maybe one Sunday I'll go. But your church sounds so big and overwhelming," Angel said.

"Just visit once. I promise, it'll be worthwhile."

"I'll think about it. I'm going to get off this phone. It's getting late. Lexi, thank you. I really needed a listening ear. I'll call you sometime this week."

"Oh, alright. I hope I helped."

"Yeah. Yes, you did. Talk to you later."

Angel had never sounded like that before and had never allowed me to talk to her about God without quickly changing the subject. I was worried.

Two of my friends were going through changes. I started to wonder if any of us were truly happy. What is true happiness anyway?

It was all starting to feel too deep, too heavy, so I decided to go to bed early again. Once I got to my bedroom, I grabbed the white fluffy teddy bear I'd gotten for Valentine's Day one year and buried myself underneath the comforter. *I'm almost 30 years old and sleeping with a teddy bear.* Part of me didn't want to grow up. I didn't want bills or responsibility. I didn't want to go to work every day. I wanted to be held, spoiled, and suffocated with love.

Then I thought about what I'd told Angel about God. I put in CeCe Winans's album *Alone in His Presence*. I wanted the soft music to fill the air. Following my own advice, I started confessing scriptures. The last words I heard before I dozed off were *"His strength is perfect . . ."*

CHAPTER EIGHT

If at First You Don't Succeed . . . .

apri, there's a delivery for you at the receptionist desk. Shall I send them up?" her assistant,
Amelia, asked.

"Yes, I guess. I didn't order anything. Is it an express package?"

"No, not quite."

"Well, OK, send it up."

"Now what could this be?" Capri mumbled to herself as she tried to recall anything she should be expecting. The deliveryman soon appeared at her door.

"Ms. Capricia Sterling? I have a delivery for you.
Can you please sign here?"

"Oh, yes."

The pink box stood about three feet high and was
about three feet wide. She opened the box.

"What? I don't believe this . . . ," she muttered as a

bundle of multicolored balloons floated to the ceiling. There was a card in the bottom of the box.

From what I've seen so far and from what little I know, I'd like to know more. Give me one chance and you'll never regret it.

Yours in Christ,

Anthony M. Stanton

"God! Men are even using Jesus as part of their rap now!"

Then she looked at the balloons and smiled on the inside. After a slight pause, she stuffed the balloons in the box and pushed them in the corner. Then she grinned.

I'll at least take them home. It's a sweet gesture, but he won't be knocking on these panties.

CHAPTER NINE

The Scoop

Lexi, Capri is on line one," Ms. Hobby said.

"Hey, girl, what's going on?" I asked as I jumped up and shut my office door.

"Hey, you'll never guess who sent me what today?"

"What? You know I'm not good at guessing," I said.

"Your friend, Mr. Anthony Stanton, sent me a balloon bouquet."

"Whaaaaaat? Capri, girl, don't blow this. What is up with you?"

"Calm down. I'm starting to get the impression that he's not like other pro athletes, but he is a man."

"*And . . . ?*"

"Well, Lex, it's complicated. I'm just not one for long-term commitment."

"Who said anything about marrying him. Just go out on a date with the brother."

"Well, I just don't know. All that attention he gets, no privacy—it's just not me. You know I'm low key except for when it comes to handling my business as a lawyer," she said. "Uh-oh, gotta go! Boss-man's ringing. I'll call you."

She hung up.

"Darn, just when it was getting good," I said as I hung up the phone.

I saw Terrance pass by my glass wall and got an instant attitude. He was always sneaking around, trying to get in my personal business.

Not in a million years. He's cool to share office space with, but he's a bit overbearing. Besides, we have absolutely no chemistry. Chemistry is very important.

CHAPTER TEN

The Closer I Get to You

Angel sat in the pale blue chair rubbing her hands together. She reached in her purse for a cigarette, realized where she was, and pulled out a stick of gum instead. She looked around the room. Following the protocol of the other patients, she buried her head in a magazine. She was nervous.

Angel hated having her annual exam because she feared they'd find something wrong. But over the past year, her cycles were becoming extraordinarily painful. Sometimes her cramps would be debilitating. She hoped it was just age.

She thought of Octavio and their plans for an early dinner after her appointment. She started to feel a little more relaxed.

Since her divorce, Octavio was one of the few male

friends she had. There were other men in her life, but she would only bother with them when she wanted to have sex. Octavio was different. They laughed and chatted freely. She was sort of his mentor. She started fidgeting.

What if something is really wrong? Maybe God is punishing me for not going to church. That's just like God, interrupting a good thing. You could be minding your own business, living good . . . and boom, He drops a bomb on you!

"Ms. Capers?"

A medium-height woman with mousy blond hair scanned the room.

"Yes, that's me," Angel said.

"Yes, how are you today, Ms. Capers?" the nurse asked in a somewhat rehearsed but sincere tone.

"I'm alright."

"Will you step back here?"

After the nurse weighed her and took her urine sample, Dr. Parish finally made her way to the room. She listened to Angel's heartbeat and began probing. Angel then assumed "the position" and stared at the ceiling. Although this was routine by this point, Angel had never really gotten used to it.

"So, how have you been feeling?" Dr. Parish questioned.

"For the most part, I'm doing fine."

Dr. Parish gave her a look.

"Ms. Capers, if you don't let me know what's going on, I can't help. Like I tell all my other patients, 'You know your body better than anyone else.'"

"Well, over the past six months my cramps have

been almost unbearable. I've had to take a day off of work during my last two cycles. I've never felt this much pain during my period."

"Hmmm, well, don't panic yet. Our bodies go through many changes. We'll see what your Pap smear says. If you need more testing, we'll do that. Are you more tired than usual?"

"Yeah, all the time."

"Have your periods been longer than usual? Any constipation?"

Angel nodded her head twice.

"Hmm. Well, could be fibroids, but we'll see. For now, try not to worry."

"Fibroids?"

"Yes. Fibroids are tumors that actually appear quite frequently among Black women. Sometimes there are no symptoms, but based on your answers to my questions, that may be the issue. Have you been under a lot of stress lately?"

"A little more at work."

"You haven't stopped smoking yet?"

Angel hesitated. "I'm cutting back."

"Angel, again, until we know for sure, try not to worry."

"I won't. I'm pretty healthy. I haven't had any major problems. So I'll just wait to hear from you. But what if I do have tumors?"

The doctor took a deep breath. "Depending on how bad they are, there are a number of treatments. Sometimes we do hormone treatments, but in severe cases, a myomectomy or hysterectomy is necessary."

Angel tried to take this all in. "Wow. That sounds extreme."

"As I said, Angel, let's wait until we get your lab work back before we hit the panic button, okay?"

"Yeah." Angel felt unsettled. *Hysterectomy? No, everything is just fine.*

"Alright. As soon as we get your results, we'll give you a call. In the meantime, try harder to cut back on the smoking."

Angel slid on her shades and jumped in her car. She dodged through the city traffic and headed toward the freeway to get downtown. She put the doctor's appointment behind her and thought about Octavio. She noticed how warm it was for the wintertime. She turned her air conditioner on low and tuned into 90.9 KTSU to hear a little jazz.

Angel parked her car and decided she would relax in the nearby park since she was early. After walking across the grass, she sat on a bench close to a huge waterfall. A slight mist from the water sprinkled her face.

She noticed a couple sprawled out on a blanket, hugging and kissing.

Please, get a room.

Then more couples and dogs paraded by. She smiled as a husband and wife with two toddlers strolled by. There was lots of carefree laughter. But loneliness deflated her body. She felt numb and tried to remember the last time she felt joy.

A child's little red ball rolled over and bumped

against her shoe. Angel held the ball just so she could look into the eyes of the child who ran to her to retrieve it.

*A*ngel studied the menu as her hunger pangs grew. She'd skipped breakfast because she was nervous about going to the doctor. Just as she looked up, she saw Octavio standing at the door of the restaurant.

The Backdoor Bourbon Street was their favorite eatery. They always craved its Cajun-style Creole food and looked forward to each visit there. The waiter pointed in the direction of her table.

As she watched Octavio walking toward the table, he appeared to move in slow motion. She also noticed other women staring at him. She'd thought he was attractive, but thought of him more as a little brother. But seeing him today stirred something inside.

His skin was a deep, dark olive, baby smooth. His black hair was slicked back and blended seamlessly into his black mock turtleneck. Clad in cream-colored pants, he had the sexiest walk and a smile that complemented his thin moustache.

"Hey, Angel," he said as he sat down.

"Hey, bud," Angel said. She rewound her mind to friendship mode.

"You look good," he said, bending over to gaze at the entirety of her outfit—a white Lycra camisole and a black pants suit.

"I do? You're tripping," she said. "You know what you're going to order?"

"You know, my usual, blackened shrimp and dirty rice," Octavio replied.

"I think I'll have the same."

"So what's up, Angel? Talk to a brother."

"First of all, you're not a brother," she retorted.

"Here we go. Well, *excuse* me. Anyway, what's been going on in your world?"

"Well, nothing really, just wanted to get out," she said.

"No, something is going on. You've been too quiet lately," he insisted. "Remember, we go back a little ways."

"You think you know me so well. Remember, you're just a baby."

"Be careful who you call a baby now. I'll show you how much of a baby I am."

"Anyway," she said, "I've just been feeling a little tired lately. I had a checkup today."

"Are you ready to order?" a tanned, collegiate-looking woman said.

She smiled at Octavio the entire time she took their order. She said she'd return quickly with their appetizers and drinks.

"Is everything alright?" he asked.

"Yeah, just a routine checkup."

"If you say so. If you need me, I'm always here."

By the end of the meal, both the food and the conversation had been satisfying. They caught up on work. They laughed about the days when Octavio was Angel's intern and reminisced about the last time they'd hung out—the Brian McKnight concert at The Woodlands.

They both agreed that their work had taken over and vowed to hang out more.

It had gotten dark by the time they walked out of Bourbon Street. It was a beautiful night. Angel wasn't ready to go home yet. She wasn't ready to face the demons in her house, to feel the negative thoughts that constantly bombarded her at home. She didn't want to be alone.

"Wanna go to the park?" she asked.

"This time of night? Don't you know people are crazy?"

"Okay, well . . . let's go hear some live music!" Angel said.

"What's up with you? You're so hyped."

"Nothing. Let's just go."

"Alright, but I'll pick the place. There's a new club called the The Red Cat Jazz Café. It's supposed to have an all-girl jazz band playing tonight."

"Is it in walking distance?" Angel asked.

"Yeah, but let's take the horse carriage."

"OK."

As Angel sat next to Octavio at The Red Cat, she felt a little protective. She almost felt like he was her man. He usually acted like he was, but until now, she would ignore his advances. But tonight, she was excited that his chair was so close to hers.

The club was dimly lit with blue lights as the women on stage finessed their way through song after song. The music was so sensual that she almost found herself

110   N O R M A L . J A R R E T T

in a daze. She felt sexy, serene. She sipped on her wine. Octavio rested his hand on her thigh. She eased her fingers in between his. It felt natural to hold his hand. She knew he felt comfortable, too.

He looked out of the corner of his eye and slightly leaned his body toward her. They said nothing and just felt the pulse of music massaging their bodies. When the set was over, Octavio grabbed her hand and wouldn't let go until they finally reached her car. It began to drizzle.

No umbrella.

Octavio stared directly into her eyes. Her back was pressed against the car. He grabbed both of her hands and gently squeezed them. The drizzle turned into rain. He released one hand and reached out to let the rain touch his fingertips. He began tracing Angel's lips with his moist finger. They remained silent.

Angel felt like a teenager. She wondered what it was like. She wanted to taste. She just stood there.

He lightly ran his finger down her camisole. She closed her eyes, not caring about the rain or whether anyone was passing by. He slid her jacket back so that he could touch her arms, then gently pressed against her. She said nothing as she closed her eyes and saw tiny stars. She felt herself reaching around his waist.

The rain began to tickle her nose. His firm hands finally grabbed her tiny waist. He hugged her and began to softly kiss her neck. She had never felt this way before. He stopped and placed his hands on her face and looked into her eyes. She could barely look at him.

"I'm not playing," he said as he directed her gaze

toward his. He took his hand and smoothed her hair back from her forehead.

He kissed her then, softly first, then deeper. They kissed passionately for what seemed like hours. At that instant, Angel felt like someone blew the breath of life into her. She knew then that she *was* alive. She knew that something in her life was about to change—dramatically.

CHAPTER ELEVEN

Sacrificial Praise

Lord, they say we can be honest in our prayers. You're my father and my friend. Sometimes I feel a little depressed, right before that time of the month. There are times when I lie on this couch and literally feel something pressing down on me. I'm scared. It seems like I always get close to the blessing, but just when it seems like I get close enough to grab the brass ring, something or someone snatches it away.

Sometimes I get tired of praying so much for everyone else. Whenever I pray for someone, it seems like You move immediately. Lord, why do You say yes to everyone else and no to me? I work so hard, for so little. Haven't I been faithful? Haven't I been paying my tithes? I see people who don't even go to church and life seems so much easier for them. How can I keep on encouraging others when I want to give up myself?

I hate being late for church.

I looked at my watch quickly. I was fifteen minutes behind schedule. I hoped Capri would save me a seat. I got in my car and tilted my rearview mirror so I could put on my chocolate mousse lipstick. I smoothed out my black slacks and hung my suit jacket on the back of the passenger side headrest. I started the car and was en route.

To pump up my mood, I turned on the radio. I switched to Power 97.5 to hear some gospel, but the music was slow and painful. The lyrics said something about *"going up the rough side of the mountain."* I quickly clicked off the radio and opted for my Frankie Beverly and Maze greatest hits CD instead. I felt a bit back in stride. I slipped on my shades and started to bob my head to "Happy Feelin's." I felt upbeat.

After a couple of songs, I switched to my Chante Moore CD. She sounded like a songbird, singing about love, the kind that you could feel deep down. I imagined myself in a music video, a diva, dressed in white on a stage glowing with lights.

Doing a complete reverse, I thought about how confined I felt when I was practicing law. I felt so conservative, so bland.

I wanted to be up again, so I slipped in Destiny's Child and went full throttle with "Independent Woman." I was pumping my fist in the air as they yelled *"Throw your hands up with me,"* when I noticed the church was only two blocks away. I quickly switched back to the gospel station. I parked and walked briskly toward the sanctuary.

Once inside, I sat behind Capri and Jewel and happily anticipated the sermon because I really needed to be lifted. I felt old and tired. Capri seemed at peace and totally focused on the music. She was always focused in church. It was like she was having a test on the sermon the next day. Jewel, as usual, appeared distracted, too busy scanning the room for potential dates.

The sermon was powerful. Pastor Graves talked about how we should praise God in the midst of our trials. He talked about the meaning of a sacrificial praise, which is when worshippers give Glory unto God despite their rough circumstances, which is why it's a sacrifice. He encouraged us to praise God, even when our feelings tell us to do otherwise. I felt utterly convicted about my lack of praise during the rough times.

The soloist sang "*I need you now . . .*," the lyrics from a song by Smokie Norful, right before the invitation to join the church. The song was really slow. The choir member singing the solo was so emotional, I felt every note. Suddenly, I was drawn into his world. I felt every pain, every disappointment and failure.

"*Not another minute, another second . . .*" I thought I was alright, but before I knew it, one tear trickled down my face. Then another. I began crying loud and hard. I covered my face with the palms of my hands. The woman next to me handed me a tissue. I couldn't believe it. I couldn't stop crying. I didn't know why. The woman rubbed my back lightly and prayed for me.

Capri and Jewel said nothing, but kept looking back to see if I was OK.

*G*irl, what was up with you at church? Was that the Holy Spirit or what?" Jewel said while lifting her glass of grapefruit juice to her mouth. Capri nudged her.

"I'm not sure," I said nervously. "All of a sudden I felt this deep emotion. It was like I had no control. When I stopped crying, though, I felt like a thousand tons had been lifted off my shoulders."

"Deep," Jewel said.

"Is anything wrong?" Capri asked.

"No. I think maybe it's just that time of the month," I said in a low voice.

"Hey, you Holy-Rollies," Angel said as she strolled up to the table. She was looking sharp as ever.

"Angel, why do you have to be so disrespectful about attending church?" I said.

"Please don't get out your oil and try to anoint me. I'm just playing," she said.

"Guys, I have an announcement," Jewel said.

Angel rolled her eyes. Capri frowned. I sighed.

"No, really. This is a real big step for me. I have decided to put myself on a budget."

"Yeah, right."

"No, really, right after this sale at Neiman's. I vowed that after the bagel slicer I recently ordered, I'd watch my money more closely."

"Jewel, I have two words for you—credit counseling," Capri said.

"Madame Capri?" Antonio slipped her a note.

"What does it say?" Jewel said.

"Mind your business."

"I bet it's from Tony Stanton. Capri, you haven't given that man any play yet?"

"Don't be so obvious," Capri said.

"Well, you're going to be sorry one day. It's not like you're all that," Jewel said.

"Stay out of my business," Capri warned.

"Where's Jermane?" Angel asked.

"She called and said she wasn't feeling well and would catch up with us later on in the week," I said.

"How are she and Rex doing?" Angel asked. "I told you he wasn't all that. He's probably cheating on her."

"Just because your marriage didn't work doesn't mean that all men are dogs."

"Jewel, you're too young to know any better."

"I beg your pardon?"

"Ya'll stop. I honestly don't think he's cheating, but his work hours are really a strain on Jermane," I said.

"Yeah, but there's not that much money in the world. He has a wonderful marriage. He needs to be careful. There are so many men in my firm who never spent time with their families and now they're divorced," Capri said.

"Well, I wouldn't mind," Angel said. "As far as I'm concerned, a man is only good for two things—his wallet and, well, I'll leave the rest to your imagination since I know you all have delicate ears. I learned my lesson. All men cheat because they're too greedy. You just have to play the game."

"I can't do it," I said. "I'm too tired for all of that. I still have hope."

"Keep hope alive, sister," Angel said as she raised her right fist.

CHAPTER TWELVE

Giving a Brother a Chance

As everyone walked out to Etienne's parking lot, Capri glanced at the note.

Meet me by the restroom at 2:30 p.m., please. A. Stanton.

She folded it and put it in her purse.

"You guys, I need to use the restroom. I'll catch up with you later on in the week," she said, stopping in her tracks.

She walked slowly to the restroom area, inconspicuously looking at her watch. It was 2:35 p.m. Tony came around the corner.

"Well, hello. How are you?"

"Oh, I'm just fine," she said as she nervously twisted the gold pearl ring her grandmother had given her.

"Do you mind sitting here for a minute to talk?" he asked.

"Just a minute. I need to go do some work," Capri replied.

"You're so stern. Do you ever relax?"

"Yes."

"Well, I finally get to have a few minutes of your time."

"Oh, by the way, thank you for the balloons."

"You're welcome."

They stared at each other. Capri suppressed a smile.

"You're an attorney, so I'm not going to play games or insult your intelligence. I'll try to be direct. I would like to go out with you if you can reserve an evening."

"Well, I guess that would be alright."

"Now was that so difficult?"

"No, it's not that. It's just that I stay so busy with work, I don't really have much time to enjoy myself."

"I understand, but life is too short. You have to take time for yourself."

"I suppose."

"So what do you like to do?"

"Mmmm, well . . ."

"Tell me. I'm flexible."

"I, uhm . . . Oh gosh. Fine. I'll just tell you. I like Disney movies."

"What?"

"Disney movies. I like Disney movies. You asked."

"Hmmm. I guess I can come up with a plan," he said. "How about this Friday evening?"

"How about Saturday?"

"Alright, Saturday. I'll call you and give you the details."

"So I guess you want my phone number?" Capri asked.

"That would help. Man, it's like pulling teeth with you. We're going to have to do something about that," he said. She wrote down her home number on her business card. He slid it into his wallet. "I believe on the inside of that hard exterior is a very warm, compassionate person."

He stared at her again. Capri caught herself looking into his eyes for an instant. But then she realized she hadn't gazed into a man's eyes since Ty and quickly looked away.

"Well, I have to be going. It was nice talking with you, Mr. Stanton."

"Don't be so formal. Please call me Tony."

"Good-bye, Mr. Stanton," she said as she grabbed her purse and raced out of the lobby.

CHAPTER THIRTEEN

Reality Check

Jewel jumped up in response to her blasting alarm clock. She looked at the time and realized she must've hit snooze twice.

"I'm late *again!*"

She jumped up, rushed in the shower, and got dressed as quickly as possible. *I'm definitely not going to call ahead. I don't feel like hearing Melvina's mouth.* Just as she was about to walk out the door, the mailman brought her a certified letter. She signed for it, quickly scanned the outside of the envelope, and tossed it on the couch.

I bet I bounced another check.

In the back of her mind, she knew she was running short on funds this month. She could take back that pants suit she'd bought two weeks ago since it still had the tags on it. That would cover at least two of her checks and the bank fees. She just didn't want to ask any of her friends. She already owed them money and didn't want any lectures, particularly after her declaration about being on a budget.

"I just like to treat myself well," she said to herself as she sped along with the traffic.

Then she looked over to the right and almost swerved her car into a ditch. It was the deliveryman Kevin. He looked at her, shook his head, and motioned her to get off the highway.

"What the . . . ?" she mumbled. "I'm already late."

Jewel followed his truck to the exit and into a gas station. She pulled alongside him and they both got out.

"I'm flattered. You almost had an accident for me," he said with his arms folded.

"Please. I just happened to recognize you and it caught me off guard."

"So, where are you headed?"

"Work," Jewel said.

"Hmmm, either you have flextime or you have it like that," he said, trying not to stare at her chest.

"Well, I do sort of have it like that," she said.

He started to swing his arms back and forth. "So, here we are, two people . . ."

"Yeah, yeah, here's my number," she said as she reached into her wallet and pulled out a preprinted card with her personal contact information on it.

"Now this is really tripping me out. Don't you think this is a little presumptuous? Anyway, Ms. Whitaker, I'll let you go."

"Alright, because I really need to get to work. They

can't seem to function without me," she said as she got in her car.

She put on her shades and whipped out her cell phone. Kevin watched her speed off and laughed to himself. He took the card and slid it in his wallet. He shook his head and jumped into his truck.

Jewel slid past her supervisor's door. Just as she was about to ease into her cubicle, she heard a loud and piercing voice.

"Ms. Whitaker, may I please see you," the voice blared.

Darn!

Jewel slowly rose from her half-seated position and walked toward the door of her supervisor, Melvina Jefferson.

"Ms. Whitaker, please, have a seat."

She sat in the chair directly across from Melvina. As she watched her dark brown nostrils flare, Jewel tuned out the familiar sermon.

"Jewel, what is your problem? You have two degrees and still can't manage to get yourself together. There are others here who are dependent upon you. If everyone else can get here on time, so can you."

Jewel sat still and stared at this healthy woman dressed in African garb with salt-and-pepper braids. Although Jewel respected her supervisor, at this moment she wanted to bless her with a familiar finger gesture.

Suddenly, Jewel was out of excuses. Suddenly, she

realized she was broke and addicted to shopping and generally late to work.

"Is that *clear*, Ms. Whitaker?"

Startled, Jewel snapped back into reality.

"Uh, what was the last thing you said?"

"I don't believe this. Ms. Whitaker, if I have to speak to you one more time about your tardiness, you will be out of the job that didn't exist in the first place. You're on probation for the next two months."

Jewel took a deep swallow, nodded, and fought back her tears. She couldn't believe how weak she felt at that moment. As she slowly wandered back to her cubicle, she felt insignificant, like a child who could never do anything right. It was the same feeling she had back in law school when professors would call on her. She'd generally give some off-base answer. She felt like sliding under her seat.

When would she ever be taken seriously? She thought about Jermane, who was sweet, sophisticated, worldly, and rich; Lexi, so solid and dependable; Capri, smart, no-nonsense, with business savvy; and Angel, independent and tough. And then there was Jewel Whitaker: the shallow, spoiled, immature one.

The more she thought about it, the worse she felt. Just as she was about to turn into her cubicle, she went in the opposite direction and briskly walked to the restroom. Once inside a stall, it all came out. She put her hand over her mouth to muffle the sound of her sobs. After crying for five minutes, she felt a little better, but her spirit was still troubled.

She eased out of the stall, relieved that no one had

come in. She fixed her makeup, then walked back to her cubicle, and began the paperwork that had accumulated on her desk since the morning. She vowed that this would be the day that she would become more responsible than she'd ever been.

CHAPTER FOURTEEN

The Mark of Zorro

ermane rolled over and turned off the alarm clock. She ran her hand through her hair and covered her eyes. "Monday just rolls around too fast," she said as she let one leg fall from underneath the covers.

She turned around and saw the other side of the bed was empty. She looked at the clock. It was 7:45 a.m.

"Rex, are you in the shower?" She felt the warm moist air from the shower that had traveled into the bedroom. The dampness of the air was scented with the cologne she'd purchased for Rex when they vacationed in Paris. She noticed the cotton boxers that had been left on the floor without regard. Rex had already left.

She lifted her head halfway up and decided she'd just lie there. She reminisced about the times when she and Rex would make love in the morning, how he'd snuggle his nose behind her ears and grab her waist and pull her close to him. He'd taught her everything she knew about sex.

She realized Rex must almost be at the office. She vaguely remembered the light kiss he planted on her forehead before he left and smiled faintly. She tried again to convince herself that marriage was about sacrifice and that she needed to be a little less selfish.

After she showered and dressed, Jermane made a grocery list for Myra. She grabbed her books and her shades and slid into her Mercedes.

She didn't feel like herself. Before she pulled out of the garage, she checked herself in the rearview mirror. She removed her tortoise shell headband and ran her fingers through her hair like a comb to let it swing loose. She was beginning to look more and more like her mother every day.

She noticed how crisp her white buttondown shirt was. For as long as she could remember, her shirts were always starched to perfection. She opened a couple of the top buttons. She noticed how snug her slim-fitting khakis were. She opened her pillbox purse that was tied with a silk patterned scarf and pulled out her burgundy lipstick, but then stopped and put it back in her bag. As she looked at the lizardskin brown belt that wrapped her waist, she felt disgusted by her conservatism.

She breathed, took a moment to compose herself, put on her shades, opened the sunroof, and zipped out of the garage as soon as the door was high enough for the car to escape. As she was driving down the highway, she decided to get off at the next exit and head toward the Java Stop. She convinced herself that she merely wanted a cup of coffee and a pastry before class, since she needed to read anyway.

Jermane sat in the parking lot of the café and stared into the rearview mirror again. She started tugging at her clothes and checking her makeup. "Just an innocent cup of cappuccino," she reminded herself.

She opened the car door and slid out in her normal graceful manner. As she walked toward the door, she inconspicuously scanned the window for Black Zorro.

"Jermane!"

Startled, Jermane turned around. Standing about two feet away was a stout man wearing a cowboy hat, seersucker suit, and white shoes. A cigar hung from his mouth, and smoke wafted around his slightly sunburned pink skin.

"How is my gal doing?" he said in a voice Jermane had always hated.

"Oh, I'm doing just fine, Judge Randall," she said.

"You have grown up to be such a princess. How's that father of yours?"

"Daddy's fine."

"It's been a while since I've seen him. The last elections I believe. Your daddy's a fine man. Too bad there aren't more like him," he said as he wiped his forehead with a handkerchief. "He's a very upstanding citizen. How's that Rex of yours?"

"Oh, he's fine."

"I've always admired that young man's work ethic.

Ever since he clerked down at the courthouse, I've had nothing but respect for him. You done good with that one. Then again, he hasn't done badly, either."

"Yes. Uh well, I need to go. Just stopping in for a quick cup of coffee," Jermane said.

"Yeah, I just stopped in to get the Missus some of those, uh, what do you call 'em, those passion muffins. I guess you could say she's got a passion for 'em. Heh heh. The woman sent me all the way down here for some muffins. Well, I'd best be off," he said as he tipped his hat and waved his bag.

Jermane, relieved, headed into the café and sat down, happy her conversation with Judge Randall was over.

"I'll have a cup of cappuccino and a passion muffin," Jermane said to the waitress who came over.

"Surely. Will be up in a few minutes."

"Oh, miss, is there a . . . oh well, never mind." She frowned. She didn't have the guts to ask about Zorro.

It was for the best anyway. What would it have looked like, considering she was married?

Jermane had decided that she wasn't going to class. She would go see Lexi at her office or take in a movie. There was a new romantic comedy out she hadn't seen that looked hilarious. If she waited for Rex, she'd never see it.

As she was about to take the last bite of her muffin and close the book she was attempting to read, she noticed a man walk briskly into the backroom of the restaurant. He came back out.

It was *him.*

She tried to look down at her book. He looked back toward Jermane. Jermane looked up, and their eyes locked.

He started to walk over. She wanted to hide under the table.

"Well, hello. How are you, lady?"

"Hi," she said as she quickly looked around.

"How's your coffee?"

"It's very good."

"Do you mind if I sit for a moment?" he said hesitantly.

"Oh, uh sure, I mean no, have a seat," she said.

"So, how's your day going?"

"Oh, just fine," she said, and looked at her book.

"Hmmm, let me see. Law student?"

"No, I already have my law degree. I'm working on my L.L.M. That's the degree after law school. I want to . . ."

"You want to teach. My sister's a lawyer," he said, and gave a half-grin.

"Oh, I didn't mean to insult you," Jermane said. "So, are you working today?" She wanted to stare at his buffed golden-brown chest peeking through his red tank top, but she didn't. She wouldn't.

"No, just came to pick up my first piece of check. I just started a few days ago. I go to school part-time and dance at night."

"Oh, what kind of school?"

"Visual arts. I'm in an interior design program."

"Oh, that's great! Maybe . . . maybe you can redo one of the rooms at my house."

She immediately looked downward again, embarrassed—and stunned—by her remark.

"Anytime," he said, staring at her hand. "That's if your husband doesn't mind."

Jermane was silent.

"Well, it was nice talking with you," he said. "I'm on my way to class. I work at the café during the afternoon on Tuesdays, Thursdays, and the weekend."

"Oh, yes, well, the next time I'm here on one of those days, I'll ask specifically for your services, oh, I mean you," she said. He grinned.

"You do that. Oh, and my real name is Naegel, Naegel Foster, though you can call me Black Zorro if you like."

Jermane giggled.

"Nice to meet you, Naegel. I'm Jermane Richmond."

"Jermane. That's unique, for a woman. It's beautiful on you. I wouldn't expect anything else."

Jermane noticed the whiteness of his teeth and the prominence of his cheekbones. He was an Adonis. She swallowed and shifted in her seat. His eyes made her uncomfortable. She felt like she was drowning in a pool of hazel water. This man was so sexy, she couldn't stand it. No man besides Rex had ever made her feel this way.

"Take care," he said, then walked away.

Jermane was terrified, paralyzed. She looked down yet again. She found herself smiling at her passion muffin.

CHAPTER FIFTEEN

Drama Alert

aw office," I said while in the middle of research on my computer.

"Lexi, this is Jermane."

"What's up?"

"I need to talk to you, dear. 911 emergency. Can't
wait."

"Go ahead. I'm just doing some research. Aren't
you supposed to be in class?"

"Yes. Well, I guess I can talk here."

"Where are you?"

"In my car on my cell phone. Guess who I just had
a conversation with?"

"Who?"

"Black Zorro," Jermane said.

"Jermane, I cannot take any extra drama today. It is

too early in the week," I said as I froze in the middle of my research.

"I know, but you're the only one I can talk to. I saw him at the café."

"Yeah, but aren't you supposed to be in class?"

"Yes, but I just decided to take a break today."

"Must be nice."

"Lexi, I don't know what's happening to me."

"Jermane, don't put yourself in any compromising situations," I warned. "I know you love Rex. You're going to have to talk things out with him."

"Lexi, I've tried. I feel so unattractive and useless right now."

"Jermane, please, you're beautiful. Men fall out all over you."

"It's not the same. I can't describe it."

"Jermane, all I'm going to say is don't do something you'll regret. You have a beautiful home, husband, and . . ."

"And what? What about my own needs? I have always been in the background for someone else. Rex doesn't appreciate me. He thinks work is the most important thing in the world. Lexi, I am miserable."

"OK, just relax. I'm not saying you don't have a right to feel the way that you do. All I'm saying is don't do anything stupid. You have too much sense for that."

"That's just my problem. I'm sensible Jermane, always doing the right thing. I feel like I'm about to explode. I'm having fantasies and crap, and I can't take it anymore."

Whoa, drama alert! Is this Jermane I'm talking to or Jewel? "I thought you and Rex had a great sex life?"

"We used to. He's just tired all the time. When we do make love, he only stays up long enough to satisfy himself."

"Gosh," I said.

"Lexi, I know that maybe this seems hard to understand since you're not married . . ."

Alright, rub it in. I know you're going through it, but can a sister be a little more sensitive?

". . . but nobody seems to pay me any attention. I feel like I'm invisible."

"I do know how that feels. I'll tell you what. Why don't we have lunch Thursday and talk more about it. This sounds really serious."

"It is. I have a better idea. Let's go to the day spa and make it an afternoon."

"Why do you and Jewel have to always take things to another level?" I said, still fixated on the computer screen.

"Come on, my treat. We'll get the works," Jermane said enthusiastically.

"Well, I guess that's an offer I can't refuse," I said. "Let me check the calendar right quick . . . I'm free after 1:30."

"Alright. I'll see you then!" Jermane exclaimed. We hung up.

Why does everybody rely on me for the answers to their problems? One day I'm just gonna explode . . . Jermane is married and still has more options than I have. I can't even attract the type of man I want to be around. I've got some issues.

CHAPTER SIXTEEN

Firm Foundation

C apri sat at her desk, trying to remain engrossed in a summary judgment on an employment discrimination case. She was losing concentration. She stood up and looked out the window of her office at the Houston skyline. She took a deep breath and continued to stare. Some would say she'd already made it, but she was waiting for the day when she got to run her own practice before calling herself a success.

She thought about Anthony. All she could do was smile. *He's just too sexy for his own good.* Her smile grew wider. *I know millions of women would love to be in my shoes. But I'm gonna play it real careful.*

Then she thought about Ty, or Flip as they called him. Just thinking about his name made her touch her heart and feel engulfed in sadness. She thought back to when she was seven, to the day when she found out her parents had been killed. She couldn't conceive of such a thing. Then Flip had been taken away from her as well. She shook her head.

Young, handsome, a basketball star . . . One stray bullet . . . We were supposed to make it together, God. Lord, Anthony is Flip . . . How can you ask me to love again?

She'd made a vow to wear a breastplate over her heart for as long as she could. No one, and she meant no one, was going to hurt her.

Her intercom buzzed.

"Ms. Sterling?"

"Yes?"

"Richard Levinson has asked me to tell you that there will be a small meeting in his office today at 3 o'clock. He said you need to readjust your schedule, no matter what it is. Your attendance is mandatory."

"Levinson?"

"Yes."

Whoa, he rarely includes me in a meeting. "Sure, I'll be there."

"Very well. I'll forward the message."

Capri put her hands on the side of her face and did a mental check. She began wondering why one of the head partners wanted to see her. As far as she knew, she hadn't dropped the ball on anything. She was caught up on her entire caseload. She had more than enough billable hours. She began pacing back and forth, rubbing her forehead.

"What the heck could they possibly want? This always happens. No matter how good you are, they'll eventually find something."

She looked down at her calendar. The message for the day said, "The Lord is my light and my salvation; whom shall I fear."—*Psalms 27:1*

She stopped in her tracks and said a silent prayer.

God, I know You wouldn't have brought me this far to leave me. Lord, I realize I'm not perfect, but I've tried to be diligent, as if I'm working for You. I don't know what this is about, but bring peace to me right now. Help me to trust You. Send angels of peace to surround me right now so I may continue my work. Thank You. Amen.

She felt calm and assured. She glanced at the clock. It was 1 p.m. "This is going to be a long two hours," she said as she sat in her chair and resumed her work. She still felt a little uneasy.

Time flew. She looked at the clock. It was 2:50 p.m. She decided she would start moving toward Levinson's office. Since his office was near the top floor, it would take a few minutes to get there.

By the time she got off the elevator, Capri felt more curious than nervous. She walked up to the receptionist desk.

"Ms. Sterling, Mr. Levinson said to send you right in," the receptionist said as if she had rehearsed their brief encounter.

She turned the corner and knocked on the door. She heard several voices as the door opened slowly. Then the room became very quiet.

"Come in, Capricia," a short bald man behind the desk said.

"How are you, Mr. Levinson?" she asked as they both reached for a handshake at the same time. She noticed there was only one other woman in the room,

Sarah Applegate, one of the two female partners at the firm. She couldn't figure out if Sarah was on her team or not. Sarah appeared to have taken Capri under her wing, but like everyone at the firm, she was careful whom she trusted.

The rest of the partners all had plastered grins on their faces and were probably as anxious as Capri to get this meeting over with.

"Please have a seat, Ms. Sterling," Mr. Levinson said. "Now, I know you're wondering why you've been called to this meeting."

"Yes."

"Well, I'll get right to the point," he said. "I want to congratulate you."

"Congratulate me?"

"Yes. First, for your hard work on the Technoforce copyright case. Second, Fast-Trak Sports has decided to retain our firm for several future business ventures. Your work was an integral part of the deal."

"*My work?* But I didn't do that much. Just a few contracts and transactional work here and there."

"Yes, but the powers that be at Fast-Trak specifically mentioned you."

"Wow. I'm stunned."

"Do you remember Etta Henderson?"

"Yes. I sat with her at a fundraising luncheon a month ago."

"Well, she remembers you also. She was very impressed with your background and how well you spoke of the firm. She's general counsel at Fast-Trak."

"I remember."

"She also had a little something to do with this," Mr. Levinson said. "Ms. Sterling, if you continue this type of activity, we may have no choice but to put you on our accelerated track to be one of our youngest partners. Fast-Trak is a sizable client."

Capri sat there, stunned and overwhelmed. "I don't know what to say," she said in an uneasy manner.

"Don't say anything until you see that bonus in your next check," another partner said.

Capri swallowed and just remained speechless.

Everyone in the room walked over to shake her hand. Slightly paralyzed, she was only able to raise her arm up and down in a slightly robotic manner. Then there was a knock on the door, followed by a man rolling in a silver cart with champagne and a large cake. It had Fast-Trak's logo on it.

Capri tried not to get caught up, but for a moment she felt pretty good. After a toast was made and a few pieces of cake eaten, Capri felt like it was time to make her getaway.

"Uh, Mr. Levinson, I need to get back and finish up some projects."

"Always thinking about business, Capri. You need to take a break sometime. We can't use any burned-out attorneys. Besides, you have enough billable hours to lend to a few of these other associates."

Capri slightly tilted her head back and gave one of her "firm laughs," then smiled.

"No, truly, sir, I have to get back to tie up some things before I go."

"Alright, I guess we can let you go. Oh, by the way,"

he said as Capri walked toward the door, "we're having a small cocktail party at Fredrico's in about three weeks with several attorneys and other Fast-Trak people. I'd like to see you there. You'll get an e-mail soon," he said, peeking out over his glasses.

In other words, another mandatory meeting.

"Sure, I'll look for the invite. Thanks again," she said as she made her exit from the chamber.

"Congratulations, Ms. Sterling," the receptionist said with slight enthusiasm.

"Oh, yeah, thanks," Capri said, focused on the elevator button. "Thanks a lot."

Capri stepped into the elevator and wondered what had just happened. She felt so relieved to be in the elevator, alone. Her heart resumed its normal pace. She looked in the mirror and realized she was starting to get caught up in the firm life. She was starting not to despise the partners so much. She liked her desk and the view in her office. And then, on top of all this, she had the nerve to actually bring in a top client, or start "rainmaking," as the partners called it.

She felt like she was losing her principles.

Something has to change. I'm winning at this game and I don't like it . . . or do I?

CHAPTER SEVENTEEN

Touched by an Angel

Angel opened the door to her condo and rushed to turn the air conditioner on. No matter what time of the year it was in Houston, it felt like summer. The first thing she did was remove her stockings. Even though she always wore stockings and garters instead of pantyhose, she always felt a great relief when they came off. She sorted through her mail and noticed a letter from the doctor's office.

Probably a statement of my bill. I'd hate to be poor and sick in this country.

She decided to go to the refrigerator and pour herself a glass of wine before she read the letter.

"We have been trying to contact you to schedule another appointment . . ."

Once she read the letter, she placed it on her coffee

table. She assured herself that it was nothing too serious. She grabbed the bottle of chilled Chardonnay and stretched out on the sofa.

She removed her damp red lace bra. The phone rang, as if on cue. She looked at the caller box to see if she wanted to be bothered with whomever was calling.

"What's up?"

"Hey, girl. What you doin'?" Lexi said.

"Just got in. Like I said, I've been working pretty late hours lately."

"Well, I know that feeling. At least you get a regular check."

"Getting a regular check is cool, but I have to answer to several people. Right now, they are *all* on me," Angel said, feeling the pressure even as she spoke. "I think they know I could care less about all this political crap. I just want to do my job and go home," she said as she positioned her feet up on the couch and grabbed the remote.

"Yeah, I hear you."

"Lex, remember when I told you I went to the doctor's the other day?"

"Yeah. You are alright, aren't you?"

"Well, I suppose so. They've been calling me but I've been too busy and tired to get back to them. Then they sent me a letter that said Dr. Parish wanted to discuss my Pap smear results. I'm supposed to call them to set up an appointment for further testing."

"Hmmm, well everything will be alright. Don't panic. I'll be praying for you."

"Is that your answer for everything?" Angel asked, sounding somewhat irritated.

"Yes, as a matter of fact, I guess that is my answer for everything," Lexi said with conviction.

"Well, whatever. You and your faith thing," Angel said. "Have you ever called one of those psychics?"

"Psychics? Girl, no! That's not from God!"

"Here we go again. It's not a big deal. It's all in fun. Some sound legitimate, like they know what they're talking about."

"Yeah, the enemy knows us well, too, and he uses people," Lexi said.

"The *enemy*? Really, Lexi, you're really starting to get weird," Angel said.

"Well, just promise me that before you call a psychic, you'll call me first and we'll talk about it or pray."

"Alright, if you insist. I promise," Angel said. "Anyway, I would love to enlighten you with more stimulating conversation, but I need to get some rest."

"Before you go, what are you doing Wednesday?" Lexi asked.

"I don't know. What's up?"

"Jermane and I are going to Ladies and Gents Salon around 1:30 p.m."

"Well, first of all, some of us work all day," Angel said sarcastically.

"Angel, please. You know you find time to get those toes done and eyebrows arched when you want to," I said.

"Yes, but I told you my supervisor has been checking

on me lately. I don't know what the deal is, but they've really been in my business. Besides, Lex, even if I had the time, I wouldn't want to spend it at any bourgeois establishment that Jermane or Jewel hangs out at."

"Angel, I know *you* of all people are not talking. Anyway, if you change your mind . . ."

"I won't. But I will let you know what happens with the doctor."

"OK. I'll see you at brunch if we don't hook up before then," I said.

Angel continued to rest on the couch, switching channels with her remote even though the television was on mute. She'd brought files home with her but refused to go near her briefcase. She refused to worry about work or her body. She switched to a channel that had a tall, good-looking Black man in a tailored suit moving quickly back and forth across the stage.

Not another religious fanatic. He's probably made a fortune off of weak people calling in making pledges for some miracle.

Just as she was about to turn the channel, the man pointed at the screen. She released the mute button to hear what he was talking about.

"Do you need to be made whole? Do you feel like there's a void in your life that needs to be filled? Come to Jesus. Come, just as you are. God knows we're not perfect. If you just come, He'll get you right. If you knew that today would be your last day on earth, can you honestly say you would go to heaven? Don't let another moment pass by without surrendering your life to the Lord!" the excited preacher shouted.

Angel watched as people came down the aisle—some

crying, some running, others in hesitation. She listened and wanted to change the channel, but she didn't press the button. The man's words pierced her body. Something wasn't right in her world.

She quickly turned the channel to *BET* and watched music videos until she dozed off. An hour later, the phone rang.

"Hello?" Angel said in a semi-groggy voice.

"You sound out of it. Want me to catch you tomorrow?"

"Octavio?"

"Yeah, baby, it's me."

Baby? Oh yeah, I forgot. I am his baby now.

"Hey, what time is it?"

"8:30."

"Wow. I didn't mean to doze off for that long," Angel said.

"Are you OK?"

"Yeah, yeah, boy. I'm hungry," she said as she wrinkled her forehead.

"Get that frown off your face," Octavio said.

"How do you know I'm frowning?"

"I just know," he said.

"You think you know me so well."

"I do. So, do you want to get something to eat?"

"You know if I hook up with you tonight, I'll have a hard time getting up in the morning for work," Angel said.

"Can't come out and play because it's a school night?"

"Very funny."

Angel felt good until she looked at the doctor's envelope on the coffee table.

"Well, if you can't come out, I'll come over," Octavio said insistently. "How about some of Drexler's barbecue?"

"This late? I can hear my stomach crying."

"Well, what do you have a taste for?"

"Umm, how about some salad or pasta," Angel suggested.

"Sweetheart, I need a meal."

"Well, barbecue is fine. Whatever you want. I just won't eat a lot," Angel replied. "Oh, but they do have some great cheesecake. Could you get me a slice?"

"Sure thing. I'll be over in about half an hour," he said. "And make sure you call the security people downstairs. It's like Fort Knox trying to get up in that ivory tower of yours."

"Just get your behind over here with the food."

"Alright, sexy. See ya."

Sexy?

Angel jumped up and into the shower in what seemed like one movement. She lathered herself with perfumed soap gel and washed her face. She got out, applied papaya lotion all over, and rubbed petroleum jelly on her dark maple-colored shoulders and knees. She moisturized her face and put on a hint of makeup. She applied some moisturizer to her hair and brushed it slightly, giving herself a mental pat on the back for choosing to cut her hair. She got so much more attention with shorter hair. Octavio loved it.

As she was getting dressed, she remembered the

stockings and garter left in the middle of the floor and reminded herself to pick them up before Octavio got there. She slid on her jeans and a black tank top with thin straps. She remained barefoot, wanting to expose her French pedicure. Finally, she brushed her teeth and freshened her breath with mouthwash. She lit a few scented candles and turned on her old-school Sade CD. She relaxed as the timeless lyrics of "Your Love Is King" oozed into the room.

She walked back to the mirror and looked herself over. She did a half-turn and noticed how her jeans hugged her hips. *A twenty-two-year-old has nothing on me!*

The intercom rang. She walked to the door and told the doorman to let him up. She felt a nervous excitement inside her stomach. If this had been any other man, she would have him over without any emotional attachment. Octavio was different.

A knock at the door caused her heart to jump slightly.

"Hey, baby," Octavio said as he slid through her door.

"Hey, how are you doing?" Angel said as she grabbed one of the bags from his hands. She walked to the kitchen, placed the bag down, and grabbed some plates.

"This smells good. I'm famished," she said.

Octavio was paying no attention to what she was saying. His eyes were focused on her waist. Then he noticed the slight cleavage that peeked from her black tank top. He was turned on by the simplicity of her outfit. Everything fit just right. He loved the way she moved.

She was tough, yet tender. She had a hard edge, but
would soften at the right word or touch. He knew how
to handle her, but wasn't about to let her know that.

"Octavio!"

"Yeah?" he said, trying to camouflage his thoughts.

"Didn't you hear me? I said how did that deposition
go today?"

"Deposition? I don't want to talk about that now."

Angel thought that if she kept the conversation on
work the atmosphere wouldn't be too uncomfortable.
She was fooling herself. She looked at Octavio and noticed again how fine he was. And he always made her
feel beautiful.

It was the opposite with her ex-husband. He always
made her feel like she was never good enough. "WHY
ARE YOU WEARING THAT OUTFIT . . . THAT HAIRCUT
MAKES YOU LOOK OLD . . . YOU CAN'T COOK . . ."
Thoughts of his loud, harsh voice still pierced her,
even now.

Octavio couldn't take his eyes off Angel. She was
trying to pull out a couple of trays to put the food on
and he jumped up and grabbed them for her.

"Thanks," she said, trying to ignore his body rubbing up against hers.

"This is Sade?"

"Yeah," she said.

"I love her. She is such a beautiful and sensual
woman. I wish she would make albums more often,"
Octavio said.

"Yeah. I love her music, too."

"So are you," he said, licking his already moistened lips.

"So am I what?"

"You're beautiful and sensual, too."

"*Anyway*," she said coyly.

Angel sat down next to Octavio and admired his casual elegance. He had on a pair of khakis and a white Banana Republic T-shirt with brown leather mules. As they began to eat, Angel grabbed the remote and turned on BET's *Comic View*.

"This guy is hilarious," she said as she felt barbecue sauce drip down her chin.

"Angel, look at me," Octavio said softly.

Thinking he was going to kiss her, she froze.

"You have barbecue sauce on your chin," he said as he grabbed a napkin.

Just as he was about to wipe her mouth, he grabbed her chin and placed his lips over hers. Then he lightly kissed around her mouth and licked the barbecue sauce. His mouth soon found his way back to hers.

Angel couldn't believe the intensity of their kiss. She wanted to fight it so hard, but felt like all she could do was surrender. Angel felt his hands move softly and gracefully along her shoulders down to her hands. Her shoulders went limp to his touch. Then his right hand glided to the very top of her tank. He started to sigh, sweetly, softly. She melted.

He slipped off the thin straps that graced her shoulders. They could hear the faint laughter of the *Comic View* audience. While continuing his maneuvers, he grabbed the remote and tried to turn the television off, but clicked the mute button instead.

He kissed the top of her forehead and then moved around to her ears and neck. He grabbed her jeans, she jumped slightly.

"What's wrong?" he asked as he stopped immediately.

"Nothing."

"Well, don't interrupt me when I'm working," he said with a smile.

"It's just that . . . you're freaking me out," she said. "You just make me feel *so* good."

"Isn't that the whole point?"

"I'm just scared."

"Of what?" He rubbed his forehead.

"Of losing our friendship."

"Angel, I can't continue to just be your friend. I have tried and tried, but I'm extremely attracted to you. No other woman turns me on like you do. You have something special, and we have the friendship on top of it. You have to admit, this kind of chemistry doesn't happen every day."

"Octavio, I just don't want it to be like this."

"Like what?"

"Just bump and grind and there you have it. With us, it's different."

"Different. How?" he asked.

"Well, I think if we start having sex, things will get all deep. Then things will start to get too emotional. I just can't take all that right now."

"Angel, do you realize most women spend their en-

tire lives looking for a chance to fall in love with someone who will love them back?"

"I know, but the last time I truly loved someone, it
hurt beyond words."

"You're talking about your ex-husband again. He's
truly making my life miserable. Let him go!"

"Look, you just don't understand. Things always
start out good and . . ."

"Angel, I care about you. Why is that so hard to accept? It'll be impossible to run me off, unless you do
something ridiculous."

"Okay then, we won't have sex. Just eat your barbecue."

"You've got some issues," Octavio said as he turned
up the television.

"I never said that I didn't want to," Angel said.

He scanned the channels, found a late-night car-
toon. They ate in silence for a few minutes.

"Well, I guess I better let you get some rest for tomorrow," he eventually said.

"What?" Her heart jumped at the thought of him
leaving.

"Yeah, I'd better go."

"See what I mean?" Angel said, as she grabbed her
cheesecake and placed a forkful in her mouth.

"What? You were the one who said you had to get up
in the morning?" he said.

"Well, you can stay. I can make you a place on the
couch. Just stay," she softly pleaded.

Octavio looked into her eyes and saw the little girl
that Angel worked overtime to hide.

"Alright. I don't know about this couch stuff, but I'll try. Let me go downstairs and get my overnight bag."

"Overnight bag? Aren't we sure of ourselves!"

"Like I haven't spent the night with you before," he said as he walked out the door.

"Yeah, but this is different," she said as she noticed how firm his behind was.

Angel looked at the clock. 3:15 a.m. She couldn't sleep. She just lay in bed, looking at the ceiling. She slowly eased from under the covers to go to the bathroom. She didn't want to wake Octavio up. Then she quietly walked into the kitchen to grab some juice and began to walk to her room. She stopped and looked at Octavio lying on the couch. He had one leg hanging from under the covers. His hairy calf caused her to pause. She placed her glass on the counter and moved closer. She noticed a half-smile on his face. *Whatever he's dreaming about must be good.*

She stood there a little longer, then leaned over and kissed him softly on his lips. He woke up, but didn't move. The only light was from the bathroom down the hall. She lifted up her white satin gown, climbed on the couch, and straddled Octavio's body. She began to sprinkle him with featherlike kisses. He wrapped his arms around her back. Soon his legs embraced her, too.

"I don't think you realize how beautiful you are," he

said as he took in the silhouette of her body with his eyes.

She got up and grabbed his arm. He stood, then lifted her from the floor, and carried her to the bedroom. He lowered her onto the bed, and she released his neck. Once under the covers, they kissed, tenderly and passionately.

Suddenly, Angel stopped and rolled over.

"Babe?" he whispered in her ear, then wrapped his arms around her, and pulled her close to him.

"Yeah," she said slowly.

"You OK?"

"Yeah." She closed her eyes and felt the warmth from his skin.

He rubbed her shoulders, deciding not to press her. He squeezed her a little tighter.

For Angel, his touch was subtle reassurance. Octavio understood she just wanted to be held, touched. She rolled over and lay her head on his chest. As she dozed off, a peace and security she'd never felt lulled her to sleep. For the moment, they were both satisfied.

CHAPTER EIGHTEEN

Letting Off a Little Steam

I saw Jermane's car pull up, so I grabbed my tote bag and got out the car. She was wearing blue jeans, rare for her, with a starched white shirt and a silk Chanel scarf tied around her neck.

Just like Jermane. She even dresses up jeans.

I threw up my hand to get Jermane's attention as she stepped out of her car. She waved back and walked toward the entrance. Jermane was obviously very comfortable walking into the lavish salon. I tried to look like I was a regular.

Quite frankly, for all this money, I could probably make my own treatments at home. That Essence *article had great tips on how to make all natural scrubs. I could get some brown sugar, honey . . . but I guess I'd miss out on the ambiance.*

The salon was actually a huge, renovated Victorian house. I scanned the lobby with its chic decor. Golden pillars framed black-and-white tilework. Small ivory statues were perched on pedestals and huge mahogany doors surrounded the front hallway.

The who's who of Black Houston made it their business to come to Ladies and Gents on their lunchbreaks to get their shoes shined, beards trimmed, manicures, pedicures, and massages. There was a hair salon, massage parlor, health bar/café, and even a barbershop and cigar shop. It was becoming a trend for men to get facials and massages now, and I couldn't help but notice all the fine brothers who had stopped in for grooming. Women serviced the men and men serviced the women, unless otherwise requested.

The host came out to greet us.

"Good afternoon, Mrs. Richmond. How are you today?"

"Just fine, Julian," Jermane said.

"And you Madame?"

"Oh, I'm fine," I said.

"What will we be having today, Mrs. Richmond?"

"A purifying body mask, facial, and full body massage."

"And you Madame?"

I hesitantly looked at Jermane and remembered this was her treat.

"I'll have a manicure, facial, and half-body massage," I said.

I still wasn't used to the idea of a full body massage. Since I'd been holding out on the sex thing, I was extremely sensitive. It could really be *très* embarrassing.

After we signed in, the host came down with white

terry cloth robes and towels. We headed for the parlor and dressing room. The men's salon was to the left. It was packed, with a hint of cigar smoke in the air.

A short distance away, I could see people in the health bar/café sipping flavored coffee, shakes, and smoothies. I made a mental note that I would indulge in a health shake before I left.

After my facial, I felt like a ton had been lifted off my face. I ran my fingers over my skin.

Didn't think all this junk would make a difference. My skin does feel kinda soft and clean. Guess I have to reconsider the home remedy stuff . . .

"What's next?" I asked with the enthusiasm of a child at an amusement park.

"Steam room," Jermane said.

"I thought the massage was next?"

"I figured we can relax and talk first," Jermane said.

"Alright," I said, recalling this venture had a purpose.

I sat in the steam room and felt like I was in the opening scene from this old television show *Sisters*, where four sisters would sit, sweat, and philosophize about life.

"Lex, I've been feeling weak," Jermane said, looking at the ceiling.

"Are you sick?"

"No. I mean I feel like I'm losing self-control," she said.

"Jermane, you're probably just going through a phase."

"Call it what you want, but someone had better take me seriously, and soon."

"OK, OK. I see this is a cry for help. What's really going on? I know you're not talking about the stripper."

"Naegel."

"Who?"

"His name is Naegel. Naegel Foster."

"Jermane, be for real. All these years you've seen millions of attractive, successful men, and now all of a sudden you're turned on by some fool in a Zorro costume. Do you not realize how ridiculous that sounds?"

"I'm serious, Lexi. I don't know what it is," she said, lowering her voice, seemingly forgetting that we were the only two in the room.

"Did you go out with him?"

"No."

"Phew, thank God. There's hope for you after all. What do you even know about him? What has he said to make you think you should risk your marriage over gyrating hips?" I asked.

"I can't explain it. It's not even about that. We have this unexplainable chemistry. I felt this heat when he stood near me, this intense rush in my body. And his eyes, they are so deep . . . Rex has never made me feel that way."

"*Never*? Come on, Jermane, you're in love with Rex. Ya'll used to be inseparable."

"Please, Lexi. Yes, Rex used to make me feel like that . . . but this is different. Besides Zorro, I mean

Naegel, seems so attentive. I can't describe it. I can't put it into words . . ."

"Let me help you. It's called LUST, Jermane! You know, sin! The big scarlet letter . . ."

"Come on, Lexi, seriously. It's not exactly that. I'm just telling you how I feel. I don't plan on acting on my feelings."

"I'm serious. There's no way you can justify having a sexual relationship with this man."

"I just said I haven't done anything."

"Yes you have. You've thought about it, and that's where it starts. Temptation begins with a thought. First there are subtle acts, then big acts, and the next thing you know—BA-BOOM! Everything just blows up in a big explosion and . . ."

"LEXI! I get your point. Calm down. I just don't know what to do. I'm lonely and I'm frustrated. I'm depressed. I don't feel like doing anything. My father has taken over my husband and my life . . . again."

I tried to think of something to say. This was big. I'd never dealt with this type of issue.

Lord, please help me to help Jermane.

"Jermane, all I know is you have to be strong, God is on your side. You know marriage is in His will. I don't know Jermane, when you're married, does it really mean you'll feel good all the time? You took those vows, remember?"

"Just because I'm married doesn't mean I have to put up with everything Rex does. You just can't relate to what I'm going through. Just because you'd give anything to be married doesn't mean you can say a few

magic words and everything will be OK. It's just not
that simple."

Well, just stab my heart with a dagger and twist it around. The
nerve of her . . . I'm taking a whole afternoon off to listen to her self-
imposed drama and all she can do is insult me. See what I mean, Lord?
I don't know if I'm ready for this kingdom living. I really want to tell her
she's being a little selfish, spoiled, overly pampered strumpet. How
could she be so insensitive?

Jermane was silent. She bit her bottom lip and hesitated before she spoke. "Lexi, I'm so sorry. I didn't
mean to go off."

"It's alright. I guess you're just frustrated. You're
right, I don't completely understand what you're going
through, but I can only tell you what my spirit is telling
me. Jermane, you need to just work on your marriage
and talk things out with a spiritual counselor, if need
be. Don't give up on Rex and don't take the easy way
out. Just be patient."

"And I guess I can relate a little to what he's going
through," I continued, "since I'm trying to build a law
practice. I sometimes work twenty-four seven too, and
I know that could be hard for a partner to deal with.
But once trust in a relationship is broken, you may
never get it back. You may not think what you and Rex
have is worth saving, but it is."

"I know Lexi, I know. I really don't want to lose Rex,
but I need him now. We've been married less than five
years and haven't had a chance to truly enjoy our marriage. It's like we immediately went into overdrive. He
knows how much I used to talk about my father and how
I never saw him. He was there for the big events, but it's

the everyday, little things he missed. My father doesn't listen to anyone. He just talks and dominates, and Rex has fallen right into his trap. He's exhausted most of the time, talking about this case or that case. I'm really starting to hate the law."

"Why don't you try talking to your father?"

"Yeah, right . . . he'll just find some way to shoo me off like a little child. He doesn't realize I'm a woman."

"Well, Jermane, just consider the consequences of your actions. I know you love God. It's a sin to commit adultery."

"I didn't say I was going to do anything. Besides, God forgives sin," Jermane said as she pulled her towel tighter.

"Jermane, that's a cop-out and you know it. What's so special about this man anyway besides the attraction?" I asked.

"He's focused and gentlemanly. I feel like he knows me already. He didn't give me any indication that he wants to have sex with me."

"None that you were aware of," I said. "Jermane, just trust me on this. Don't do anything you'll regret. It may seem tempting, but in the end, you'll hurt just as much as Rex. I know you have better sense than that."

"That's the problem. I'm too sensible."

"I'm not going to say anything else about it."

———

I was a little uneasy about having a male masseur, but I became more relaxed after I saw how handsome he was. He had a very soothing voice and I was at total peace. I found my thoughts drifting.

I hadn't thought about marriage for a while. I still couldn't understand why I wasn't married yet. I'm attractive and smart and dependable. So what was up?

I peeked out of one eye toward Jermane, who was getting a massage to my left. *Everything just fell into place for her. She must be out of her mind to even think about jeopardizing her marriage. Heck, I would kill to even have a man consistently from one birthday to the next.*

I felt myself getting mad and frustrated. I wondered why I always had to be there for everyone. Even my ex-boyfriends called about their problems.

That's it. I'm tired of training men for other women. Lord, until it's right, help me to hold on to my feelings and my advice. I wish I could be tough like Angel. She has men eating out of her hands all the time. It baffles me. It seems as though the nicer I am to men, the worse they treat me. All the fragments of my heart are spread out among past lovers. I promise myself that I'll wait on God. No more disappointments.

But even after my prayer, the wounds in my heart lingered.

"Lex, you almost finished over there?" Jermane asked.

"Yeah, I'll probably be done before you. I'll meet you downstairs in the café."

"Alright."

As I showered, I listened to the piano sounds of Alex Bugnon playing over the intercom. After rubbing peach-scented lotion on my shoulders and elbows, I slipped on my long tank dress. Jermane slid into the dressing room.

"I'm finished. It won't take me any time to get ready."

"I'm heading downstairs," I said as I finished packing my bag.

I sat at a table trying to look like I was waiting for someone as opposed to trying to pick someone up, though I always had an eye out for prospects. I was about to sip on my strawberry health shake when I looked up and caught the eyes of a nice-looking young man. He had on black, cuffed slacks and a crisp white shirt with golden cufflinks and a tie. His toffee-colored baby face was warm, friendly, and his hair was slightly curly. He kind of nodded his head and gave a slight smile.

"Why can't he just come over here and say something?" I mumbled under my breath.

By the time I looked back up again from my drink, Jermane had appeared and the young man was gone.

"Oh well, easy come, easy go," I said as I signaled Jermane over. As she walked over to me, I saw several men staring at her. I tried not to be envious.

"Hey, you. What are you drinking?" Jermane asked.

"A strawberry shake."

"Is it any good?"

"Yep."

"I guess I'll stick with my vanilla-honey health shake."

"Whatever."

"What's wrong with you? You're not mad at me, are you?" Jermane asked as she settled in her chair.

"No, it's just that . . . oh never mind," I said, not wanting to expose my disappointment.

"OK. Well, don't say I didn't ask what's bothering you."

"Yeah, uh, I won't," I said, scanning the room for my lost prospect.

"We'd better get ready to go. We've spent all afternoon getting beautiful," Jermane said.

"Yeah, back to reality."

I walked through my door and felt the emptiness of my apartment. I smiled when I saw the vase that held the bouquet of flowers I picked up at the grocery store yesterday. One day, I would come home and hear noise from that special someone who would buy a bouquet especially for me.

I did my routine walk toward the caller ID, taking off a piece of clothing with each step. Soon, I just stood at the phone table in my underwear.

Capri called.

I went into the bedroom, threw on my sorority T-shirt, and plopped on the living room couch. I felt extremely relaxed. I figured after watching a couple of shows, I'd call Capri, and then finish doing some work. But the phone rang.

"Hello?"

"Hey, it's Capri."

"Hey, what's up? I was going to holler at you later."

"Where have you been all day? I called the office."

"I told you that I was going to meet Jermane today at Ladies and Gents."

"Oh, yeah. I forgot all about that little escapade. What forced you to go there?"

"Jermane paid for it."

"I knew it. How was it?"

"It was pretty nice. I could get used to it. There were a lot of fine men!"

"You meet anybody?"

"No, girl."

"Speaking of men, guess who I'm going out with Saturday?"

"Mr. Stanton?"

"Yeah."

"Well, it's about time, don't you think?"

"All right, smart-A."

"So what are you going to do? Where are you going? What are you going to wear?" I asked anxiously.

"Girl, calm down. This is not the president."

"Well, I'm just saying, the man has it going on and . . ."

". . . and so do I! I'm not tripping. I'll tell you about the details after the date. Besides, I told you that I don't like to date athletes," Capri added. "They act like they're God. It's our fault. We build them up that way. They usually have two or three women and act like they can walk on water. The last time I checked, only Jesus could do that!"

"I don't know, Capri. Tony seems different, so down to earth."

"They're all like that in the beginning. Then their big head gets the better of them."

"Well, just give the man a fair chance."

"Yeah, well life isn't too fair, now is it?"

"Capri, why do you have to be so cynical?"

"Trust me. I've dated athletes before and they're nothing new under the sun."

"Well, just let me know how your date goes. I'm pulling for my man Tony."

"Yeah, yeah, don't give him his props too soon."

"Have you heard from Jewel?" I asked.

"Yeah, she called bugging me on my job today. I swear, that girl has some issues. She was complaining about her supervisor being on her case, and how she's just jealous because Jewel is a size five and she weighs 300 pounds. The woman has told Jewel several times that she needs to take responsibility for her tardiness, but Jewel, being Jewel, just doesn't seem to get it. No one is going to just take care of her."

"Don't be so rough on her. She's spoiled and shallow, yes, but there's something underneath all of that that's true and loving. By the way, she talks about Anthony Stanton all the time. It's just killing her that you're dating a pro basketball player."

"I am *not* dating him!"

"Not yet."

"Girl, let me get ready to get off this phone. I need to finish up here and head home. I'm exhausted," Capri said.

"Sounds like somebody is trying to make partner."

"Please. You know what the plan is."

"Alright. I'll talk to you soon."

I got off the couch, went to get a cold eye mask from the refrigerator, placed it over my eyes, and laid back. The mask felt soothing to me. I blindly reached for the remote and turned on the TV. I heard Brian McKnight's tenor voice fill the room and imagined he was singing to me. I reminded myself that God had someone special coming my way.

When he shows up, he'll be especially made for me. He will pamper me, remember every holiday, and my favorite color. He'll send me flowers and will meet me for espresso at midnight, just because. He will love the Lord. He will love me, despite my less-than-perfect feet. I imagine that when I look sad, he will know and care enough to cheer me up. He will pull the car up to the curb when it rains, and he will be all mine.

But I was in the here and now, by myself, so I removed the eye mask, got up, and ate the leftover pizza from the refrigerator.

CHAPTER NINETEEN

Not a Girl, Not Yet a Woman?

ey, rough day?" Toliver inquired, peeking out his front door.

"Toliver, do you work?" Jewel said as she was about to unlock her door.

"Yes, I work. I'm a graphic arts designer."

"Well, it seems like the only thing you've designed in the last year was that house and your porch because you're always here."

"Check yourself before I wreck you, little girl!"

"Toliver, I'm really not in the mood today."

"What's the matter, you actually had to work a full day? You didn't have time to do your nails?"

"Whatever."

"You'd better be nice to me or I won't give you your package that came today."

"Toliver, don't play with me. Give me my package."

"Ask me nicely."

"Toliver, if you don't give me my package I will kick your *little* . . ."

"No need to get funky about it."

He reached out with a package in his left hand. Jewel snatched it and walked inside her townhouse.

She listened to her messages and recognized Kevin's voice on the answering machine. At first, she smiled. Then, she reminded herself to keep her feelings in check. She had to be realistic about his potential; after all, he couldn't be anything more than a default man with his deliveryman salary.

She decided to return his call before the weekend just in case he wanted to take her out to dinner. After she showered and ate a frozen dinner, she turned in. She slid between her satin sheets and started to read a magazine article about Denzel Washington when the phone rang. Looking over at the caller ID, she saw Kevin's name and number. She thought about not answering it.

"Hello," she said, in a rehearsed, sexy tone.

"Hi, Jewel, this is Kevin."

"Kevin?" she asked.

"Yes, I saw you on the freeway the other day and . . . girl, you know who I am. Stop playing games."

"Oh, alright. So how are you?"

"Oh, I'm just fine. It's been a long day. I'm just getting settled and thought I would make sure that you gave me the right number."

Jewel knew he was the one playing games now, since

she'd seen his number on the caller ID, which means he must've heard her name on her voicemail.

"Let me assure you, if I didn't want you to have my number, I wouldn't have given it to you. I don't have time to play *those* types of games."

"So how's your week been so far?"

"It's been kind of hectic. My boss is trying to fire me."

"What makes you think that?"

"Well, I think it's a jealousy problem. She resents me because I'm young, beautiful, and . . ."

"Modest?"

"Very funny."

"So, what do you do, Jewel?"

"I'm the Coordinator of Special Affairs at Westwood School of Law."

"That sounds like one of those overstated jobs that doesn't really mean very much."

"I perform a very important function at the law school!" Jewel responded.

"Oh, really?"

"Yes, really."

"What exactly do you do?"

"Well, I plan and manage any major events for the law school, like dinners, banquets, and alumni functions."

"Oh, so you're a party planner."

"No, I am not a party planner. Don't insult me."

"That's not an insult. Party planners make good money."

"Good money to you probably isn't very much."

Silence.

"You'd be surprised. Well, Miss Party Planner, I'm not going to keep you any longer. It was nice talking to you. Maybe one day we'll go out. Take in a movie or something."

"Yeah, right. Talk to you later."

Jewel hung up the phone, miffed that he wanted to get off the phone first, and so quickly. That was *her* job.

He has some nerve, calling my job insignificant. It's very important. As Jewel lay in her bed, she tried to get a mental picture of what Kevin looked like. She ran down her mental list of must-haves, and he was far from her ideal. He was short, didn't wear a suit to work, drove a delivery truck, and couldn't be making six figures.

Wrong, wrong, wrong! But I am still attracted to him. He does have a take-charge attitude. He seems like a man's man. But he just doesn't worship me enough . . . right now. There's potential.

She began thinking about all the men she'd previously dated, wondering why her relationships seemed so meaningless. She thought about Rex and Jermane. Jermane had the Prince Charming Jewel was looking for—good credit and all. She wished some fine rich man would come and pay off all her charge cards and other bills so she could stop working.

She'd give anything to be in Jermane's shoes. Jermane could shop at any store, eat at any restaurant, and have all the guilt-free sex she wanted because . . . *SHE'S MARRIED TO A FINE, BLACK MAN . . . GOD, I AM MAD AT YOU!!!*

Okay, Jewel, calm down. But it was hard. She was very, very unhappy. She wanted company, to be comforted. She looked at the clock. It was 10:15, too late to make a call to her best friend.

She slumped. No one took her seriously. And, she had to admit, her job really was not that important. She was indeed a mere party planner.

Jewel started crying uncontrollably and shouted, "I am a party planner . . . I am a party planner . . . a party planner!"

Just then, the phone rang. Without looking at the caller ID, she picked up the phone, trying not to sound like she'd been crying.

"Hello."

"Hey, baby, how you doing?"

"MAMA!!!"

"How are you, sugar?"

"I'm fine, Mama. I was just thinking about you . . . but you're usually asleep by now."

"I know, but I had a restlessness in my spirit. Are you doing OK?"

"Yeah, Mama, fine. I don't want you to worry about me."

"Well, I just felt that something was going on with you."

"Umm, just a little stressed with work. How's Daddy?"

"Just fine. He's downstairs on the couch watching reruns of *Sanford and Son*, or *Sanford and Son* is probably watching him."

Jewel laughed as she pictured her father asleep in his favorite easy chair with his hand propping up the remote.

"Baby, are you sure that you're alright?"

"Yes, Mama," Jewel paused. "Mama, are you proud of me?"

"Am I proud of you? Baby, you have to be kidding

me! Do you know how many young women out there have broken their mother's hearts? You're a healthy, strong, beautiful young woman. You've never disappointed me. Sometimes you may get your priorities a little out of order, but you're making it on your own. Don't you put any extra pressure on yourself, baby."

"You aren't disappointed because I'm not married or practicing law, are you?"

"Jewel, what has gotten into you? Lord, chil', is it time for me to come visit?"

"No, Mama. Maybe you can come for my birthday, but it's not urgent."

"Jewel, life is hard and it's not fair. You have to give your best at whatever you do. Just realize that everyone has a different path to walk and your path is not the same as everyone else's. Just try to make sure you don't create any extra obstacles for the Lord to do His work in your life. By the way, how is that boy . . . Samuel?"

"Mama, that was three boyfriends ago!"

"Oh, well, I can't keep up with them. He was a nice boy though. And fine, too."

"Mama, what do you know about a man being fine?"

"Your mama had it going on back in the day. And so did your daddy. Why'd you think I got with him?"

"OK, Mama, I get it."

"You need any money?"

"Mama, I'm grown. I'm supposed to be taking care of myself."

"Yes, but you're my only child. You're still my baby. Besides, if I have it, you have it. Don't fool yourself.

Other people help their children all the time, even after they're grown. Jewel, you know we're not poor.
Your daddy would have a fit if you needed money and
didn't ask."

"OK, Mama, you can send a little cash. Can you
wire it tomorrow?"

"It'll be there tomorrow. Good Lord, Jewel! What
do you spend your money on? Clothes, I bet."

"See, Mama, you're making me feel bad."

"Well, you know the Lord wants us to be good stewards over our money. Have you been tithing like you
should?"

"Yes."

"Well, I'll tell your father you said hello."

"Mama, don't tell him about the money, alright?
He won't do nothing but fuss."

"Baby, when you get married, you'll realize you tell
your husband most things, but never *everything!*"

"Mama, pray for me . . . whatever the spirit leads
you to pray about."

"Baby, the Lord already led my spirit to pray for you
earlier . . . Mama knows. How do you think you
passed that bar? The question is, have you been praying?"

"Yes, Mama, but you have that powerful prayer
thing going on."

"Baby, we all have the same access to God. You just
need to pray more consistently. Jewel, you give up too
soon. It takes time to build a relationship with the
Lord. You can't be so impatient. Everything is beautiful in its own time. I had to wait nine months for you,

and look how beautiful you turned out. My baby is the most beautiful woman in the world!"

"Mama, please!"

"I'm just telling the truth."

"What did you cook tonight?"

"Roast beef, candied yams, greens, pinto beans, and cornbread."

"That's enough. I can't take it anymore," Jewel said, still feeling her frozen dinner in the pit of her stomach.

"I hope you're not eating those frozen dinners or acting like those folks who eat chicken without skin, steamed vegetables, and all that crap. We've been eating like this all our lives. As soon as people tell us it's not healthy, we start having all these heart attacks. The good Lord didn't tell me personally that I couldn't eat fried chicken and pinto beans. Trust me, I would know because you do know He talks to me. He ain't said nothing about that yet. So, until He does . . ."

"Mama, Mama, stop. I get the point."

"Oh, you know how your mama can talk. How's my other babies—Lexi, Jermane, and the other two."

"They're all fine."

"Lord, I don't know why that child's mama named her Jermane."

"Mama, I explained that before. They thought they were gonna have a boy. Once they saw it was a girl, they figured the name would make her distinguished."

"Still. Oh never mind. Folks have the right to name their children whatever they want."

"Well, Mama, it's getting late. Give Daddy a kiss for me."

Jewel felt herself on the verge of tears again as she

hung up the phone. Her mother was a strong, ener-
getic woman. Her father was the kindest, most handsome man she'd known. He would do anything for her
mother. Jewel wanted that kind of love.

Still, they had their moments, like the time her
mother got mad because he came home late and locked
him out and put his favorite chair out on the porch.
Just then, her mother's voice interrupted her thoughts.
She realized that before she dozed off, she needed to
get on her knees and pray.

*Lord, thank You for another day. Thanks for my mom and dad.
Thank You for all You've done for me. I know I don't pray as much as
I should, but I'll try harder. Lord, I can only tell You what's in my
heart. Right now, I'm feeling incomplete. I'm feeling very lonely. I know
that You're my company keeper, but even Your word says "it's not good
for man to be alone."*

*Lord, You said we should pray for our enemies. Well, I pray that my
boss becomes more understanding. I pray, Lord, that You help me to
keep my job. Please show me what I'm supposed to be doing with my life
right now. Everything just feels out of whack. I have been going to
church, but things seem to be getting worse instead of better. Everyone
else's life seems so great. Please send me my soul mate. I know life would
be so much better with him.*

I love You. Amen.

CHAPTER TWENTY

Love and Basketball

apri found it hard to concentrate on her work. She placed her pen down next to the petition she was attempting to draft. She took a deep breath, then leaned back in her chair. She couldn't believe how excited she was about meeting up with Tony. The phone rang.

"Ms. Sterling, this is Mr. Stanton. How's your day been going?"

"Oh, uh, I didn't expect to hear from you."

"Well, I just wanted to see what time you wanted to get together tomorrow."

"I guess seven o'clock would be fine."

"Would you like for me to come and pick you up?"

"You mean you're not going to try to impress me and send your driver?"

"I thought you would enjoy more personal service, and I didn't want to scare you off or be pretentious."

"It depends on what you have planned."

"I'd really like to talk to you, get to know the real you, so I don't want any major distractions. Can I surprise you?"

"I don't know."

"You could cooperate. It's the least you could do since you made me wait so long to go out on a date with you."

"Well, OK."

"What kind of food do you like?"

"I like just about anything, but I'm crazy about Cajun food."

"I'd like you to come to my place first. If you feel more comfortable driving your car, I understand."

"Yeah, that would probably be a good idea."

They talked for a little while longer, cementing the plans. As soon as Capri hung up, the phone rang again.

"This is Attorney Sterling."

"Hey, bud, this is Lexi. Ready for that hot date?"

"Girl, would you calm down. I must admit, though, I am just a bit excited."

"Girl, do not, do you hear me, do not give this man a hard time. This could mean more tickets to basketball games or the *Essence* Awards or who knows what else."

"You're starting to sound like Jewel, God forbid."

"Am I? Well, I guess I have to live vicariously through the rest of y'all since my love life is at an all-time standstill. What are you going to wear?"

"I don't know. I was thinking about a pants suit."

"Capri, loosen up! Stop being so anal."

"I'm not trying to give it away on the first date. I told you, he's probably a dog anyway. I don't get easily excited."

"At least wear something a little sexy. What about that black, strapless, cocktail dress?"

"Too dressy. He said to wear something kind of dressy-casual, whatever that means."

"How about your long, slender-fitting taupe skirt and the black top that has thin spaghetti straps. That really fits you well, girl. It has just the right hint of sexiness."

"I guess. You don't think that top hugs my breasts too tightly?"

"If it does, so what? It's the perfect little outfit for a first date."

"I guess so."

"And make sure you do your hair. You wear it pinned back so much. You have beautiful hair."

"I'll wear it down if you do it for me."

"As much money as you make, couldn't you make a hair appointment?"

"I was so busy this week. To tell you the truth, I *was* going to wear it slicked back in a pony tail."

"I'll be over tomorrow at 5:30 p.m."

Capri followed the directions to get to Terracotta Plains, the subdivision where Anthony lived. She

pulled up to a security station that sat in front of a large
wrought-iron gate.

"Yes, I'm here to see . . ."

"Anthony Stanton?"

"Yes."

"Can I see your license, Ms. Sterling?"

"Yes."

The security guard made a brief phone call and
came back to the window. He surveyed her car and
wrote down what looked like her license plate number.
"Okay, Ms. Sterling, you have a good evening."

The huge, iron gate opened and Capri drove
through. She was happy it was still fairly light outside so
she could see the house numbers, which were so far
from the street. She admired the manmade lakes and
fountains that were part of the landscape. She'd heard
that several corporate executives and pro ball players
had houses here. A whole little community behind an
iron gate. It was so serene. All of a sudden, Capri
wanted a house, a huge one.

"There it is," Capri said to herself as she found 1916
Halliburton Lane. She pulled in the half-circle driveway and quickly checked her makeup. She grabbed her
small black purse and stepped out. Before she took a
step, she admired the architecture of Anthony's huge
one-story house. The outside was made of white adobe,
and there was a long red brick walkway leading to the
front door's huge white stone archway. Before she could
get halfway up the path, the door opened, and there was
Anthony, clad in a maroon silk shirt and black slacks.

He stood there with the sexiest grin Capri had ever seen. She tried to look unimpressed.

"Hi. I'm glad you made it," he said with a sexy assurance.

"You gave excellent directions."

"Come on in," he said as his eyes subtly scanned her from top to bottom.

Her hair had loose curls and layers that grazed her shoulders. She had a low part on the side and the front swooped sexily across her brow.

Her skin glistened from the moisture in the air. Her skirt accentuated her figure. He looked down at her black strappy sandals and noticed her perfectly maincured feet.

"You look very nice," he said in a low voice as he looked slightly away from her body.

"Thank you . . . you do, too," she said as she stood, waiting for instructions.

"Could you wait here for a minute . . . ?"

Before she could answer, he walked off, which gave her a chance to look around. A half-table and a mirror trimmed in gold stood against one wall. A floral arrangement sat on top of the table. In the middle of the hallway stood a glass case with three crystal statues—each of a man and woman in passionate poses—on each of its shelves. To the left were double mahogany wood doors with brass handles. To the right looked like the kitchen, but the lights were turned off. Just as she was about to peek around some more, she heard Anthony's voice.

"Capri, close your eyes and hold your hand out," his voice said from a short distance.

"What's going on? I don't like games."

"Remember, you said you'd cooperate."

Capri closed her eyes and held out her hand, expecting him to put something in it. Instead, she felt his hand slip in hers. She could smell his cologne.

"Walk this way and don't open your eyes."

She heard him open the double doors she'd just surveyed. She walked several feet and through another door. She was tempted to peek, but she didn't. Once they went through the other door, she felt the open space of the room. Anthony let go of her hand. Then she heard the sound of liquid pouring into a glass. A chair slid out. He held her hand again and told her to sit down. She awkwardly slid into the chair. She felt a table in front of her. Then she heard music.

"You can open your eyes."

She was in a mini movie theatre. To their left were several rows of chairs. A linen-covered table was set with wineglasses and a fresh floral centerpiece. A spotlight was over the table. She looked up at the screen and *The Lion King* was playing. Her heart jumped. She just looked at Anthony and smiled.

"I also have *101 Dalmatians, The Little Mermaid*, and any other Disney movie you want. I rented a stack of them." Before she could say anything, a man eased into the room and approached the table.

"Mr. Stanton, dinner is ready. Would you like to eat at this time?" a short man dressed in chef's attire said.

"Capri?"

"Yes, let's eat. What's on the menu?"

"Shrimp scampi, Cajun fish, and etoufée."

"That sounds *so* delicious."

"Would you like a salad?" the chef asked Capri.

"Yes, please."

"I'll be back with the bread and salad."

Capri was overwhelmed with excitement, but continued to try hard not to show it.

"This was really nice of you, Anthony. I know it sounds strange, but since I was small I've always loved Disney movies. Sounds corny doesn't it?"

"No, it shows me that you're a human being. You have a sensitive side."

Capri allowed herself to smile softly. Although the room was dimly lit, she couldn't help but notice the sincerity of Anthony's face. He always gave her his full attention when she spoke. She liked that. She also liked that he didn't appear intimidated by her. He seemed totally at ease with her *and* himself.

"So, do you miss New York?" Anthony asked.

"Well, I miss my family, but not the city. Everything is so congested. The cost of living is way too high. You can't beat their hot dogs and pizza, though. We used to call them dirty dogs."

"I know what you mean."

"What do you know about New York?"

"I'm from Mount Vernon. Didn't your girl tell you?"

"Who?"

"Lexi. I cornered her the night y'all came to my club, and she told me a little about you."

"I didn't know you were from New York. You came down here to play for the Meteors?"

"You got it. How'd you end up here?"

"Law school. I have a grandmother and sister still in New York."

"What's your sister's name?"

"Trina. She goes to New York University."

"Where are your parents, if you don't mind me asking?"

"They're not living. They both died when I was seven."

"I'm sorry. Let's not talk about it."

"Well, I can deal with it now. I'm just thankful for my grandmother. She raised Trina and me. She made sure I made it to undergrad, so I help her and Trina out as much as I can."

"Do they ever come to Houston?"

"They came out here for my law school graduation, but haven't been here since then. So, you're a client of the firm?"

"Yeah, they handle the majority of my endorsement deals and other related matters."

"You know, if we were to become more than friends, there may be some conflict of interests for the firm."

"I don't know anything about all that conflict of interest stuff. Regardless, you have to have a life."

"Yeah, but the firm may not look at it that way."

"The firm? You're starting to sound like you are programmed. 'The firm' this, 'the firm' that . . ."

"Excuse me, but I do take my job seriously. For as long as I have to be there, I don't really want to cause any problems. It can be a lot of pressure, but one day I'll be able to start my own firm."

"So you do want to go into private practice."

"Yes, that's what I wanted to do from the start."

"Why didn't you?"

"Like I said, I have some obligations I need to take care of, so until then, I'll continue to work at the firm."

"We need strong minority law firms in Houston."

"Well, I know I could do it, it's just bad timing. Do you mind if we don't talk about this anymore?" she said, grabbing a roll from the basket of bread the cook had sneaked in.

"You know, it takes a certain type of man to appreciate a woman like you."

"I'm glad you recognize that," she said with a semi-serious face. "So, how does it feel to be such a public figure, to have women following you everywhere and throwing themselves at you?"

"Honestly, I love playing basketball, but I hate the lack of privacy. I'm very much a homebody. I'll admit, it is tempting to get caught up in all the hype people make about you. So if you don't have some type of foundation to ground you, you can start to believe that it really is all about you."

"So what's your foundation?"

"God, family, and friends."

"Hmmm. Good answer," she said.

They ate and chatted, becoming more familiar with each other. As they became more relaxed, their New York accents became more overt.

"Capri, can I ask you a question?"

"What am I supposed to say. No?"

"Do you find it hard to give a brother a chance to treat you like a woman?"

"What do you mean by that?"

"Well, it seems like you're so used to handling things by yourself. Don't get me wrong. You're the ultimate woman, but you seem like you don't have time for a man in your life."

"Tony, that's not really it. I just don't have time for games. I'm a little burned out on promises and happily ever after."

"Have you ever been in love?"

"Umm . . . uh, yeah, once."

"What happened? Did he hurt you?"

"No, he didn't. He's the only man to this day I could have ever seen myself with."

"So, why didn't ya'll get married. Did he move away? Were you too young?"

"No, none of those things," she said, finding her eyes getting slightly watery. At that moment, she felt transparent, like he could see the story written all over her face. Anthony reminded her so much of Ty. At that moment, it was too painful to look at him.

"I'd rather not talk about it. Maybe I'll tell you another day," she said, focusing on animals singing on the screen.

"*Another day*? Does that mean you have plans to see me in the future?"

"We'll see. Just for the record, I am capable of being treated like a woman. I let you open the door for me a couple of times, didn't I?"

"I ain't talkin' about that. That's a given. I mean

really being treated like a woman," he said, staring directly into her hazel eyes. "Are you afraid of that?"

"Please."

"I'm talkin' about me taking care of you."

"I'm doing a pretty good job of that."

"Yeah, you are, but I'm talkin' about going beyond just your everyday needs. I'm talkin' about giving you what you can't give yourself. Like, I want you to have someone to really listen to you. Someone who won't cut you off when you're talkin'. Someone who doesn't mind rubbing the small of your back until the fatigue is gone. Someone to remember the things that make you special, your favorite perfume, your favorite music, your birthday, what makes you smile. Someone you can be comfortable with in a room full of people or cuddled up on a couch, not saying a word. I'm talkin' about *intimacy* and . . ."

"Mr. Stanton, what is it about me that you find so appealing, considering you don't know me?" she asked, cutting him off.

"Capri, I don't make decisions quickly. I do like you, but I'm also careful about who I let into my life. I've been watching you. I like the way you carry yourself. You have a sense of confidence and self-assurance that makes you mad sexy. You move like a cat. You're intelligent and have the most beautiful legs I've ever seen. I've watched you and you look like you can handle just about anything, but there's a side to you that you don't let folks see. I'd like to see that side."

"And what side is that?"

"The part of you that's alive, unpredictable, uncensored! When I look at you, I see a person always on schedule. Always with a plan. Everything has to fit into your regimen."

"You're somewhat right."

"That's a good thing, when it comes to business, but what about your social life? Life's too short not to enjoy it."

"I enjoy life. I have a great job, wonderful friends, and God in my life."

"All that's great, but when's the last time you did something that had nothing to do with work?"

"Well, the party where we met."

"Long time ago. What else?"

"Well, I'm a homebody. I'm not a party person. Besides, life *is* serious business. That's what's wrong with our people. They don't take life seriously enough."

"Capri, I'm just sayin' life should be a balance. I know life is a serious matter, but I feel much, much better when I can laugh or enjoy sharing the things that I dig with someone else."

Capri was silent for a moment.

"Hmmm, I guess I see your point. Is that what you wanted to hear?" she said.

Tony chuckled. "Did you enjoy your food?" he asked.

"It was delicious. I'm glad I decided to grace you with my presence."

"Funny."

"No really, this was really thoughtful, and, to be honest, I am enjoying your company."

Capri looked across the table and had to mentally

pinch herself. She knew she could really like this man and wanted to savor every minute of this euphoria. Then she remembered again that he was a client at her firm. She gave herself a mental smack upside the head for carelessly overlooking the "small" detail that could eventually become very big.

"So how do you like having Pearson Carrington handle most of your work?"

"Well, I really wanted a Black attorney and I wanted one of the best. Pearson is extremely sharp. So far, we have a great working relationship. If I'd known you before I retained Pearson, though, I would have requested you."

"Yeah, we definitely would've had problems then."

"We would've, huh?"

Tony stood up and Capri couldn't help but scan his body. Her hormones went haywire. It had been years since she'd been this close to a man in a room with candlelight. He walked around to her chair, lightly placed his hands on her shoulders, and bent down.

"Let me get your chair for you," he said softly, close enough for her to feel his breath on her neck. "We can have dessert in our theatre seats."

"None for me. I am so full."

"Alright, but you'll miss out on some slammin' cheesecake."

"I love cheesecake," she said with regret. "This is amazing. How often do you come in here?" Capri said as she saw the proud lion, Simba, saunter across the screen.

"Every now and then. I like to watch movies. It relaxes me."

They watched the rest of *The Lion King* in silence. Capri felt a certain comfort sitting next to Anthony. She tried hard not to allow her skin to touch his, but then he softly placed his hand on top of hers. She turned her palm upward, signaling to him it was permissible to hold her hand. Tony was right; it was OK for her to loosen up.

After watching *The Little Mermaid* and *Bambi*, Capri started dozing off. It was almost one o'clock in the morning. She came to and noticed she had placed her head on Anthony's shoulder. She quickly sat up, at attention, as if someone had scared her.

"You OK, babe?" he said.

Babe? "Yeah, I'm alright. I guess it's time for me to go."

"Well, uh, I don't wanna offend you or nothing, but do you think it's safe for you to be driving this late?"

"Yeah, I'll be fine. I have a lot of work to do tomorrow."

"Sunday? Do you ever stop?"

"I'm just trying to stay ahead."

"That work will be there. Why don't you just stay? I know this may sound crazy and this is your first night here, but I have an extra bedroom. I won't be at peace if you left this late at night. I would have to follow you home."

"Well, why don't you do that?" she said, genuinely not realizing how much he wanted her to stay.

He looked back at her with a face that said "Me and

my bright ideas." He pictured his size fifteen foot in his mouth. "Alright, if you think that would be best. Let me get my keys."

As Capri stood there, satisfied with the sensible decision she'd made, there was a sudden jolt in her body. She wished it wasn't her first date. She actually wanted to stay, but knew it would be stupid to be so comfortable so soon.

But she was always so planned, so predictable. She thought of the most unpredictable person she could think of at that moment.

What would Jewel do? What am I doing? Why on earth would I want to do anything Jewel would?

"OK, I have my keys," Anthony said in an accommodating tone.

As Capri got to the door and was about to grab the knob, she hesitated. She pulled her hand away. She silently prayed, *Lord, don't let this fool be a maniac.*

"Babe, are you ready?"

"Well, I was thinking, since you have an extra bedroom, maybe I could . . ."

"Stay the night," he said calmly.

"Yeah, I guess I'll stay the night; *but* I have a few rules."

"Look, Capri, I respect you. This has been a great evening. I don't want to ruin it just because I'd like to spend some more time with you. I'll give you some of my pajamas and whatever toiletries you need. We can stay up and talk or if you're tired, you can turn in now. I promise I won't try anything. When you get up in the morning, we can have a big breakfast so you'll be ready to do all that work you have to do. Can you deal with that?"

"Yeah, that sounds good, except . . ."

"Except what?"

"You won't talk about me if I have morning breath?" she asked.

"I keep a spare toothbrush. It's just a habit of mine. Whenever I'm purchasing toiletries, I usually buy several of them."

"Sure, sure. I mean, you never know how many 'guests' you'll be having in a given week, right?"

Tony held his chest with a face that said, "You're killing me!"

Capri smirked.

"Well, alrighty then. I guess I'll be staying at the Stanton Inn tonight."

"I do have to give you one warning though."

"What's that?"

"Once you stay, you might not want to leave. This could end up being one continuous date," he said and winked his eye.

Capri didn't say anything.

She woke up and saw a bright beam of sunlight blasting across the bed. She felt like she was miles from the floor in the huge canopy bed.

She was thankful she was still there in one piece. She still felt safe, like she had spent the night at an old friend's house—albeit one who was very well off.

She heard a knock.

"Come in."

"Hey, sleepy head," Anthony said, as he stuck his head into the room. "Were you planning on joining me today?"

"It can't be that late," Capri said, sitting up.

"It's nine-thirty. I've been up since seven."

"Doing what?"

"I run in the mornings. I've already run five miles, showered, and I'm ready to eat. I've been waiting for Sleeping Beauty to wake up."

"Mmmm, something smells good."

"Yeah, breakfast."

"Oh, I have to hurry up and . . ."

"Hurry up and do nothing . . . can you take a day off for a change? That's what the weekends are for," he said.

She looked over at her clothes hanging neatly on a hanger. "I need to get dressed."

"Not until you have breakfast."

Capri stopped and noticed how sexy Anthony looked in his tank top and matching shorts with rubber sports sandals. He looked so refreshed and at ease. His presence made her feel relaxed, too. He walked over to the bed and started gently pulling her arm.

"Alright, alright. I'm getting up."

He plopped alongside her and brushed her hair away from her face.

"Capri, you know what?" he said in a soft voice.

"What," she said, realizing this was going to be one of those sentimental moments she wasn't ready for.

"You might want to stop in the bathroom and get

something for that dragon breath," he said, and burst out laughing.

"You just think you're funny, huh?" she said. "Ha, ha, ha . . . well, I'll take care of my breath if you rub some lotion on them ashy boat feet of yours."

He looked down at his feet and then gently tackled her. He wiped her hair out of her face and kissed her lightly on her lips. She kissed him back.

"I guess your breath ain't that bad," he said.

"Yeah, your feet don't look *too* rough," she said.

"The bathroom has plenty of towels, soap, and whatever you need. Hurry and wash up, babe."

"I can't wait to see what you cooked for breakfast," she said as she slid from the bed.

"Cook? I don't know how to cook. I just fried the bacon. I was waiting on you to come help me with the rest."

"I should've known," she said, rolling her eyes.

"Hurry up, woman, so *we* can finish cooking breakfast."

"Uh-huh. Anthony, I can tell you're spoiled."

"Maybe a little. But if I'm spoiled, I don't mind reciprocating."

"I see. Well, since you were such a gracious host, I guess we can try to work this breakfast thing out, but you need to learn how to cook, boy, if you're gonna be swinging with me."

"I have other important business to take care of."

"And? So do I."

She turned around and proceeded to leave the room. He smacked her behind as she walked past him.

"Look, don't get carried away," she said, trying to sound serious.

"You know you like it."

Capri turned away from him. She smiled. She *did* like it.

CHAPTER TWENTY-ONE

Answered Prayer?

I got up, washed my face, and felt depression coming on. I turned the radio to the gospel station and they were playing one of my mother's favorite old songs, "No Charge." I turned it off. To match my mood, I decided to wear a dark pants suit to church. I knew I should give the Lord my best, but right now, I thought I would do well just to get to church. After I showered and dressed, I decided to grab a bagel and some coffee, although I was already behind schedule.

These brunches are getting to be costly.

When I got to church, they were just at the part of the program where they were doing the welcome. Normally, this was my favorite part, but today I didn't feel like being hospitable. Nevertheless, I put on my best Christian smile and proceeded to greet the other

people who were waiting to get into the sanctuary. I
tried to look for Jewel and Capri but figured they were
already inside. I wondered how Capri's date with Anthony went.

I looked around and saw lots of attractive couples in
their Sunday best. I pacified myself by thinking *everything that looks good isn't always good*.

During the prayer, I couldn't help but say my own
silent prayer for God to deliver me a church partner,
someone who would place his arm around the back of
my chair during the sermon, or someone I could hold
hands with while walking outside the church. Someone
so fine, all the single women would be staring and
drooling.

Alright Lexi, get a hold of yourself, I thought after the
prayer was over.

Just as I lifted my head, I felt a slight touch on my
shoulder. I turned around, and a handsome man with
slightly curly hair smiled and said, "I think I know you.
Weren't you at Ladies and Gents last Wednesday?"

"Yes," I said, remembering the brief glances we exchanged that day. "Are you a member here?" I asked.

"Yes, I joined about two weeks ago," he said, walking alongside me as we entered the church sanctuary
from the lobby.

I prayed he was going to sit next to me. I didn't say
anything because I didn't want to appear too interested. I gave myself a silent kick in the butt for not
wearing a nicer outfit. I turned into my row and he followed me. We sat down together. I looked up.

Thank You for answered prayer.

At the minister's instruction to greet your neighbor, he shook my hand and seemed genuinely interested.

"Kyle."

"Lexi."

For the rest of the morning, he made little, thoughtful comments about the sermon. When the service was over, I walked at an inconspicuous pace, hoping he would follow me out, and he did.

"That was an excellent sermon, wasn't it?" he asked, calling my attention from the perusal of his outfit. I had to catch myself, because I love a man in a nice pin-striped suit. His teeth sparkled, and his wire-framed glasses were the cutest thing.

"Oh, yes, it was a good service."

Just then, I noticed Jewel in the far corner. *Please don't come over here. I just want to get my groove on in peace.*

Then I heard a slight buzzing sound. His pager was vibrating.

"Wow, this is rare. I need to get to a phone. I really enjoyed bumping into you like this. This church is so big, you never know who's a member. I have to apologize for being brief, but let me give you my card. We can talk a little more if you'd like," he said, searching through his wallet. "I hope you don't think this is inappropriate."

"Oh, no, it's quite alright," I said as I took his card and discreetly slid it in my purse.

"Remember . . ."

"Remember what?"

"You asked for me." He winked his eye, turned, and walked away.

My heart stopped. *Did he say what I think he just said?* Just as I was about to bask in the moment, I heard a familiar, irritating voice.

"Girl, who was that?"

"Jewel, you don't miss anything do you?"

"Well, girl don't hold out. Where have you been hiding him?"

"I just met him. His name is Kyle, Kyle . . ." I pulled out the card and looked at it. "Kyle Morris. He's a certified public accountant," I said. "Let's go eat. My bagel has worn off."

Angel waved to us as we walked to our favorite table.

"Hey girl, what's up?" I said as Jewel and I sat down.

"You're here on time for once," Jewel said.

"Very funny. I really didn't get enough sleep last night. I thought I'd be tired, but for some reason I got up early," Angel said as she lifted her coffee cup to her mouth.

"And *why* didn't you get enough sleep?" Jewel said.

"Wouldn't you like to know."

"Probably with that Julio person," Jewel said.

"Octavio."

"Julio, Octavio, Antonio . . . what's the difference?" Jewel said, diverting her attention to the breakfast table.

"Here comes Capri."

"Oh, no, miss. I hope you don't think you're just going to stroll in here and not give an explanation as to why you were not in church. Could it be the morning-after effect?"

"Jewel, if you must know, I overslept," Capri said as she sat in her seat. I couldn't wait to talk to her about Tony when we had a moment to ourselves.

"Yeah, OK. I'll let you slide for right now," Jewel said. "Hey. Ohmigod!! That's Kevin!"

"Kevin?" we chimed in unison. She was glaring at a short man who'd walked in with a woman and a little girl.

"Kevin Eastland," Jewel said. "I met him when he delivered my . . ."

"Your what?" I asked, my eyebrows raised.

"Never mind. He works for the parcel service."

"Jewel, be for real. You won't even look at a man if he's not an athlete or some other professional," I said.

"I told you, I just met him. I'm not even interested."

"Is that why you're killing yourself trying to find out who he's here with?" Capri asked.

"Shut up," Jewel said, clenching her teeth as she watched him walk toward the buffet room. "He's here with a woman and a little girl. The nerve of him, if he's married. I am going to *have* to call him out. He's not even all that fine."

"They don't have to be fine to be a player," Angel said.

"He looks fine to me," I said and shook hands with Capri.

"I cannot believe him," Jewel said.

"Jewel, you just said you weren't interested. It's time to eat. Let's go to the buffet," Capri said.

"Wait a minute, Miss Thing. You're not off the hook. I heard you had a date with Mr. Stanton. We want details," Angel said.

"Lexi, you're on my list," Capri said, glaring at me.

I shrugged innocently. Jewel, who normally would've jumped on this news mercilessly, was so undone by Kevin that she didn't react.

"Well, I have to admit, we had a nice time. No, let me just be honest." She paused. "He is the bomb y'all."

"Did you have sex with him?" Angel asked.

"No, Freakmaster, we didn't have sex," Capri said.

"I beg your pardon. I'm a reformed woman. Anyway, let me ask you this, Ms. Innocent, what time did you go home?" Angel asked.

"None of your business."

"I know you spent the night because I tried to call you this morning," Angel said.

"I had my ringer off, Smarty Pants."

"Lying on a Sunday, Capri. Tsk, tsk," Angel said.

"I'm going to get a plate," I said.

Everyone got up except Jewel, who sat there with her lip poked out.

"Jewel, stop acting like a baby. You shouldn't play so hard to get," Capri said.

"You're talking?" Angel said. Capri rolled her eyes.

"Like I was saying, Jewel, don't start tripping until you find out what the deal is. She could be his sister, so don't let the brother know you're pressed. Get up and get your food," Capri said.

A little while after we'd returned from the buffet, Kevin walked over to our table.

"The nerve of him. I can't believe he's walking over here."

"Hello, Jewel. How are you?" he asked.

She looked over at him. He had the prettiest little girl with him. Her hair was neatly pinned up in a pony-tail with tendril curls hanging down. She had on a cream taffeta dress with matching ribbons and bows.

Jewel stood up and put on a forced smile. She grabbed his arm. "Hey, Kevin," Jewel said.

"Good morning, everyone," he said, waving to our table. "This is my daughter, Aja."

"Hi *Aja*, I'm *Jewel*."

The little girl grabbed her father's leg, hid her face in it, and smiled. She looked about five.

"Your daughter, huh?" Jewel placed her hand on her hip, neglecting to introduce us.

"Yes. How are you ladies doing? I'm Kevin East-land. I'll overlook your friend's rudeness today." He was purposely ignoring Jewel's obvious inquisitive ex-pression and reached for Capri's hand as he spoke. We all introduced ourselves.

Then Jewel whispered something in his ear. He just gave her a look, smirked, and then began to pat her on her back. Jewel's brow creased.

"Well, I guess Aja and I should get to our table. It was nice to see you, Jewel. Nice to meet everyone."

"Yes, yes, Kevin, it was nice seeing you, too. And it was nice meeting you, Ms. Aja," Jewel said as she looked down at the little girl. Aja came from behind her father and had a big smile on her face.

"So what did you say to him, Jewel?" I said, making sure they had walked away.

Jewel sighed. "I asked him who was the woman. You saw how he reacted. That's his problem. He's just so condescending!"

"I thought you said you could never date a man with a child," I said.

"I didn't say that exactly. I said I *prefer* not to date men with children. I want the experience of giving a man his first child. When another mother is involved, there are always headaches."

She placed the napkin in her lap and sliced a piece of cantaloupe.

I took a sip of cinnamon coffee. "Well, it just depends on the situation," I said. "It could be benefical if you really don't want to have children yourself. You can have a ready-made family without the stretch marks. Besides, if you love a man, what's important to him should be important to you."

"Thanks, Ms. Idealistic."

"Personally, I can't be bothered with all that," Angel said.

"What a surprise," Jewel said.

"I don't know. I have to take it on a case-by-case basis," Capri said as she scooped the whipped cream from her apple pancakes.

"So, Lexi, what was up with Mr. Suave at church?" Jewel asked as she sliced a piece of French pastry.

"I told you, I've never met him before. I think I saw him briefly at Ladies and Gents salon with Jermane."

"Speaking of Jermane, where is she?" Angel asked.

"Oh, I forgot. She called and told me she wasn't going to be able to make it," Jewel said.

"She's been acting strange lately. Has she said anything unusual been happening with her?" Capri asked, looking at me.

I sliced my warm blueberry muffin. "No, nothing lately," I said, keeping my confidentiality vow.

"She sounds kind of depressed, if you ask me," Jewel said.

"Jermane doesn't have real problems. Her biggest dilemma is when one of her cars breaks down or when she runs out of golf balls," Angel said.

"Everybody has problems," I said. "You can't take people's problems for granted. We don't know what's going on in her life."

"I agree. We shouldn't take anybody's problems lightly, except Jewel. You know she's the drama queen," Capri said, then chuckled.

"See, why don't you all ever take me seriously?" Jewel asked, folding her arms.

"I'm just joking Jewel," Capri said.

Jewel continued to sulk as she glanced over at Kevin. She got up and headed in the direction of the ladies' room.

"Don't think you're getting off the hook, Lexi. You

should be ashamed of yourself, picking up men in church," Capri said.

"I did not pick him up. He just started talking to me. The next thing you know, he was sitting next to me."

"What does he do?"

"He's an accountant."

"Oh, no," Angel said.

"What?" I asked.

"He's going to bore you to death." She took a sip of coffee, then refilled her cup.

"Well, let me go out on a date with the man first. One good sign is that at least he's not afraid to come to church."

"Yeah, well that doesn't always guarantee he'll act right," Angel said in a cynical tone. She leaned back slightly and patted her stomach. "I'm full. God I ate too much."

"How's Octavio?" I asked.

"He's alright. We've been hanging out a lot."

"I'm back," Jewel announced.

"Did you get a good look at the woman who stole your man?" Capri said, chuckling.

"She did not *steal* my man. Kevin is *not* my man. He's just someone I met. Besides, she wasn't even cute. I could see her hairweave tracks from a mile away and she had a cheap suit on. Dare I say . . . *polyester*!"

"Alright, Jewel. Well, I hate to call it a day, but I have some work to do," Capri said as she slid from the table.

"Yeah, it's about that time," Angel said.

We paid and got up. As we walked out, I noticed

Jewel taking one last look back at Kevin. Then she turned to speak to me.

"I'm sure he'll give me a call, and that's when I'll find out who that woman is."

"Maybe you should give him a call, Jewel. I think he's a cutie."

Jewel pursed her lips.

"Maybe you're right, Lexi. Maybe I should."

CHAPTER TWENTY-TWO

The Afterglow

apri found herself daydreaming about her night with Tony. She usually hated Mondays, but the memories were making her feel good. Her work didn't feel like a chore. Her phone rang and she picked it up.

"Hey, babe," a deep voice said.

"Yes, this is *Ms.* Sterling."

"I just wanted to tell you good morning and let you know I was thinking about you."

"Alright, well you've done that. Now I have to get some work done."

"You are mad cold."

"Alright, Mr. Stanton. How are you this fine morning?"

"I'm pretty fine myself. I just hadda let you know I really enjoyed your company this weekend."

"I enjoyed myself, too." Her voice grew more relaxed.

"I wanted to see if we could do lunch this week?"

"I'll have to see. What day?"

"I have to meet Pearson up there on Wednesday."

"Well, it probably wouldn't be good if we met anywhere close to here."

"Why not?"

"Anthony, since you're a client, me seeing you is not the most ethical move."

"You're not my attorney. Pearson is."

"Yeah, but since I'm a part of the firm, theoretically, you're my client, too."

"Well, how are we going to get around this?"

"I really don't know. I've been trying not to think about it, but I can't ignore the issue."

"Well, if things work out the way I'd like, you may not need to work there at all," he said.

"Oh, so you got this all planned out. Don't I get a say so in this?" she said indignantly.

"Umm, not really."

"A little cocky, aren't we?"

"Just spoiled. My mother never worked and . . ."

"First of all, what makes you think, if we ended up being serious, and I mean that with a big *IF*, I'd just want to sit at home. I was raised to take care of myself. And furthermore, I like my job. I just met you and don't know how long you're going to be around."

"Whoa, time out! I'm just kidding. Seriously, I just think you'd be the type to own your own firm."

"Well, you and me both, Mr. Stanton. For now, I gotta do what I gotta do."

"Anyway, Ms. Sterling, I plan to be around for a while. You can't stop fate."

"Fate, huh, you think so?"

"Yes. Anyway, what're your plans for the weekend?"

"Not much, but I have to go to this company function on Friday night."

"My agent said I'm supposed to meet him at Fredrico's on Friday."

"Probably the same function. This should be interesting."

"Yeah, well, we'll talk about this later. Anyway, babe, I really want you to have a good day, alright? I'm gonna call you at home tonight."

"Alright, I'll talk to you later." Just as she hung up, as if on cue, there was a knock on her office door.

A short young Black man in a gray suit peeked in. "Hey, Ms. Sterling, how's it going?"

Recognizing the voice, she looked up quickly. "Hey, Pearson, how are you?" she said, trying to look busy.

"I heard congratulations are in order."

"It's nothing."

"Well, I guess you're on the partner track," he said.

"I don't know about all that."

"I'll let you get back to work. By the way, I believe we have a mutual friend," he said.

"Who?"

"Mr. Stanton."

"Oh, yeah, I just met him recently. How did you know we were friends?"

"I saw you two talking one Sunday at Etienne's. Besides, he's mentioned your name a couple of times. I'm glad you two had a chance to hook up."

I am going to kill him.

"Well, Pearson, we have not hooked up. He just introduced himself to me and we're just friends."

"Yeah, friends. Well, I have to go. I'm on my way to depositions."

Snake. "Take it easy," she said, trying to remain cool. She planned to chew Tony out when he called tonight. Capri had warned him to be extra discreet about their "friendship" for the moment. She didn't need any complications.

CHAPTER TWENTY-THREE

Designer Pink Slip

Jewel sat at her desk and commended herself for being only fifteen minutes late. She was happy because Melvina's office was empty and the lights were off.

"Ms. Whitaker, may I see you?" said a heavy voice from behind her.

Jewel turned around. It was Melvina.

Darn, darn, darn . . .

"Ms. Whitaker, shut the door behind you and have a seat."

Jewel followed her orders.

"Ms. Whitaker, did we not recently have a talk about your tardiness?"

"Yes, but . . ."

"Ms. Whitaker, I am speaking. It seems as though you're not taking me seriously."

"I am . . . but . . ."

"No, you're not. I told you that you were on probation. I also told you that if you were late one more
time, your employment here would be terminated."

"Yes, but . . ."

"Well, the time has come for you to learn one of
life's lessons, responsibility. Your grace has run out,
Ms. Whitaker."

"What?" Jewel said in disbelief. "What are you saying?"

"Ms. Whitaker, I am going to have to let you go."

"No, not now. Please give me another chance,"
Jewel said, about to cry.

"Ms. Whitaker, I have given you several chances,
but you seem to take us for granted. You have a job to
do, and you're never here on time. I'm sorry to have
to do this, but the situation has gotten out of hand.
I'll discuss your severance package with human resources."

"I just don't believe this. I was only five minutes late
and you're going to do this?"

"Jewel, it's nothing personal, but you're going to
have to take responsibility for yourself."

"I got your responsibility, Melvina."

"Ms. Whitaker, I am losing my patience. Please
clean out your desk and go."

"Gladly," Jewel said as she got up and slammed the
door on her way out.

She tried to keep the tears from rolling down as
she approached her desk. She tried her best to ignore
the curious stares of her coworkers as she quickly gath-

Reality hit hard as she walked to her car. She started to panic. She wanted to run home and get underneath the covers.

What am I going to do about my bills? She sat in her car and didn't move. *Who can I call?*

She couldn't manage to lift the cell phone to her ear. She imagined the embarrassment she'd feel over having to admit what happened to any of her friends. Then she thought of Kevin.

He'll probably criticize me, too. She took out her palm pilot and looked up his number, happy that she had taken it down from her caller ID. She didn't know why she was calling, figuring he was probably at work anyway.

"Hi, you have reached the right number, but unfortunately, at the wrong time, so . . ."

I knew he wouldn't be there. Just as she was about to hang up, he picked up the phone.

"Hello."

"Hey, umm, may I speak to Kevin?"

"This is Kevin."

"Hey, Kevin. This is Jewel."

"Oh, Ms. Jewel. To what do I owe this distinct pleasure?"

"Well, I just happened to think about you and decided to give you a call."

"What's up? Your voice sounds a little funny."

"Yeah, I'm fine. What are you doing right now?" she asked.

"It's my day off. Right now I'm not doing anything, but this afternoon I'm going by my daughter's school."

"Oh, well, umm, I know this is short notice, but do you mind meeting me for a cup of coffee?"

"Uh, I was planning to run some errands this morning, but I can spare an hour."

"Oh good. Do you know where the Java Stop is?"

"Yup. That's not too far from my daughter's school. Do you want to meet there in about thirty minutes?"

"Yes, that would be great."

"Are you sure you're OK?"

"Yes, I'm sure," Jewel said, taking a slight breath.

As soon as she arrived at the Java Stop, she found a window seat. She gazed out the window and watched the people go by. She started wondering why she was put on earth. The more she thought about her job, the more she didn't care about getting fired. She actually felt liberated, yet she was still confused.

She watched the waitress. She seemed so enthusiastic and happy. She couldn't be making more than minimum wage plus tips, yet she had a big smile on her face.

She's probably gettin' some good lovin' . . . The walls could be falling down around you, but if you have someone who makes your toes curl, life seems great. She stared at her cup of espresso. She jumped when someone tapped her shoulder.

"Hey, don't be so tense. What's up?"

"Hey, Kevin. How'd you sneak in without me seeing you?"

"Well, you looked like you were totally in another

world. Excuse me, I'll have a cup of cappuccino," Kevin said, stopping the waitress before she walked past the table.

Jewel noticed how sweet his smile was. He had on a mustard-yellow polo shirt with baggy jeans and a pair of white tennis shoes. He *was* a cutie, like Lexi said, and it lifted her spirits to see him.

"I just have some things on my mind," Jewel said.

"So, why am I so privileged to have your company today?" he asked, slightly leaning forward and folding his hands on the table.

"Nothing really. I just wanted to talk with you for a moment since the last time we saw each other we were both preoccupied. You didn't tell me you had a woman," she said.

"Jewel, that wasn't my woman. I knew you would get to that sooner or later. Guess it was sooner. What about you? Are you attached?"

"Well, not really."

"What does that mean? Either you have someone or you don't. You're a grown woman. Stop playing the games."

"Games? You have some nerve. You show up at Etienne's with a date *and* a child and don't even have the decency to tell me who they are."

"Uh . . . if I remember our last conversation correctly, I don't recall you having much interest in me. But if you must know, that woman was my ex-wife."

"You've been married before?"

"Yeah, and you already know about my daughter, Aja."

"Well, what happened? How come things didn't work out?"

"It's complicated."

Jewel had an intuitive hunch.

"Are you raising your daughter yourself?"

Kevin sighed. "Yeah. I don't usually tell my business to just anyone, but for some *stupid* reason, I feel like telling you."

"Gee, thanks. I feel so honored."

"You asked, so I'm telling you. My ex-wife had a problem with drugs."

"Wow."

"Yeah, tell me about it."

"And I thought I had problems."

"You're so tactful."

"That must have been hard." She leaned in toward him and touched his shoulder.

"Yeah, to see someone you love just throw away everything. It hurt a lot."

"How'd she get hooked?"

"Well, she started messing around with other guys while we were married. One guy she messed with was into all sorts of drugs—acid, heroin, coke. She started seeing him on the regular and fell into using as well. She became hooked. I really don't want to go into details, but it was hell dealing with it. I tried to hold out for as long as possible, but I couldn't have Aja around a drugged-up mother. So Aja and I moved in with my mother. That scared the hell out of my ex and made her take stock of her situation and check herself into rehab."

Drama!

"Kevin, I'm so sorry."

"Thanks, but you know, we all have our crap to deal with. Anyway, once she was clean, it just didn't work any longer. I wanted us to try and rebuild, but she just wanted to start from scratch. Have a brand-new life, away from the reminders that she'd messed up so badly. She filed for divorce 'cause she thought it was the best thing to do. I fought it, but it takes two people to stay together."

"How is she now?"

"She's much stronger. She's a born-again Christian. She's about to finish her degree and is getting it together little by little. I try to be there for her when she needs me. I also try to make sure Aja spends a lot of time with her."

"Aja. That's a beautiful name. She is so precious."

"Yeah, she's my heart. I'm supposed to go to her school today and read to her class. Gotta do the parent thing."

"I really admire you."

"For what? I just do what I gotta do. Aja is my responsibility."

"Yes, but it takes a lot of strength to do what you're doing. You know how many Black men don't take care of their children. Besides, you seem so positive, considering the circumstances."

"I don't have a choice. All I can say is what was meant for evil, God took and made it for our good. But enough about me. You called me here for a reason. You sounded kind of down on the phone."

"Well, it was nothing in particular. I guess I just wanted to talk to you. I realize our first conversation didn't go too well. Sometimes, when I'm going through different emotions, I take it out on other people."

"You're a little moody, huh?"

"Well, I guess I am a little."

Then they traded stories about their childhood. Jewel, being an only child, could barely imagine what growing up was like for Kevin, who was the oldest of five children. To Jewel's surprise, he liked to travel, so they talked about a few places they'd both visited.

Jewel's excitement rose as they talked about her trip to Paris, a college graduation present from her parents. He'd gone there for his honeymoon.

And they both liked to shop: Jewel was the Galleria's resident shopaholic and Kevin was a major bargain hunter at Katy Mills Outlet. Jewel was pleasantly surprised at how much they had in common, while also feeling enticed by their differences. For a moment, she'd forgotten about the ex-wife drama.

"Hey, I really want to continue our conversation, but I'm going to have to take off," Kevin said. "I apologize, but I have some errands to run and then I need to go to Aja's school. So I'd better be taking off."

Jewel wanted to ask if she could go with him, but caught herself.

It's too early for all that. Besides, I need to think about this conversation.

"If you're not doing anything Saturday, maybe we can go to the movies or dinner."

"Yes, that sounds nice."

"I'll give you a call before then, though."

"OK," Jewel said, realizing that when he left she would be alone.

She watched him walk out the door and put her head in her hands. When she looked up, she thought she saw a familiar frame getting into a car. It looked like Jermane from the back. It was definitely her car, but she couldn't make out who was in the driver's seat. It certainly didn't look like Rex. She put her hand over her mouth.

Jewel, don't assume the worst.

She had enough problems of her own right now. Still, she was happy she'd decided to call Kevin.

God, could he be the answer to my prayers?

It sure didn't feel that way. She slumped back in her chair.

CHAPTER TWENTY-FOUR

Risky Business

Jermane felt a little nervous. Although what she was doing wasn't technically wrong, she didn't feel completely right being alone with someone else besides Rex.

She looked over at Naegel and couldn't believe she was in her car with him, on their way to her condo in Galveston. She looked out the window at the coastline.

"Let me know when we get close to the place," he said.

Jermane began giving him specific directions. They finally arrived at her condo. She pushed the garage door opener and they pulled in.

All of a sudden, it became real to her. She was with this man, and he was not her husband. Rex was out of town with her father, and she probably wouldn't hear from him until tomorrow. She got out of the car, and Naegel grabbed the groceries.

She opened the door and cool air surrounded her body. She opened the blinds and headed for the kitchen. When she turned around, she noticed Naegel standing at the window, resplendent even in a cream turtleneck and jeans. He stooped down, untied his laces, and removed his hiking boots and socks.

"Do you need some help putting those groceries away?"

"No, I'll be fine. It's not that many."

He opened the sliding door and started to walk out on the deck.

Jermane's eyes shot up. "Naegel, um, where are you going?"

"I was just going to go outside for a minute," he said.

"Well, I just think it'd be better if we just stay inside," she said, hoping he'd get the hint. She didn't want to take the chance of anyone seeing them.

"Oh, OK. I see. That's cool. I'll just chill out in here," he said as he stepped back inside. He left the door slightly open.

Jermane, relieved, took a few minutes to gaze out of the window. *It is a beautiful day.*

The winter chill had set in, and there was a slight breeze in the air. Jermane could feel the dew's gentle tingle on her skin. She started to think about Rex and the special evenings that they'd spent here. She felt nervous again.

Naegel eased into the kitchen and stood behind her. "Hey, you," he said, causing her to jump. "I'm sorry. I didn't mean to startle you. You seem uncomfortable."

"No, not really. I was just thinking of Rex."

"Jermane, I told you, I'm not trying to sleep with you. I asked you if this was all right. I thought you just needed someone to talk to. I respect you. I realize that you love your husband very much and I'd never do anything to hinder that."

"I know, but it still doesn't feel right. I was certain this was an OK idea since we're not doing anything. It's just that I feel like I'm cheating."

"Well, we can leave. I won't be upset."

"No, we have a whole day planned. I want to see your design ideas."

"Well, I just don't want to offend you. I can see how you feel. I'm not even sure why I'm here. I just know that I enjoy talking to you and, right now, you need a friend. I guess I just want to be there for you in some way. It's strange. You're beautiful, but I'm not attracted to you in that way. You're almost like a porcelain doll, too delicate to touch." He allowed his finger to wipe a strand of hair from her eye.

Jermane's body trembled slightly. It had been a long time since someone had touched her so gently. The gesture felt so warm to her, almost intoxicating. She moved toward the sink in a sharp movement, signaling her discomfort.

"I brought some CDs, mainly jazz and classical music. I love classical music," she said.

"I like classical. I don't know it well enough to tell

who the artists are, but it makes me feel good," he
said.

"It's so relaxing. Let's not do anything right now,"
Jermane said.

Jermane sat on the chaise lounge and crossed her legs.
She watched as Naegel sat on the couch near the chaise.

"What does it feel like?" he asked.

"What does what feel like?"

"What does it feel like to be among the young, rich
African Americans?"

"I'm not sure. Right now it feels kind of numb."

"Numb?"

"Yes, numb. I don't really have a hunger for anything. I don't even know what I'm about. I'm twenty-
seven years old and I feel like an old woman in a young
woman's body."

"Hmmm."

"What's that supposed to mean?"

"Nothing in particular, just thinking. When your
husband makes love to you, what do you see? Do you
see anything, or do you just feel your soul being lost?"

"I'm not sure what you mean."

"Never mind. We should stay away from that conversation."

"No, it's alright. I'm just not sure what you mean."

"If you have to ask, we don't need to talk about it."

"My husband and I have tons of chemistry. Still, in
the beginning, sex wasn't so great because, well, Rex *was*
a bit awkward and stiff. But now he knows exactly what
makes me feel good."

"I envy you," he said.

"Why?"

"Because you can make all the love you want and you won't be living in sin."

"Hmmmm. OK."

"I mean, I love making love, but I always feel so guilty afterward. I know sex outside of marriage is a sin, but my body just, I don't know, can't go without it."

"I really don't know what to say. Do you have someone special in your life?" Jermane asked.

"Well, I am seeing someone . . . she's a little younger. She's a model."

"It doesn't surprise me you're with someone gorgeous."

"Don't be impressed. I think it's just a sexual thing for her. She's intelligent, but I'm not sure I see a future for us. She's a great lover, but something's missing. She doesn't challenge me."

"In what way?"

"I don't know. I can't describe it. She's a bit manipulative, too."

"If you don't love her, why do you stay with her? I've never understood why men stay in relationships with women who aren't good for them."

"You know, when you share your body with someone and the connection is great, it's hard to just throw that away. I have to say, the sex is hot! Plus she worships me, and I haven't really met anyone else I'm interested in."

"Well, don't complain if you get trapped in the relationship and it's too late to get out. People need to be wise enough to recognize when they're staying in a relationship for the wrong reasons."

Naegel didn't respond.

The room became so quiet that they could hear the breeze coming through the screen door. Each wanted to say more, but gave up their urge to speak to the moment's serenity. Jermane was quietly shocked that he kept his word and didn't try to touch her. She heard tiny drops of rain and closed her eyes. The last thing she recalled before she dozed off was a warm and calm hand stroking her hair. She entered a place far away from her own.

CHAPTER TWENTY-FIVE

The Waiting Game

I hated this part. I waited a week and a half to call Kyle, making sure I saw him in church a second time before giving him a ring. I detested the formalities of getting to know a man. So many games were played. I already wanted to give up, but decided I had nothing to lose. Besides, I had to continue to be brave.

I picked up the phone in my office and called him. It rang three times. I wanted to hang up rather than leave a message, but before I knew it, the machine clicked on. "You've reached the voice mail of Kyle Morris, I'm unavailable at the moment . . ."

I have to leave the perfect message. Nothing too wordy or anxious.

"Hi, Kyle. This is Alexis Parker from church, just giving you a ring. You can return my call at 713-555-5234. Take care and I'll talk to you soon."

Now I had to go through the pain of wondering

when or if he was going to call. One thing was for sure—
I was not going to call before he did. I tried not to get
my hopes up. I felt like I had to have control. So I dismissed him from my mind.

After about an hour of working, the phone rang.

"Hey girl, what's up?"

It was Angel.

"Not much. Where are you?"

"In my car. I had a doctor's appointment today."

"That's right. Everything fine?"

"Hard to tell. They took more tests and said they'd
get back to me. It's a good thing my insurance pays for
all this crap."

"Hmmm, you said 'crap' instead of a curse word.
You're making progress. Are you sure that you're doing OK, girl?"

"Yeah, I'm a little nervous, but you know me. I try
not to worry unnecessarily."

"Where are you on your way to now?"

"Just home. Octavio's going to meet me there."

"So what's up with that? Y'all have been seeing each
other pretty tough lately."

"Well, he's cool. We've been friends for a while, but
I think he's starting to get a little too attached. I've been
giving him too much of my free time."

"Angel, I don't know what it is you do to these men,
but whatever it is, let me in on the secret."

"The secret is to never let them know exactly how
you feel. I don't care how good their intentions are.
Men are conquerors. As soon as they know they have
you, that's it."

"Well, so many men say they want someone kind and attentive . . ."

"That's a bunch of bullsh— I mean crap. Lexi, you've got to learn how to control your emotions. You meet a man and want to cook him dinner and pull out all the goodies on the first date. Let him work for the prize."

"I don't know. It makes more sense to me that they'd want someone calm and sweet."

"Lexi, you'll get it one day. Sweet is nice, but after a while, men get bored. I don't think they're satisfied unless they have a little drama in their lives."

"You could be right. I know too many men dating obsessive fools."

"See what I mean? I'm not asking you to go slashing any tires, but just cool out a bit."

Maybe I am too nice.

"I can only be who I am. I can't help it if I'm warm and sensitive."

"OK, 'Warm and Sensitive.' If what you're doing isn't bringing you the results you want, you need to change the formula."

"I hear you."

"Well, I have to go."

"Take care, Angel. Tell Octavio I said hey." We hung up.

I thought about what Angel said. It must have had some truth to it because it seemed like every man Angel dated was all caught up with her.

The loud ring jolted me out of my thoughts.

"Ms. Parker?"

"Yes, this is she."

"This is Kyle Morris. How are you doing? I got your message."

"Oh, hi. I didn't expect to hear from you so soon."

"Yes, I've been very busy, but I wanted to take a quick moment to return your call. I can't talk long, but I wanted to know if you were free for lunch this Friday?"

"Well, yes, I am."

"I'll call you back tomorrow and we can pick a place and a time to meet."

"That sounds fine, Kyle."

"I'll talk to you then."

I hung up and shimmied my bootie a bit in my chair.

Okay, don't get too hyped. Remember what Angel said. Cool and calm.

I had to take it easy. I just didn't want to hurt anymore. The little excitement I felt from Kyle's call was suddenly extinguished by the wave of heartbreaks I'd previously suffered. My eyes started to water as I thought about how broken I sometimes felt, about how much of a disappointment all the men I'd dated had turned out to be. I just couldn't take another heartbreak. I promised to avoid it at all costs.

CHAPTER TWENTY-SIX

Too Close for Comfort

Angel felt the emptiness of her apartment. She looked at her caller ID. Octavio had called twice. She was behind schedule and figured she'd call him when she was running out the door. In the shower, she started to think about her doctor's appointment and felt overwhelmed by anxiety. The doctor's news had shaken her. She couldn't believe she had to face the option of not having children. Her knees grew weak at the thought. She'd never had any type of surgery, and, until the doctor's report, she'd never even known what fibroids were. She touched her lower belly, as if she could feel them or make them dissolve.

Then she thought about Octavio again and felt even more anxious. She was getting dependent on him. He made her feel special, loved. She loved the way he smelled, the way his hair was slicked back and always glistening, the way he said her name in Spanish—Angelita, his "Little Angel."

I cannot get caught up with this man. Not now.

She suddenly felt uncomfortable. She longed to see him tonight, but also felt like she needed to be alone. As she got out of the shower, the phone rang. She grabbed her robe and reached for the cordless.

"Angelita, que pasa? Where've you been?"

"I had to run some errands. I'm dripping wet. I just got out the shower."

"Oh, so you're that excited about seeing me."

"Well, I was thinking, I'm really worn out from the doctor's. I wanted to see if we could postpone our date until the weekend."

"Oh, alright. If you're feeling tired, I *guess* I understand."

"What do you mean you guess?"

"I didn't mean anything by it, really."

"Well, I'm really tired. I think you need to be a little more considerate based on the circumstances."

"Angel, I know you may be a little on edge about your appointment, but chill out. Anyway, I wanna talk about how your appointment went. You OK?"

"Yeah, I'm fine. Anyway, I gotta go. I'll talk to you."

Angel hung up the phone, quickly stifling her feelings of guilt. She couldn't deal with Octavio right now.

The next thing she knew, she was crying slow, continuous tears. She couldn't stop. She wiped the tears with the sleeve of her robe.

She got down on her knees and said nothing. She
bowed her head. At that moment, nothing could
soothe her. Old pain poured out uncontrollably.
She cried and cried until there was nothing left inside.

God, please help me!

Angel succumbed to her tiredness and fell asleep.
She woke up in the morning on the living room floor,
curled up like a baby.

CHAPTER TWENTY-SEVEN

Be Anxious for Nothing

I was sitting in the Blue Moon Bistro, waiting for Kyle to arrive. I'd been fashionably late, but he was even later. I twisted my napkin back and forth. I tried not to stare at the entrance too long. I started to think I'd been stood up. Then I heard a voice from behind.

"Lexi, how long have you been here?"

I turned around and breathed a mental sigh of relief.

"Oh, for about ten minutes."

"I'm sorry. My office paged me and I had to go use the phone. You look beautiful."

"Thank you," I said, trying to sound relaxed.

"So, how's your week been?"

"Not bad. Really busy. I just got a couple of new clients," I said as I reached for my water.

"So, have you been here before?"

"No, this is my first time. What do you recommend?" I asked, picking up the menu.

"They have excellent pasta dishes."

"I love pasta."

Kyle looked like he was about to ask me a question when the waiter appeared.

"Mr. Morris, how are you today?" the waiter said.

"I'm doing great, especially since I have such great company."

I tried not to blush.

"I'll have the penne pasta and chicken with alfredo sauce and the lady will have . . ."

"The same," I said.

"Very good, Mr. Morris." The waiter walked away.

"So, you're an attorney. Very impressive."

"Well, I guess you could say that. It's not all it's cracked up to be."

"It must've taken a lot of hard work to accomplish that. Don't take it lightly."

"Yes, finishing school and passing the bar was a lot of work, but now my biggest challenge is establishing a business, and it takes a lot out of me sometimes, particularly finding paying clients."

"I'm quite sure you're well on your way. You seem very savvy."

"Thanks, Kyle. The feeling's mutual."

"I hope you don't mind me asking this, Lexi, but do you have any kids?"

I smiled. "No, and I've never been married."

"*You* don't have any kids and have never been

married? What's wrong with you?" He laughed. I
forced a smile.

*If one more man asks me that, I'm gonna scream. I'm supposed to
be the majority, not the minority. I'm tryin' to do things the right way.*

"I know you didn't just ask me that. The million-
dollar question. Well, the million-dollar answer is
'nothing.' Have you ever been married?"

"No. No kids, either."

"Well . . ."

"What's wrong with me? Nothing. I hope I didn't
offend you. I'm just surprised an attractive woman such
as yourself hadn't been snagged by some lucky man
much earlier."

He got more points for that.

"So do you enjoy being an accountant?"

"I'm a CPA, and yes I do enjoy it. I've always been
good with numbers. So what do you like to do, Lexi?"

"Plays, movies, traveling, concerts—I'm pretty
open. I just like to stay active."

"Well, we'll have to make sure we find plenty of activities to indulge in as we get to know each other."

Lord, YES!!!

"That sounds fine to me, Kyle."

As I ate my food, I tried not to look like I was sizing
him up. But it was hard not to. He was smart, articulate, a professional, polite, sexy—and he went to
church! I thought about how "Parker" would sound hy-
phenated with "Morris." Then I came back to earth.

*He seems like such a keeper. Lord, don't fool me now. I am tired of
false prophets.*

After we ate and talked some more, he walked me to

my car. He said he'd call me to see if we could coordinate going to church together on Sunday. I calmly smiled and said "sure" as my heart did flips and cartwheels. He gave me a hug and kiss and walked away. As I got in the car, I pretended to look for my keys so I could see what kind of car he drove. I watched him get into a black Mercedes.

I can work with that.

CHAPTER TWENTY-EIGHT

The Clean-Up Woman

Angel drove through downtown on her way home, choosing the route to bypass highway traffic due to an accident. Her mind was in five different places.

She'd never really thought about the possibility of not having children. All the negative things she used to say about children weren't really true. She'd felt in her heart that she would eventually remarry and have kids. She was just scared.

The possibility of having a hysterectomy at such a young age was crushing. She felt like God was punishing her for talking so much about not having kids.

The pain in her heart was indescribable. She felt incredibly alone. She wanted to talk to Octavio, but felt ashamed because she'd been pushing him away so much the past few weeks. She was afraid that if he found out that she may not be able to have children, he would no longer want to be with her. She was confused, and terrified.

And then there's his age. But then again, there's a trend going on. Look at Demi Moore. She's forty or so and that guy she's dating is at least fifteen years younger. Since when do I care about what people think anyway?

I wonder what his family would think about us? Won't they be looking for him to bring some nice, young Hispanic girl home? But no other man has ever treated me so well. It doesn't matter now anyway, since we're not speaking. Angel took a deep breath. *I really do miss his friendship.*

She almost ran into the back of the car in front of her when she saw Octavio coming out of Ruggles, another of their favorite restaurants, with a slender Hispanic woman. She looked to be about twenty-seven years old. She tossed her dark wavy hair as they laughed and walked arm in arm.

Who in the heck is that? Angel thought as her nostrils flared.

She didn't know whether to be angry or hurt. What could she do? She reminded herself that *she* was the one who'd started pulling away. But Angel couldn't deny the extreme jealousy she was feeling at the moment. She was mad. Mad at everything. Mad because her first marriage failed. Mad because God didn't stop her from getting married in the first place. Mad because she was sick. Mad because everyone thought she was so tough and she wasn't. Mad because she thought she'd made it professionally, but now was disappointed in being at the top. Mad because she'd been talking to God lately, and it seemed like He didn't have a word to say. Mad because she didn't understand why her friends went to church every Sunday and still had problems. Mad because Octavio was with another woman.

I'm out of control. She turned on her radio. She put a halt to her silent rage long enough to listen to the lyrics of the song playing.

She listened carefully to the words and decided she was going to keep on praying until she heard from God. He couldn't possibly ignore her if she continued to bother him. All these people couldn't possibly be lying. She continued to listen to the radio, hoping they'd announce the singer of the song she'd just heard.

"That was 'Just a Prayer Away,' by Yolanda Adams. I know it's unusual for us to play gospel this time of day, but I figured at rush hour, our listeners need something to slow them down. Remember, He knows what you need before you really know it, so be encouraged and remember that God is still on the throne," the radio announcer said with reassurance.

Angel took a detour and stopped at the record store.

CHAPTER TWENTY-NINE

The Other "Other Woman"

J ermane was excited about her new project. She was determined to bring some much-needed life and change to her home. As she drove up to the Java Stop, she anticipated seeing Naegel so she could tell him the good news. She reasoned that having him decorate two rooms in her house would give him experience and exposure. Yet she also knew she was flirting with fire.

When she walked in, she froze. A tall, reedy, dark-skinned woman stood in front of Naegel. Her hair was pulled up into a high ponytail that bounced with the slightest movement of her head. She had on a long black lycra skirt and a white sleeveless v-neck top with a black sweater tied around her thin waist. A small, totelike black purse hung from her thin arm. The woman's back was to Jermane and she was facing Naegel. Jermane wanted to turn around and walk out, but Naegel had already spotted her. He stopped talking.

"Jermane," he called.

Jermane, halfway startled, walked over.

"Hey, how are you?" he said.

"Good," she said.

"This is Kenya," he said.

Jermane noticed how exotic Kenya's features were. Her skin was very dark, with an almost charcoal tone to it. She had high cheekbones and thin lips. Her eyebrows were neatly arched. Her lips were stained with a hint of cherry color. The rest of her face was completely bare with a slight glow of moisture. She looked no more than twenty-five. She was extremely poised, like a statuesque flower.

"How are you?" she said with an accent, tilting her head gracefully. Jermane remembered that Naegel said she'd been born in Trinidad, but was raised as a French Canadian.

"Oh, great," Jermane said.

"I have heard a lot about you," she said, looking Jermane up and down.

How much?

"Oh, yes, I've heard a lot of wonderful things about you as well," Jermane said after a slight pause.

"Well, sweetheart, I am going to be off. I have a shoot this morning. Ciao," Kenya said as she kissed Naegel quickly on the lips. "Lovely to meet you, Jermane. Ciao." She gave Jermane an air kiss, whirled around, and pranced away as if she were a dancing horse.

Jermane tried to regroup so she could tell Naegel

about the decorating project, but she was thrown off by
this unexpected scene. She was surprised by the im-
mense jealousy she was actually feeling, hoping and
praying it wasn't showing on her face. As much as
Naegel talked about their lack of compatibility, he
seemed pretty comfortable with Kenya.

"So, are you having the usual today?" Naegel said,
interrupting Jermane's thoughts.

"Uh, oh yeah," she said, snapping out of her trance.

"You're here a little earlier than usual," he said.

"Yes, I wanted to discuss a proposal with you," Jermane said.

"Oh, really? I'm all ears," he said.

"Well, I talked to Rex about doing some redecorat-
ing, and naturally, I thought about you. This will be a
way to build up your clientele. If you do a good job, we
know a lot of people we could refer you to," she said in
a serious tone.

"Wow, that would be great. It would be an excellent
addition to my portfolio!"

"Yes, I thought it was a good idea."

"Well, when could we get together to discuss some
ideas? And I need to look at the space," he said.

"What about this weekend?" Jermane asked.

"Do you have some time during the week?" he said.

"Sure, I just said the weekend because I thought it
would be better for you."

"Normally it is, but Kenya just mentioned some
last-minute plans for this weekend."

"Well, alright. I don't have any classes on Thursdays. So how about this Thursday at 11 a.m.?"

"Sounds great."

"I'll write down the directions for you," Jermane said as she pulled out a pen.

"Cool. I'm going to get your cappuccino," Naegel said.

Jermane sat there and wrote out the directions. She couldn't help but play back in her mind the scene that had just occurred. She felt like she was losing her mind. She had no business feeling jealous of Kenya and fought hard to suppress those feelings. There was a special bond with Naegel, but she had to draw the line with her emotions. She convinced herself she was in total control of her feelings and continued to write the directions to her house.

CHAPTER THIRTY

"Where Two or More Are Gathered . . ."

As soon as I walked into the house, I pulled off my pantyhose. My day had been very long, a reminder of how I worked too hard for too little. I was feeling pretty discouraged.

There was a revival at Living Truth tonight, but I was so tired, I couldn't even make it to the revival to get revived.

I checked my messages and noticed Capri had called, but Kyle had not. If he didn't call by Wednesday to confirm our date for Friday, I was going to have to ignore his calls for the rest of the weekend. I really didn't want to do that.

I slipped on my leggings and an old T-shirt from Reggie. Although I was hungry, I didn't have a taste for anything, so I decided to order pizza. I was breaking all the diet rules, but at this point, I really didn't care.

I thought about Angel and reminded myself that before I went to bed tonight, I really needed to pray hard. Just as I reclined on the couch, the phone rang. Thinking it was Kyle, I jumped up and grabbed the phone from the coffee table.

"Lexi, hey. It's Capri."

"Oh, hey girl, what's going on?" I asked. My question wasn't merely rhetorical, since Capri's workload had gotten even higher of late. Between work and her romance with Tony, she hardly had time to speak during the last few weeks. She'd even been missing our brunches.

"I had a really bad day."

"Join the club, girl. I am so tired. I did all this rushing to get to court and couldn't find a parking space. I had a hearing in Judge Hinkle's court. You know how moody she is. Anyway, I got there and the clerk was so nasty. For no reason at all, she gave me major attitude. I don't know if it's because I look so young or what, but I'm sick of getting no respect. Anyway, I got there after all this rushing and sweating and the hearing had been reset. No one bothered to notify me. Then on top of things, I haven't heard from Kyle in a week. I am so tired of people just thinking they can take my kindness for weakness. You know what they always say, 'the squeaky oil gets the wheel.' "

"You mean 'the squeaky wheel gets the oil.' "

"You know what I mean!"

"Well, I guess this isn't really a good time to burden you with any extra bad news," Capri said slowly.

"I'm sorry, I just got off on a tangent. Is everything alright with you?" I asked.

"Uhm, things are generally fine. By the way, how's the crew? Sorry about missing brunch."

"Everyone's hanging in. By the way, did you know that Jewel's stopped actively looking for a job?"

"What?"

"Yeah, she said something about taking time to 'find herself.' I don't know how she's making ends meet. I really can't worry about Jewel right now. I guess we just need to let Jewel be Jewel and pray for her."

"What's up with her and that Kevin guy?" Capri asked.

"I don't know. He seems to really like her and she seems to really like him. They've been spending a lot of time together. Jewel's even been cooking for him and his daughter. Jewel is just crazy about Aja. I heard his ex-wife was a nut though, so I told her to be careful."

"Unbelievable," Capri said. "Who would've thought Jewel would go for his type."

"Well, maybe Jewel is maturing," I said. "Anyway, before you get too excited, let me tell you about her birthday plans. It's major."

"She's planning something major for her birthday? She's not working."

"Regardless, it's her special day. She's planning a '70s party, girl, with Afros, pimps, and platform shoes. The whole drama."

"Lexi, I really need to talk about something serious. My grandmother isn't doing too well. She tries to pretend like everything's all right, but Trina called me today to say she has to stay overnight in the hospital for some tests. Her treatments don't seem to be making that big of a difference. Then on top of that, I told Pearson Carrington, Anthony's attorney, to 'go directly to hell' on the way out of my office today. I've never lost my cool like that at work. I just don't trust him. I believe he knows I've been seeing Anthony and keeps on dropping slimy hints. And remember that big Fast Trak client I brought in?"

"Yeah?"

"Well, they had endorsement deal talks with Tony. They wanted him to sign this waiver of conflicts agreement so the firm can represent both him and Fast-Trak. I saw the agreement, Lexi, and it doesn't appear to give Tony the best protection. I can't believe Pearson would advise him to do it. Something funny is going on."

"Maybe Pearson's not on the up and up?"

"I don't know. But I think I need to talk to Tony about it," Capri said. She let out a sigh. "This is getting so messy."

"Capri, I'm sorry. Are you going to go home to see your grandmother?"

"Well, I did talk to her today and she insists that I shouldn't worry and should stay put. But I can't help it. She's my second mom," Capri said.

"Have you told Anthony about your grandmother?" I asked.

"No, not yet."

"Capri, you need to open up to him more."

"I just don't like to burden people with my problems. Anyway, have you talked to Angel this week? I called her tonight and she seemed out of it," Capri said.

"Oh yeah, I have. She's probably just tired. She's been working a lot of extra hours."

"Whatever happened to her hot romance with Octavio?" Capri said.

"I'm not sure. You know Angel. She doesn't believe in getting too attached. I think she really does care for him, though."

"She needs to stop pushing men away. She's missing out."

"Excuse me? Look who's talking!"

"Now, Lexi, you have to admit that I am giving Tony a big chance, at great professional risk, might I add," Capri responded.

"Well, if worse comes to worse, you could always quit the firm," I said.

"It sounds easy, but I don't want to go out like that. If I leave, I want it to be on my terms. Besides, having this money is really a big help to Grandma and Trina," Capri said.

"I know, but you can't stay chained to a situation forever. Tony really makes you happy. Sometimes in life you have to make choices. If you decide to leave the firm, God will provide. Besides, if you think something unethical is going on, you may not want to continue doing business there. Everything you've done so far at the firm has been legitimate. You've had success and maintained your principles. You don't want to undercut yourself," I said.

"Yeah, but I'm not being so legitimate now, am I? I'm dating one of our clients."

"Well, you never now why God has brought Tony into your life. Maybe if you hadn't met him, you would never think about leaving the firm. Before you know it, you would look up and the years would've gone by. You would have all this money and no life. Yes, Capri, you have a great job. You've proved that you can hang with some of the toughest lawyers, but life has other things. I'm quite sure God has a plan. You have to just pray and ask for wisdom so you can know what to do next. Still, I think in this instance, you need to follow your heart."

"I don't know. It's kind of scary," Capri said.

"What?"

"Just letting go of the control you have over life and putting it in God's hands. I can do it really well in some areas, but in other areas it's hard," Capri said.

"I know exactly what you mean. But it gets easier the more you let go. Anyway, girl, I'm really tired, but before we get off the phone, let's pray," I offered.

"Pray together?" Capri asked.

"Yes. I'll pray. You don't have to say anything if you don't want to."

"OK."

Dear heavenly and most gracious Father, I just want to thank You for another day. I want to thank You for Your tender mercy and for-giveness. We give You all the praise. I ask that You cleanse us with the blood of Jesus Christ. Give us a fresh spirit, for we know that we have sinned and fallen short of Your Glory.

First Lord, I want to uplift our families. Touch them, meet all of their needs according to Your riches and glory in Christ Jesus. Second Lord, I want You to bless all of our friends. Those who are unsaved, we ask that they come to know You as their personal Savior.

Lord, I especially pray for Capri. Give her wisdom for every area of her life. Lord, You said if we want wisdom, "all we have to do is ask and You will give it to us freely." Whatever is not right at her job, reveal it to us, Father. As for her grandmother, Lord, I know that You are the ultimate healer. According to First Peter 2:24, You said, "By His stripes, we have been healed," so we speak healing in her grandmother's body right now. We also ask that You put a hedge of protection around her sister while she is at school. Lord, we say a special prayer for Jewel as well. Give her guidance and wisdom. Help her finances. Help mine as well. Help us to be good stewards over our money.

Finally Lord, I pray for myself. You know my deepest desires. You said in Your word, in Psalms 37:4, "If we delight ourselves in You, You would give us the desires of our heart." You know my desire is for my business to prosper. Lord, I also desire a good relationship. You said You would not withhold any good gifts from Your children. Lord, we thank You and give You all the praise. And as always, let Your will be done. In Jesus' name we pray. Amen.

"I never knew you could pray like that. That was very powerful. Thank you so much," Capri said.

"You're welcome. I just said what came to mind. I believe God's heard our prayer and is going to do something miraculous," I said.

"I hope so."

"No, believe so," I said affirmatively.

"We're going to have to do that more often. Anyway,

I'm going to try to turn in early. Tony and I talked about going to San Antonio this weekend, just to get away, but I might go see Grandma. I'll let you know for sure what my plans are either way," Capri said.

"Alright. I'll talk to you before the week is over."

I thought about Capri and Tony. It was clear to me that Capri didn't have to guess about their relationship. Tony was a man who knew exactly what he wanted. I realized that there were men out there who were mature enough to put their feelings on the line.

Kyle and I had been seeing each other for several months now, but he was still calling me his "friend." He still turned his ringer off when we were at his apartment and I had hardly met any of his friends. Whenever I invited him to hang out with my friends, he cancelled at the last minute. Then he always told me what I should wear, as if I don't have taste in clothes.

Plus, we had started to go out on actual dates with less frequency and he was starting to push for sex, even though he wasn't ready for the committed-relationship talk. In fact, the last time we hung out, I refused to go there sexually, which might explain his current missing-in-action status. This situation was starting to look sadly familiar. Yes, his credentials were great, but that was becoming irrelevant because he was failing to realize what he has in me.

Still, the last time we saw each other, he had invited me to a job function on Friday, which gave me a glimmer of hope. After thinking about my drama with Kyle, I felt even more tired and dozed off. I said a quick silent prayer for Angel right before sleep hit me.

CHAPTER THIRTY-ONE

Layin' Down the Law

Angel was nervous. Her next doctor's appointment was at 2 p.m. the next day and she was trying not to think about it. It had been another long day. She had had to sit in on several long, boring depositions relating to the case she'd been working on. Her caller ID showed that several people had called. After checking the numbers, she decided not to call anyone back because she just wanted to be alone. She baked herself some chicken and steamed some vegetables instead of eating her usual greasy treats. Her last few visits to the doctor had given her the revelation that she wasn't twenty-one anymore.

Just as she took a second bite of chicken, the phone rang. It was Octavio. She hesitated for a moment, then answered.

"Hello."

"That was a crazy message you left on my machine," he said.

Angel flashed back to the message she'd left. "Hi, Octavio . . . as I should've known, you've turned out to be a trifling, insincere piece of . . ."

I let the green-eyed monster out. So unlike me. She wished she could've erased the message.

"Oh, yeah, I forgot about that," she said.

"Give me a break, Angel. Have you lost your mind?"

"Well, I was just a little stressed out that day. Then I saw you downtown with that woman."

"Angelita, what is up with you? If I recall, you were the one who cut me off. You knew how much I was starting to care about you," he said.

"You just don't understand," Angel replied.

"How much more understanding do I need to be? I tried to be a friend to you. I respected your space. After three years of friendship, if I don't have your trust by now, I'll never have it. I'm tired of working like a racehorse trying to get women to take me seriously and trust me. If you want me, Angel, you're going to have to let me know."

"Well, I've explained to you, I've been hurt . . ."

"Angel, I don't want to hear anymore of this 'I have been hurt' BS. We've all been hurt, but you have to let it go. Stop being a baby."

Angel was silent and a bit shocked by Octavio's bluntness.

"And the girl you saw me with was Liz. We went to high school together, and her job relocated her back here recently. I do like spending time with her, but we haven't established a relationship. So, the burden's on you. If you want to give us a serious chance, get rid of that baggage and step up to the plate. Otherwise, I'm proceeding accordingly."

Angel was stunned. "I guess I really need to think about what you just said."

"I said what I had to say, Angelita." His voice softened and he took a deep breath, "Umm, how have you been feeling lately? I mean physically."

"I'm hanging in there. I have a doctor's appointment tomorrow," she said, relieved that he cared enough to ask.

"Well, if you need me, you know where I am. I'm always here for emergencies. You take care of yourself," he said.

"Bye."

Angel sat back and absorbed their conversation. He was so serious. And certain. She had to really think about her next move. She couldn't mess with Octavio unless she was serious about him.

A part of her didn't like his ultimatum because it felt like she was no longer in control of their relationship. But another part felt charged and turned on by his assertion. She had a lot to think about over the weekend. But one thing was for sure—she missed him dearly.

CHAPTER THIRTY-TWO

Get to Steppin'!

I looked at my watch and saw it was almost two o'clock. I'd spoken with Kyle the night before, and he said he would call me before one o'clock today, but I didn't see any messages from him. I sighed and continued to put away the files I was working with. When I was just about finished, the phone rang.

"Hey, Lexi. This is Kyle."

"Hey," I said in a less-than-enthusiastic tone.

"What's wrong now?" he said sarcastically.

"What do you mean by *that* comment?" I said.

"You don't have to say anything. I can hear it in your voice," Kyle said. "Well, I was calling to tell you to meet me at Mosaic's on San Felipe."

"I thought you were coming to pick me up."

"Well, it's just easier for you to meet me there. A

couple of guys from the office are going over early, and I'm going to head over with them. You won't even be finished with your work yet," he said.

"I work for myself. I can leave when I want to. Never mind, Kyle. I'll meet you there at about 5:30," I said.

I felt frustrated already. Kyle and I weren't on the same page. But I was tired of spending Friday nights at home. I worked so hard, I deserved a night out.

As five o'clock approached, I finished up the Request for Admissions I was working on and began packing my things up. I went into the restroom to freshen up and reapply my makeup. I didn't feel very confident.

I took the elevator downstairs and saw the new security guard with the gold tooth who always flirted with me. He flashed his tooth and tipped his hat as I walked by. He really got on my nerves sometimes, but it was nice to know someone appreciated me.

After I arrived at the restaurant, I heard music and saw people who appeared to have started the party way before I arrived. I finally tracked Kyle down in the crowd. He was deep in conversation with a group of his coworkers and looked like he'd been enjoying the festivities for some time. When he finally noticed me, he waved his hand for me to come over and join his circle of coworkers. I walked over. He didn't introduce me or grab me closer to him. He just kept on talking.

After about ten minutes of him running his mouth, his circle dispersed. Two of his coworkers remained.

"Who is this young lady?" one of them asked.

"Oh, I'm sorry, this is Lexi," Kyle said.

"Hi, nice to meet you," I said in a monotone.

"So, is this the future Mrs. Morris? She is very pretty," the other coworker said.

We both took a deep breath. I was slightly embarrassed.

"We're not quite at that stage yet. As a matter of fact, I don't really know where we are," I said, knowing this statement was going to be discussed later.

Kyle changed the subject. I stood there and realized I didn't really want to be there. After about an hour of making small talk with people I had to introduce myself to, I pulled him to the side and said I was going to make it an early night. He seemed concerned and offered to walk me to my car.

"Sweetie, I warned you that you might be bored," he said.

"I was only bored because you paid me no attention."

"You have to be more sociable."

"What? I just forced myself to mingle with folks who don't know me from Adam! I was just picking up some very negative vibes from you," I replied.

"Well, I'm going to call you when I get home. You drive safely," he said.

I barely got in the car before he shut my door and headed back toward the restaurant. I felt discarded, dismissed, and disregarded. I decided I was going to stop on the way home and rent a movie, something funny to take my mind off his trifling behind.

———

*M*y nap was interrupted by the phone. I looked up and realized I hadn't finished watching even half of *The Best Man*.

"Lexi, this is Kyle. Were you asleep?"

"Sort of. What time is it?" I asked.

"It's eleven," he replied.

"Where are you?" I asked.

"I'm on my cell phone. I'm about five minutes away and wanted to stop by," he said.

"No, Kyle. It's too late."

"Come on, Lexi. I promise, if you let me come over, I'll go to church with you on Sunday," he said.

"Kyle, don't do this to me. I'm angry with you anyway," I said.

"Lexi, please. I really can't drive home," he said.

"Kyle, don't give me that. You don't even drink that much," I said.

"I know, but tonight I did," he said.

"Well, you can come by long enough to sleep off whatever it is you had to drink," I said.

"Alright," he said quickly.

When Kyle came in, he went straight to my bed. He passed out like a rock. I sat up and watched television. The more I thought about him, the angrier I became. I was serious. He *was* going to church with me Sunday, or that was it.

Around 2 a.m., I climbed in the bed and left Kyle on top of the covers. About an hour later, he rolled over and grabbed my waist. This felt nice at first, but then I remembered that I was still mad at him.

The next thing I knew, his hand was up my

nightgown, attempting to caress me. This felt really good too, especially since I had been celibate for a while now. He started kissing my neck lightly. This was definitely one of my weak spots.

But my body was starting to give in. He knew it, because he started to roll on top of me. I pushed him away.

"Kyle, get up."

"What?"

"*I said get up!* How do you think you're just going to come over here and act like this? You barely talk to me, and then you come over here drunk to get some!?!"

"I don't believe this," he said as he sat up. "This is why we will never be in a relationship. You're too freakin' uptight. All you do is nag and complain about this, nag and complain about that."

"Well, I'm sorry you feel that way. You're just mad because I won't put up with your arrogant attitude. You think you have it going on just because you have a decent job and a nice car. But guess what? You don't have any character. You're such a hypocrite."

"What do you mean hypocrite?"

"Never mind, Kyle, just go home," I said as I rolled over.

Without saying a word, he got up and fumbled his way over to the door. I heard it slam. I honestly didn't care. As I dozed off, the only discomfort I had was the thought of having to see him in church from now on.

Promises, Promises

J ermane sat in the study and finished her reading for the next week. Then she pulled out the jacquard and silk fabric swatches that Naegel had left for her to look at last Thursday. She was already pleased. *It's amazing how well he knows my taste*.

He was creative, yet tried not to stray too far away from her personality. She enjoyed working with him and was glad she chose him for the remodeling.

"Hey, sweetheart. How is your reading coming along?" Rex asked.

"Oh, I'm done," she said. She looked up and noticed how sexy her husband looked. She liked the way his drawstring cotton pajama pants rested at his waist. His chest was bare, and he was walking around barefoot. He looked natural, uncomplicated, casual—such a rare look for Rex.

"So have you decided how you want the bedroom to look?" he asked.

"No, not yet," Jermane replied.

"Oh, I meant to tell you, Jewel called today," Rex said with a smile. "She wanted to make sure we received her birthday party invitation. She's having a seventies theme celebration."

"Yes, I know. Jewel never ceases to amaze me," Jermane said.

"It might be fun," Rex said.

"You're planning on going?" Jermane asked with surprise in her voice.

"Yes. I was told about it far enough in advance to make time in my schedule," Rex replied. "So, where did you meet this Naegel?"

Jermane paused. "He was a referral. He's a student at the interior design school downtown."

"Oh. Well, I hope he does a good job."

"Yes, I'm quite sure he will," she replied.

"When will he be back?" he asked.

"Sometime next week," Jermane said.

"Maybe I'll hang around." Rex paused. "I realize I need to try harder than I have. When we first moved into this house, we picked out a lot of things together," he said.

"Yes, we did a lot together back then."

"Yeah . . ." he replied, sounding distant.

"Rex?"

"Hmm?"

"Do you think I'm being selfish? Is this how marriage is really supposed to be? I really miss you," Jermane said.

"Sweetie, I have been thinking a lot about that lately. I finally had a chance to slow down the other day. I'm waiting until the right time to talk to your father about cutting back on my caseload."

"Will you please?" Jermane pleaded like a disbelieving child.

"Yes, I promised myself I would," Rex said as he grabbed and embraced his wife.

"I love you," Jermane said, losing herself in his embrace.

"I love you, too, Jermane," he said softly. "Now please, honey, I've heard you. Things will be different," he said as he pulled away gently. "After I finish a little work today, I promise we'll do something."

"OK," she said quietly. She felt her stomach tighten a little as she watched him walk out the door. *Promises, promises.*

CHAPTER THIRTY-FOUR

Life Is About Change

Jewel grabbed Aja's hand and walked her to the buffet table so she could fix their plates. Kevin watched them from our table. I could tell that he cared a lot for Jewel. I had to give Jewel credit. She was maturing.

She was also smothering Aja, who is Kevin's heart. I think he liked Jewel so much because she was so good with his daughter. Jewel said they were taking her to Kid's Mountain after brunch. I don't know if I could deal with all that noise—one million screaming children!

"So where's Capri?" Jermane asked. "We never see her anymore."

"Oh, she went to San Antonio with you know who," I said.

"Oh, well, that's nice," Jermane said.

"So what's been up with you lately?"

"Nothing much. Rex and I are having the bedroom and the study remodeled."

"Oh, really. And who might be doing the decorating? Not one designer by day, stripper by night?"

"Do you mean Naegel?"

"Yes, I mean Naegel."

"Lexi, he's an interior designer. I thought he would do a good job. And so far I'm right."

"Has Rex met him?"

"No, not yet, but he will. Naegel is a total professional. We're just friends. As a matter of fact, I met his girlfriend the other day."

"I'm not here, and I'm definitely not hearing this," Kevin said as he stuffed his face with pancakes.

"Kevin, I don't know what Lexi is implying. Don't pay her any attention," Jermane said.

"I have just one thing to say—a man knows when someone else has been dipping in the Kool-Aid."

"I beg your pardon. You have me mistaken for someone else."

"I'm just being real with you."

"Can we change the subject?" Jermane asked.

"Lexi, is Angel coming today?" Jewel asked, returning with Aja.

"I haven't heard from her."

"What is up with her and Octavio? I saw him the other day with some Hispanic chick."

"Now she didn't tell me anything about that. I'm going to have to call her. I think she's just been going through some things lately."

"Lexi, I know you're holding out," Jewel said.

"Jewel, you wouldn't want me to tell any of your business, would you?" I said as I sipped my espresso.

"You're right," she said, quickly dismissing the subject.

"Ms. Jewel, can you take me to the restroom?" Aja asked, finally finding a break in the conversation.

"Sure." Jewel got up and helped Aja out of her chair.

"So, did ya'll hear about Jewel's party?" Kevin said after a few minutes, shifting the conversation from gossip.

"Yes, we did. Do we have to actually dress up? I will look ridiculous in an Afro," Jermane said.

"That's the whole point. Jermane, don't be so tight. Loosen up a little. Bring your husband or Naegel, whoever, and have a ball. Don't disappoint my baby," Kevin said.

I think I'm going to throw up. "You know we'll all be there," I said.

"You know Jewel. She gets overexcited. We'll have to hear about this until the day of the party. We'll probably end up having to pay for half of it anyway," Jermane added.

"No, everything is taken care of," Kevin said.

"Kevin, I knew there was something about you I liked. Anybody who can keep Jewel from mooching is alright with me," I said.

"I know you all are talking about me," Jewel said as she eased into her chair after placing Aja in her seat.

"Jewel, you're not that important," I said.

"Yes, as a matter of fact we were. We were talking about your party," Kevin said.

"Oh, yes, and if you don't dress up, you won't get in. I'm going to get more fruit. Do you want anything, Kevin?"

"No, I'm cool. Thanks, baby."

"So, when are you two getting married?" I jokingly whispered to Kevin as Jewel walked away.

"Who said anything about that? I have been thinking about it, though. I actually enjoyed being married, before things went wrong, and Jewel's my baby. I guess that's something you can't really plan. It just has to happen."

"Well, I really wouldn't know anything about that," I said in a self-pitying tone. Jewel came back and we continued with our usual gossip-fest, trying to be mindful that we had five-year-old ears at the table. Then Jewel got up yet again to use the restroom.

"I'm full. I think I'm going to head out of here and continue my regular Sunday ritual and get my newspaper and banana pudding," I said, sliding away from the table.

"Yes, I have some reading to do as well," Jermane said.

Jewel returned from the restroom only to find that everyone was leaving the table.

"Huh! As soon as I leave, the party's over."

Sure enough, I went to my favorite little grocery store for my paper and pudding. If all else failed, I could still count on my pudding to make me feel better. I was glad that God had spared me from seeing Kyle at church. I hadn't heard from him, either.

Although I thought I'd done the right thing, I was still disappointed at the idea of another failed relationship. But I didn't want to dwell on Kyle. I had to move past him and not get wrapped up in the pain.

"Hi. Are you all out of banana pudding?" I said to the counterperson after I scanned the salad bar.

"No, we made some changes to the salad bar. We're no longer going to sell banana pudding on a regular basis."

"You what? Well, who decided that?"

"Our managers."

"That's just perfect. I have been coming here on Sundays for the past two years to get banana pudding. It's my routine. I get pudding and a paper. I can't get one without the other. Do you understand me?"

"Ma'am?"

"All I ask for is just a little respect and a little banana pudding. That pudding wasn't hurting anyone, and it was good pudding, too. I don't have time to make it. Besides, the kind in the box just isn't the same. Do you have any idea how serious this is? Of course you don't because . . . well, never mind. Get me the manager."

The woman at the counter stood there in disbelief. Then she moved in a sudden motion to call the manager over the store intercom. He was there in about ten seconds.

"Yes, ma'am, is there a problem?"

"Is there a problem? Is there a problem? Oh yes, there's a problem all right. Evidently, you don't realize the problem you people have caused. Did you check with anyone before you made this decision?"

"I'm sorry. I'm not sure what you're talking about?"

"Don't play dumb. I'm talking about the banana pudding. You all decided, all on your own, to remove the banana pudding. Like this would be a *good* thing.

You see me here every Sunday. I pick up my paper and I get my pudding. You have ruined everything. Just, just . . . never mind. I'm a customer and we have some rights, you know. From now on, I'm boycotting this store. I'm gonna search high and low for a store that sells fresh banana pudding, and by God, I will not stop until I find it! You have a blessed day," I said as I stormed out.

I sat in my car and realized that, yes, I had gone completely off the deep end. I put my head in my hands and started crying hysterically.

CHAPTER THIRTY-FIVE

Somethin' Just Ain't Right

Capri loved San Antonio, especially the River-walk. It was so romantic. On their way home she closed her eyes and thought about when she and Anthony sat outside the hotel to listen to live jazz. They had a little heater placed by their table to stay warm. She wished she could keep the feeling she had at that moment forever.

For two days, she didn't worry about anything. She didn't worry about work, her friends, or her grand-mother's illness. She needed to escape, and the week-end was perfect. Then she started thinking about work again. It just started nagging at her, and she had to say something, even though it was going to spoil the mood.

"Anthony."

"I thought you were asleep."

"I was just thinking."

"You can never rest, can you?"

"I want you to do something for me. Can you tell Pearson that you're not going to sign the waiver? He can modify the clause."

"Capri, you're worrying too much over this."

"Anthony, I'm just in a tight spot here. I can't say anything. They will definitely think I have a personal interest in the situation. I'm not even supposed to know the full details about the agreement. Just do it to be safe."

"How will I be able to explain this sudden revelation to Pearson?"

"Just let him think you talked to one of your teammates and that he talked about some problems he had with a similar situation. You have to have some protection, and, as it stands right now, you don't have any. Besides, if Fast-Trak really wants you, they'll be willing to bend a little."

"You feel really strongly about this, don't you?"

"I do."

"Well, I'll test the waters, if it'll give you peace of mind."

"Yes, it really will."

Capri leaned back and felt more relaxed as she listened to Maxwell's *Urban Hang Suite* playing. She was prepared to deal with whatever was going to happen. Her relationship was starting to become very important to her, so important that she couldn't allow Pearson to get away with possibly selling Anthony Stanton out.

CHAPTER THIRTY-SIX

Let the Weak Say I Am Strong

I sat at my desk and stared off into space. It had been a long week for me, and it was only Wednesday. I felt like I was on the verge of a nervous breakdown. I'd been having headaches constantly. And although I'd been praying a lot more than usual over the past couple of days, I still felt no relief.

My car note, insurance, and light bills were due this week, not to mention the phone bill for the office, but I could talk Terrance into paying for that. Two of my clients who promised to pay me this week failed to come through. I had money, but it was in the client trust account, and I refused to mess with that.

Things really looked bad. I wondered if I would have to borrow some money again from my girls.

Then I thought about Kyle. Although I felt a sense

of relief that I'd let him go, I felt extremely alone. I felt like I didn't have anyone who understood what I was going through.

All my friends have someone special, and it was becoming harder for me to deal with the single life. I was trying my best to stay in God's will, but it felt like He'd put me on hold for longer than a minute.

I felt beat up, exhausted. I was tired of going to court and dealing with the animosity of snotty opposing counsels in civil court who I know are giving huge amounts to the judges for their political campaigns.

Lord, You said I can do all things through Christ, who strengthens me. I really need Your help. I'm not feeling very strong right now. Despite my confessions, I'm still feeling fear. Help me to know that with You, all things are possible. I need You to show up for me.

After that, all I could do was put my head down on my desk. I remembered that tonight was Bible study at the church. I didn't feel like going, but something at the back of my mind told me to just go. The phone rang.

"Law office."

"Lexi, hey, this is Angel," she said in a low monotone voice.

"Hey, are you at work?"

"No, I'm at home."

"Well, what's going on? How was your doctor's appointment."

"My doctor gave me a prescription. She's going to see how the medication works and if the discomfort from my fibroids will decrease. If the medication

doesn't work, then it may be possible that I'll have to
have a complete hysterectomy. She's holding off on the
surgery for now."

"Well, that's a positive sign. Angel, I'm still praying
for your healing. God is going to come through."

"I don't know, Lexi. This is tearing me up. I never
thought I had these emotions. I know God is punishing me for being so mean. I used to talk about how I
never wanted kids, and now He's giving me my wish. I
never meant it. I was just bitter."

"Angel, God isn't like that."

"Well, if He loved me, He wouldn't allow me to go
through this."

"He knows your heart. He knows deep down inside
you didn't mean what you said. We don't know the reason for any of this. We just have to trust Him. We're
just going to believe in your healing. Remember, the
doctor didn't say you had to have the surgery yet, so
we're going to have to do some serious praying over this
issue."

"Lexi, all I know is that right now, everything is going wrong. God's not going to help me. I haven't been
going to church. I don't even care about church. What
can God do for me that I already haven't done for myself?"

"He can save your soul. Aren't you tired of hurting
and feeling bitter? Angel, you haven't been able to have
a real relationship since your divorce. God not only
can heal your body, but He can heal your mind and
your spirit, too. Why don't you come to Bible study
with me tonight?"

"I'm really not in the mood. Besides, most ministers seem money hungry to me. All they do is beg."

"Angel, just give my church a chance. We're supposed to tithe. My pastor is educating us on that right now. There were a lot of things I didn't understand in the Bible, and I had some of your same reservations. I always thought preachers took money for their personal use. Tithing is in the Bible and it does work. When I tithe, which I have to admit I have missed the last two Sundays, God does great things. He blesses me financially as well as in nonmonetary ways. I can't remember the last time I was sick. He has protected me and kept me safe. He has stretched the money I do have. He has given me an office where I don't even have to pay for office space on a regular basis. God just wants you to obey His word. Angel, please come tonight, it's important."

"I don't know, Lex, I'll think about it. Give me directions to the church. I'll call you back at about four o'clock to let you know if I'm coming."

"Alright."

I sat in the pew and tried not to let my thoughts distract me from the sermon. Angel hadn't called by the time I left the office, so I just came by myself. Still, I promised to pray for Angel when I got to the service.

The praise and worship portion began and I got comfortable in my seat. As I listened to the music, my spirit started to lift a little. Although I didn't feel like being there, I promised I wasn't going to quench the

Spirit. I needed to allow God to really take over my soul. Just when I was about to sing a verse of "Alone in His Presence," I happened to look to my right a few rows up and saw Kyle.

Is he with that woman? It took everything I had to keep from standing up for a better view. My eyes started to water a bit. *This hurts, God. I held out. I wanted to be the one on his arm at church. Why not me? Why can't I be appreciated?*

I choked back the tears, for I was about to blow. I found myself about to get furious at God. I was hurt, devastated. I came to church for deliverance and had gotten this.

But then, suddenly, I felt calm and peace. Something inside of me awoke!

Not my will, but Thy will be done. What God has for me, nothing can take it away, I whispered silently to myself. At that moment in my heart, I was reminded that God had someone special for me. I just had to wait.

When Pastor Graves had altar call, I almost ran up to the front. Tonight, I didn't care who was watching. I really needed to hear from God on some issues. When I got to the altar, everyone held hands at Pastor Graves's instruction. I bowed my head and listened to his prayer. Then, he instructed everyone to lift his or her own petitions to God.

Lord, I come to you now with thanksgiving and praise. God, You said to "ask, seek, and knock and it shall be given unto us." Lord, I am coming to You as Your child in a time of need. I am coming to You on behalf of my friends and others. Lord, I ask that you give my friend Capri wisdom over her situation at her job. God, work everything out for the good. I also ask that You heal her grandmother and protect her sister, Trina. Second, help Jewel to find a job. Give her wisdom also. Lord, I particularly want to say a special prayer for Angel. Please help her to receive the knowledge of Your kingdom. Heal her body. Let her know You are not punishing her. Remove the bitterness and hurt from her heart. Finally, while on others Thou are calling, do not pass me by. Please bless my law practice. I have been diligent. I haven't always paid my tithes, but Lord, I have really tried. I have tried to uphold Your principles. I have many bills due this week and I'm tired of borrowing. You said for us to be "lenders and not borrowers." I don't know how You are going to do it, but I believe You are going to honor my diligence. You know my needs. I also want to pray for a Christian mate. Lord, I want to do it Your way. Please make me a suitable helper for the man You have chosen for me. And Lord, help Jermane keep her marriage bed pure. Help Rex stand up and be the man You have called him to be. Restore the oneness in their union. All these and many other blessings I claim in Jesus' name, Amen.

I walked toward my seat and felt like a ton of weight had been lifted off my shoulders. I still felt a little low, but I knew God had heard my prayers. Pastor Graves then began preaching about tithing.

"Before God wants you to give any tithes and offerings, he wants you. You are the first offering," he said boldy.

Not this sermon again.

Tithing wasn't my issue. I had no problem with the concept, and I thought I'd heard all I needed to know on that subject. Outside of my last two checks, I'd been consistent with my tithing. But I made up my mind to receive the message.

Pastor quickly moved to talking about offering ourselves as a sacrifice. He said that no matter what level of your Christian walk you thought you were on, you must continue to grow.

I questioned myself. I knew I'd grown a lot since I'd joined the church, and I witnessed to people in my own way. However, I also knew I was in a comfort zone. In my heart, I knew God was calling me to an even higher level of maturity and spiritual development. He was calling me to trust Him with every issue in my life, including my personal life.

Just when Pastor moved into the time of invitation, I started feeling around in my purse for a mint. I looked in a zippered compartment and felt some paper. I pulled it out and it was a twenty-dollar bill that was crumpled up and obviously forgotten about. *Lord, You do hear me! You're meeting my needs.* Finding that money was encouragement. *God, You do take care of me. You are the God of miracles.* My heart was racing.

Just then, I looked up and just knew I was seeing things.

There was Angel, with a tear-stained face, walking down the aisle to give her life to the Lord.

My heart just flooded with emotion. I began to cry, too. *Lord, forgive me for doubting You. All my prayers are not in vain.* I stood up and clapped as I witnessed my friend receiving Christ as her personal savior. Others joined me and cheered as they watched their loved ones receive God.

Finally, the congregation settled down, with a few

random Amens and hallelujahs sprouting up here and there. When the offering tray came around, I placed the twenty dollars in the tray and thanked God for what He was going to do with it. That night, He had done something great again. He was becoming more real to me, and I was thankful.

CHAPTER THIRTY-SEVEN

Compromising Position

Jermane watched Naegel as he adjusted the new curtains that he'd placed in the bedroom. He'd been in there most of the morning, arranging things, painting, and creating. Jermane couldn't help but notice how sexy he looked. He had on overalls folded at the waist and a tank top, and he worked in his bare feet.

"Are you ready to take a break?" Jermane asked, pretending that she'd just arrived in the doorway.

"Well, I almost don't want to stop here."

"I have some coffee here. Or do you prefer juice, milk, or . . ."

"Do you have any wine?"

"Wine, well . . ."

"I hope I'm not being unprofessional. Wine relaxes me. It helps my creativity."

"No, that's fine. I'll be right back."

Jermane returned with two glasses of wine, some cheese, crackers, and fruit.

"What do you think so far?" he said, grabbing his glass.

"It's beautiful."

They sat at the small bistro set he had positioned near the bay window. They both remained silent.

"You were jealous, weren't you?" he said.

"Jealous? Of what?" Jermane said, caught off guard.

"Jealous of my girlfriend, Kenya. It's alright. I've been wanting to talk about it for a while now. Jermane, you hide too many of your feelings. You need to express yourself more. We've been friends long enough for you to trust me. I love talking to you and being with you."

"Naegel, I'm just not sure how I feel. I enjoy being around you, too. I love my husband. We have something special. I guess I'm just changing as a person. You allow me to grow and explore. You pay attention to me. You recognize things about me that no one else seems to realize. You let Jermane be Jermane. And, yes, I was a little jealous. When I looked at her, I knew that she loved you. I knew that despite your complaints, you cared for her, too. You two have a chemistry that almost seems electric, that I could totally feel and see. You both seem so sensual and in tune with each other."

"Yeah, we do have a lot of chemistry, like I told you. And yeah, I love her, but I just don't know if I wanna be with her forever. She's sexy, fun, and crazy about me, and I can't get enough of her. But that's the problem, because we just don't ever seem to get that deep. But you, you're different. You're so elegant and intelligent. I could talk

to you all day. Your thoughtfulness and innocence is sexy
to me. Jermane, you are a very beautiful woman."

Jermane didn't want to talk anymore. She knew she
was in danger. She also knew she didn't drink on a regular basis. She slid her chair away from the table. She
reasoned it was best to let him get back to work. He
quickly stood up and grabbed her hand. Before she
knew it, his hands were wrapped around her tiny waist.
He pulled her back toward him. He just held her.

"I've been wanting to do this for a while," he whispered into her ear.

Jermane didn't move, didn't say a word. She stood
there, letting him hold her. He turned her around
toward him, grabbed her face with both his hands, and
began kissing her softly. She wrapped her arms around
him and her hands were soon under his shirt, exploring
his back. She kissed him, gently at first, then deeper.

A rush of passion engulfed them both. He loosened
her hair and began running his fingers through it. He
unbuttoned her blouse. He lowered her to sit on the
edge of the bed. Jermane was in another world.

When she realized he was on his knees and pulling
at her pants, she snapped back into reality.

"No," she cried. "No," she said again, louder,
"please get up. Please."

He jumped up, breathing hard. "I'm sorry. I am so,
so sorry," he said as he sat on the edge of the bed, rubbing his forehead with his hand.

Jermane didn't say anything. She began fixing her
clothes. She grabbed the glasses of wine and sprinted to
the stairs, leaving Naegel alone.

CHAPTER THIRTY-EIGHT

A New Attitude

Capri nervously paced back and forth in her office. One of the partners had called an impromptu meeting at two o'clock. She told herself she was worrying over nothing. She reminded herself that the last meeting she'd had with the partners was a good thing, so she continued to work and silently pray.

When it was ten minutes before two, she decided to head upstairs to the partners' suites. Although she kept telling herself it was going to be nothing, something in her spirit was just not right.

As she reached the receptionist's desk, she was instructed to go right in. This time the receptionist was not as friendly—not a good sign. *This is it, I'm busted.* Capri knocked on Bob Lentz's door. He was one of the other senior partners.

When she walked in, she felt a sudden coolness. Only two partners were in the room. She felt strange.

"Good afternoon, counselor. How are you today?"

"Well, I'll be doing much better once we get this meeting over with."

"I know you're wondering what this is about. Would you like some coffee or juice first?"

"No, thank you. I had a big lunch."

"Well, as I was saying, Capri, we've been very proud of you. We've invested in you, and our investment has truly paid off. You're a very talented attorney. We always like to think of our firm as being different from the others, like we're a family. We want to be able to say we trust one another. Do you agree that we have provided an excellent opportunity for you to advance here?"

"Yes. But . . . well . . . can you please get straight to the point?"

"Well, we always try to be very careful. We uphold the canon of ethics. Well . . . I'll just come straight out and say it. It is our understanding that you may have become intimately involved with one of our clients."

Capri immediately gathered her thoughts. She wasn't surprised.

"Well, I, umm, Mr. Stanton and I are friends, however . . ." Capri felt her mouth take over. It was like an uncontrollable reaction. "Let me just lay it on the line. Yes, I agree. I've been given a great opportunity at this firm. But I've made the best of this opportunity. I've been dedicated and, might I add, brought plenty of money *and* clients in." She folded her arms. I've proven myself time and time again. You've gone out of your way to make me feel like the chosen one. That's a lot to live up to. Nonetheless, though this may come as a surprise to you, life at the firm is not the be-all and end-all."

"Well, Ms. Sterling, we all are chosen ones. Not everyone gets an opportunity to work in a firm like this."

"An opportunity for what? An opportunity to work myself to death? An opportunity to be forced to social-ize on Fridays and Saturdays when all I want to do is stay home and watch television? An opportunity to work for things I don't even have the time to enjoy? If you must know, yes, I am seeing Anthony Stanton. I do re-alize that it may be wrong, but I owe it to myself to be happy.

"Yes, gentlemen, I made a mistake. I got involved with a client. However, let me point out that when you thought it would be to your advantage, you didn't hes-itate to introduce us. As a matter of fact, every time I turned around, you were seating us together at your functions. I was the bait, and Anthony was the fish. Why not use me to make sure you keep his business. Then things got messy when Fast-Trak retained you without letting you know they were already working on a potential endorsement deal with Tony. Gentlemen, I appreciate every opportunity that you have given me. However, my grandmother once told me never to be so dependent upon anything that you can't walk away from it."

"Wait, Ms. Sterling, we may be getting a little too excited here and we wouldn't want . . ."

"I'm sorry, but as of today, I'm resigning from my position."

"Ms. Sterling, we just wanted to talk to you, to hear your side, to be fair. Dating a client is serious. We have to protect ourselves. We just want to prevent any problems."

"I understand, but this is not about you or the firm anymore. I realize you have to do your jobs and protect the firm's reputation. This is a decision for me. I realize how much I've been living my life for other people. It's time for me to live my life the way that I want to. Don't worry. Mr. Stanton has a lot of trust in his attorney. I'm quite sure he will continue to retain your services."

Before they could say anything else, Capri left the office and rushed to the elevator. It was good no one was in there. She began to shake violently and had to hold her stomach. *Pull it together, pull it together*. She took deep breaths, checked her face in the mirror, and straightened her suit jacket. By the time the elevator opened, she looked as though nothing had happened. She lifted her head and pulled her shoulders back. With a confident, calculated stride, she walked toward her office. She was determined to exit with dignity.

CHAPTER THIRTY-NINE

A Breakthrough

I felt like this day was going to be another bad one. Despite praying a lot this particular morning, I still felt down. I made up my mind to try to have a good attitude.

I'd been doing a lot of thinking lately about my career. I was beginning to wonder if I had what it takes to be an attorney. I wasn't talking about my actual skills, just my mental capacity to play the games that lawyers have to play at times. It was a very competitive field, and to try and do things "right" all the time made making it even harder. I wondered if I'd made a mistake. People had told me that private practice would be too hard. Others had warned that the big firms would eat me alive and overburden me with paperwork.

I was barely breaking even so far, but I wanted to hang onto my faith.

"So much for faith," I said as I began to clear off my desk. Just as I was about to sink into depression, the phone rang.

"Law office."

"Yes, I would like to speak with Attorney Parker please."

"This is she, how may I help you?"

"Ms. Parker, this is Edward Freeman of Freeman, Byers and Boles. How are you today?"

"Oh, I'm doing just great. What can I do for you?"

"Well, I'm calling on behalf of our client, Toy-Time. We're ready to make a second settlement offer on the Hudson case."

"Well, would you like to meet or would you like to make the offer now?"

"Since we have attempted a formal mediation once, we can discuss the offer verbally. Then if your client accepts, we can meet for the final details."

"What is your offer?"

"Two hundred fifty thousand dollars."

I tried to compose myself. This was a product liability case, and my client had only expected half that much. I was sure she would accept that offer. I had to take a deep breath before responding.

"Mr. Freeman, I have to reach my client. I'll have an answer for you by this afternoon. I'll give you a call then."

"That will be fine."

After taking down his direct number, I reached for my client's number. I knew exactly where my file was, because I'd been waiting on this call for a while. After

I called and received authorization to accept the offer,
I tried to call Attorney Freeman back to set up a meeting to finalize the agreement. I tried two times, but he
was in meetings. The last time I left a message. I was on
pins and needles. In the midst of my anxiety, I realized
that God had answered my prayer.

I started singing "Lord, You are good and Your
mercy endureth forever!" and dancing right in my office. Terrance knocked on the door to see if I was all
right and to remind me that there were people out in
the lobby. The phone rang, interrupting my worship. I
just knew it was Attorney Freeman.

"Lexi."

"Hey, Capri."

"Yeah, it's me."

"Girl, you'll never, ever guess what just happened.
The Toy-Time case settled for—guess? You'll never
guess so I'll tell you . . . Two hundred fifty thousand
dollars . . . and I get my *thirty-three and a third*, baby!"

"That's great, Lexi."

"I'm waiting to set up a meeting with opposing
counsel. I thought you were them calling. Wait a
minute, you don't sound too excited. I guess that may
not be a lot of money to a big-timer like you, but you
could sound a little more excited for me. I won't be
borrowing any more money for a little while."

"Lexi, I am really happy for you. It's just that I quit
my job."

"What? When? What happened?"

"Well, I had a meeting with the partners. They knew
about Tony and me. My first intuition was to be scared.

I knew that I was wrong. But suddenly, I didn't care. I
was just tired of it all. I didn't like the person I was becoming. I was starting to live my life just for the firm.
I guess meeting Tony was the best thing that could have
happened. If I'd never met him, I probably would've
never left. Despite my initial intentions, I was actually
getting a little caught up in the money and the power,
knowing I could compete with some of the top attorneys. But after all's said and done, maybe firm life isn't
what God wanted for me."

"So, are you all right? Are you feeling sad, mad?"

"Actually, I feel really relieved. I felt like I was suf-
focating in there. I felt like I was just a number, not a
person. One thing is for sure, Pearson is probably very
happy right now."

"Have you talked to Tony?"

"No, not yet. I think I might take a trip home this
weekend to see my grandmother and sister. I just need
to get away."

"Capri, you are going to talk to Tony about this,
right?"

"Yes. I just won't tell him all the details."

"Capri, you need to be completely honest with him.
That's the reason so many people get all stressed out
and lose it. They don't talk about their issues and
trauma. You don't have to act like everything is always
under control. Sometimes things just aren't."

"I know, but I just don't feel like talking about this
issue with Tony right now. I'm more worried about my
grandmother. She's been on my mind all week. I need
to go home to see her. Plus I just want to get away, clear

my head some more. I'll talk to him when I get back. Right now, I feel like my biggest priority should be figuring out how to cover Grandma's and Trina's expenses after leaving this job."

"Capri, I believe that God arranged everything that's happened so far. He is going to make sure everything is going to be taken care of."

"I know. Well, I'd better get off this phone so I can make some flight arrangements."

"Girl, I'll be praying for you."

CHAPTER FORTY

"Perfect Love Casteth Out All Fear"

A ngel interrupted her reading and stared at the telephone. She took her pencil and tapped the table, unable to concentrate on the interrogatories she was trying to draft. Although millions of thoughts were running through her head, she felt calm. Before she gave her life to God, she felt like there was a war going on inside of her. Things were changing.

She put her work down and picked up the materials from the church she'd received when she joined that night. She had to attend a new member's class for eight weeks. Personally, she thought eight weeks was rather long, but she reminded herself that she'd made a commitment. She'd been unable to commit to much of anything for a while. She flipped through the first couple of pages of a workbook, then went to the first lesson.

Before she read through it, she went to get her Bible. She started to fan through it. It had been so long since she'd read a Bible. This one was a gift from when she first got married. Angel remembered the gift-giver's voice referring to First John 4:18. She went there and read: "There is no fear in love; but perfect love casteth out fear: because fear hath torment. He that feareth is not made of perfect love."

She started thinking about Octavio. She was truly scared of him. She knew that in order to love him, she couldn't be afraid, for God had made her in perfect love. There was no place in her life for fear.

After sitting still for five minutes, she decided to take a chance. She was going to knock down every wall of fear in her life. She was not afraid of what any doctor had said. She was determined to allow herself to love and be loved, and she was determined to turn to God for her healing.

Just as she picked up the phone, reality rushed in. Octavio had started seeing someone else. She didn't want to be rejected. But she wasn't going to turn back.

"Hello, the party you're trying to reach is unavailable, please leave a message . . ."

Just as Angel was about to hang up, he picked up. "Hello?"

"Octavio?"

"Yeah, Angel?"

"Yes, uh, how are you?" she said.

"I'm alright," he said.

"Did I catch you at a bad time?" she asked softly.

"No, I had just dozed off. I was out all day and needed to take a nap. I didn't intend to sleep this long," he said.

"How is everything at work?" she asked, feeling relieved he didn't have company.

"Cool. Angel, what do you really want to talk about?" he asked.

"OK, OK. You know it's hard for me to really express myself. Well I, I really miss you, and I would like for us to try again. I mean to be together. I don't know how involved you are with anyone else, but I believe . . . I hope that we can make each other happy. I'm not afraid anymore. I'd like the chance to be there for you, like you've been there for me," she said as she took a breath.

Octavio was silent for a while. "I guess I'm shocked," he said. "I really miss you, too. I've been seeing Liz. She is very cool and beautiful, but I'm not one to just jump from person to person. So, I wasn't thinking about starting a new relationship with her. Angel, I care about *you*. I just knew we couldn't have anything substantial until you were willing to confront your fears and let your guard down. I don't blame you for being protective of your feelings, but you have to realize that the only way to fall in love is to be open to love. You can be wise and cautious and take it slow, but just don't shut down."

"A-men. I hear you," she said.

"What's this 'A-men' stuff?"

"Oh, right, you wouldn't know. I joined a church the other night. I gave my life to the Lord."

"Wha-at? Angel, that's great. I'm very proud of you," he said.

"Well, what do we do next?" Angel asked.

"Well, let's just take it a day—and date—at a time. I just can't wait to see you again. Are you going to church tomorrow?" he asked.

"Yes, at ten o'clock. Wanna come?" she said.

"I would love to go. But . . ." He paused.

"But what?"

"You won't be yelling and rolling all over the aisles, will you?"

"You never know what God might do. I might have to calm you down before it's all over with."

"Heaven help me."

CHAPTER FORTY-ONE

Healed by His Stripes

I felt especially good today at Living Truth. I looked over at Jewel and Kevin, who were just the cutest couple. I was happy Jewel had found someone who so obviously loved her for her. He was one of the few men who could handle her, knowing exactly when to let Jewel get her way and when to be firm.

I didn't know what Jewel was going to do about her job situation, but I refused to mention it until she did. Then I remembered to continue to pray for Capri. She had called to let me know she'd made it to New York safely, but I hadn't heard from her since. I was also excited for Angel. I looked over and saw her and Octavio listening to the music. Octavio seemed to be enjoying the service so far, though I imagined he was probably more happy to be there with Angel.

Pastor Graves led a short prayer. He gave us

instructions to turn to the scripture for today. "Today's teaching text comes from Psalms 103:2—3 and
Isaiah 53:5. Everyone say amen when you get to Psalms
103."

"*Amen.*"

"Psalms 103:2—3 says 'Bless the Lord, O my soul,
and forget not all His benefits: Who forgiveth all thine
iniquities; who healeth all thy diseases.' Then Isaiah
53:5 says, 'But He was wounded for our transgressions,
He was bruised for our iniquities; the chastisement of
our peace was upon Him; and with His stripes we are
healed.' I want to tag this text 'The Healing Blood of
Jesus Christ.'"

The Pastor raised his voice. "First you have to believe that God is willing and able to heal. Healing is in
God's will. I'm not just talking about physical healing,
but He can heal your mind, your finances, and your
spirit."

He went on to tell the story about the widow and the
unjust judge in Luke 18:2. "You see, this widow kept
coming back to that judge until he heard her case. It
looked bad, unseemly, but she knew if she prayed without ceasing, if she did not give up . . . God would
bring justice against her adversary."

Angel was very moved. Her eyes were fixed on Pastor Graves and she clapped and raised her hands in response.

By the middle of the sermon, the air in the room
was so thick. There was so much noise, with people
screaming and shouting. Everyone soon started to
stand up.

"I don't know why, but the Holy Spirit has commanded me to break the sermon at this point. I believe there are people here who need healing. The doctors have given you a grave report. But guess what—I know the ultimate doctor who created all earthly doctors. He holds the hands that move the world. His name is Jesus Christ. If you need healing today, without hesitation come down to the altar."

At first no one moved. Then I saw Angel get out of her seat and quickly walk down.

"I see you, sister. God is going to honor your obedience. He's healing you right now," Pastor Graves shouted.

Before you knew it, the altar was so crowded that people couldn't move. Pastor Graves began laying hands on people randomly and praying. Some passed out. I had only seen this on television. Then he laid hands on Angel. She fell to the floor as if she'd fainted. Octavio looked scared and amazed. I sat there and didn't say a word. Whatever was going on, I knew that God's anointing was heavy today. I could just feel it. So I got up and raised my hands in praise.

CHAPTER FORTY-TWO

Do Not Pass Me By

tienne's was crowded, as usual. Octavio, Angel, and I got seated quickly. Jewel and Kevin arrived a few moments later. They'd had to pick up Aja from the children's church. We were expecting Jermane to show up at any minute.

Then I saw her walking toward the table. She looked as radiant as ever in a black suit with a long slim skirt and a choker with an emerald cameo. Her hair was neatly pulled back in a bun.

"How is everyone this morning?" she asked. Just as she put her bag on the floor, her cell phone rang. "Hello. Yes, honey, I am at Etienne's. Yes, I'll be home at about three thirty. I'll call you before I leave. I love you, too. We'll talk when I get there."

Everyone looked at each other and silently wondered what was going on, except, of course, Jewel.

"And what was that about?" Jewel said.

"Nothing. That was Rex. He just felt the need to call." Jermane looked at me as if to say, *I'll explain later*. I knew it had something to do with Naegel. She had gotten busted.

"Church was so good today," I said, diverting attention from Jewel's question.

"It really was. I enjoyed it," Octavio said.

"Yeah, I saw you over there trying to sing 'Praise Is What I Do.' You didn't even know the words," Kevin said.

"I was trying, man," Octavio said.

We all started to laugh.

"I see we have guests again today," Antonio said as he eyed Octavio. "What will we be having to drink today, ladies and gents?"

Everyone around the table made their requests, then headed toward the buffet. I was the last one to get up. Just as I was about to slide from behind the table, I heard my name called.

"Lexi, hey. How are you this morning?" Tony walked over.

"Hey, how are you? I know you miss your honey," I said.

He sat in the chair beside me. "Yeah, that's what I came to talk to you about."

At that moment, a young lady with a snug-fitting black dress and shoulder-length hair interrupted us.

"I'm sorry for interrupting, but, Anthony, do you remember me? We went to junior high school together?" she asked.

"I really don't mean to be rude, but I'm having a private conversation," he said firmly.

The woman looked slightly offended and walked off.

"Yes, have you talked to Capri? I've been trying to call her for the last three days," he said.

"She didn't call you?"

"No. What's going on?"

"Tony . . ."

"Lexi, be straight up with me. I'm concerned about her."

"Well, she said she was going to call you before she left," I said.

"She left? To go where?" he asked, confused.

"She went home, to New York. To see her grand-mother," I said.

"She said her grandmother was a little under the weather, but nothing serious. That was a little while ago," he said.

"Anthony, her grandmother has cancer," I said.

"What? I didn't know it was that serious. Why didn't she tell me? Aaaaw, man! She never tells me anything," he said.

"I'm not sure. I probably shouldn't have opened my big mouth."

"No, Lex, you did the right thing. She always tries to be superwoman. It's all starting to make sense to me. That's clearly the other reason why she continued to work at the firm. I really need to talk to her. I heard she quit."

"Yeah, I know," I said.

"When you talked to her, was she very upset?" he asked.

"You know Capri. She doesn't show too much emotion. She's generally tough as nails, so she seemed fine when I talked to her about it. She thought maybe your attorney said something about you two dating."

"I talked to Pearson. I was very direct with him. He was straight up with me, too. There were some behind-the-scene maneuverings going on about the Fast-Trak deal. He told me he was starting to feel some pressure from the partners about how to handle my representation, and I definitely would've had some headaches in the future. Capri was right about that. However, she was wrong about Pearson talking to the partners about us. It was the San Antonio trip. A firm associate saw us there. Nevertheless, I've let Pearson and the firm go. It had gotten way too messy."

"Wow."

"Yeah, so I have to talk to Capri."

"Well, she'll be back in a few days, I think. She just needed to get away," I assured him.

"I'm really worried about my baby. I'm going to be on edge until she gets back."

Oh, he is so sweet!

"Everything will be fine. I would give you her grandmother's number, but it probably isn't the best idea right now. I've known Capri for quite a while now and when she takes some time to get herself together, she doesn't appreciate being interrupted."

"I guess."

"Everything is going to work out, Tony. Just have

faith. I know she really cares about you. She wouldn't have quit her job if she didn't."

"I wouldn't have fired Pearson if I didn't care about her. He's been my attorney for a while. Anyway, Lex, I really appreciate you talking to me. I owe you. Anytime you want some tickets to a game, let me know. They won't be in the nose-bleed section, either," he said.

"No problem."

"Lex, you're a really great person. I'm surprised no one has snatched you up by now."

"That's what I keep telling myself," I said in a low voice.

"Tony, how are you?" Jewel asked, surprised to see him there.

"I'm fine, Jewel."

"Tony, don't forget my party on Saturday."

"Oh, yeah, I almost forgot. I'll try to be there. I'll talk to Capri."

"Well, you know she's going to be there, so you have to be there as well. It's going to be so much fun. You must dress up, seventies style, or you can't get in. I'm coming as Thelma from *Good Times*. You know when she had an Afro and the big hoop earrings. Except I'm going to give her clothes a makeover. I can't let these wonderful legs go to waste. It'll be the ultimate blast from the past! Everyone is going to be there."

"I said I'll try my best to be there," Tony said as he eased out the chair.

"Jewel, may I ask you a question?"

"Go ahead, Lexi."

"Has it slipped your mind that you don't have a job?"

"No, it has not. Kevin's paying for the party, and I haven't gotten around to asking him to help on some of my bills. Mama and Daddy have been helping me out in the meantime."

"Oh, and you just assume Kevin has that kind of money, too?"

"I told you before," she said, making sure Kevin was still with Aja at the buffet, "Kevin has money. He saves. One day one of his ATM receipts was lying on his desk. Of course, I had to look. He has a very healthy savings account. He invests his money."

"That goes to show you, it's not how much money you make, but what you do with it. No wonder you're so in love."

"No, Lexi, all jokes aside, I've really fallen for Kevin. He treats me like a queen. He thinks I'm smart and listens to what I have to say. And he doesn't treat me like I'm some child . . . well, most of the time he doesn't. And Aja is just so sweet and wonderful."

"Well, if you legitimately care for him, then I have to say I'm very happy for you, particularly since you've challenged yourself and gone for someone's character over their riches. But you have started looking for a job again, haven't you?"

"Yes, I have. Anyway, what are you going to wear to my party?" Jewel asked.

"Oh, I don't know. I'll think of something," I said.

"Make sure you bring plenty of people because it's sure to be a stone blast, honey!"

"Oh, brother," I said. "Where is it going to be again?"

"Did you even look at the invitation?"

Not really. I looked at her and raised my eyebrows.

"At Kevin's neighborhood clubhouse. Check the invite for the exact address."

"Got it," I said.

"I just hope his ex-wife doesn't try to ruin anything. She's been a real piece of work lately, calling every minute with some trauma and drama. Kevin's been pretty tough with her. I guess that's another thing I love about him, Lexi. He is so strong and responsible, yet still so much fun. I've met men in the past with children who allow their baby's mama to manipulate them, but Kevin always lets me know that I'm important to him." Jewel was beaming in an unusual way. "So far, he's the best man that I've ever met, Lexi, right up there with Daddy. I've grown more as a person since I've been with him. Aren't you proud of me? I just love that he helps me to keep God in my life. We pray together and we study the Bible together with Aja, like a little family worship."

"Jewel, that's amazing," I said, feeling like I was in some sort of dream. "I'm so happy for you."

Although I didn't feel jealous, I couldn't help but realize that all my prayers for everyone were being answered.

While on others Thou are calling, please don't pass me by.

CHAPTER FORTY-THREE

Taking Care of Business

ermane picked up a few items to drop off at the dry cleaners before running the rest of her errands. In the process, she admired the work that Naegel had done to the bedroom.

After she loaded her car and stopped at the cleaners, she started to crave coffee. She navigated to the Java Stop. She hadn't talked to Naegel since the incident. She mailed him a check for the job he had done.

Rex had also acted particularly strange that day. He had no reason to feel suspicious. She'd quickly washed the wineglasses immediately after Naegel left. Rex came home hours after that. Maybe her friends were right. A man just knows when his woman's interest is somewhere else.

She was about to pull into the driveway of the Java Stop when her phone rang.

"Hey, honey, what are you doing?"

"Rex, hi love. I was on my way to the store," she said.

"Well, do you have anything planned for the afternoon?" he asked.

"No, I don't."

"Well, I took the afternoon off. How long will it take you to get back home?"

"About twenty minutes."

"Okay, well, meet me back home. I want to spend the rest of the day with you. What would you like to do?"

"I don't really know," Jermane said.

"We'll figure something out," he said.

Jermane was caught off guard. She headed in the opposite direction without even thinking about the Java Stop, or Naegel. As she was driving down the highway, her heart started beating with anticipation. When she pulled into the driveway, she noticed Rex had gotten home before her.

She opened the front door and saw him standing there.

"Hey," he said as he pulled out a small box and walked over slowly.

She could tell he'd rushed home because his face glistened with moisture from the Houston heat. His tie was loose and he had taken his jacket off. She walked over to him. She grabbed the box and tears started to form in her eyes. "What's this?"

"Just open it."

It was a sterling silver heart-shaped paperweight.

She read the engraving, "Rex and Jermane . . . Forever."

"It's not much, sweetie. I just want you to know that *you're* my heart. Please know you're the most important thing to me."

She stared at the paperweight for a moment, then looked in his eyes. "Thanks, baby, I believe you." She placed the heart on a table nearby. He wrapped his arms around her, grabbed the back of her head, and started massaging her neck. She reached around the back of his behind and pulled him close to her. He grabbed her face with his hands and kissed her slowly. Then he began kissing her with an intensity she'd never felt before. She started taking off his tie, then unbuttoning his shirt. Her hands moved over his chest. They moved toward the stairs, losing a piece of clothing with each step.

They tried to make it up the steps, but eventually gave in to their immediate desires. They were pressed against the bottom stairs. Jermane's eyes were closed tight. She wanted to feel her husband. Rex obliged and showered her with an outpouring of kisses and gentle caresses all over her body. After what seemed like an eternity, he stood up, lifted her in his arms, and moved toward the couch. He delicately put her down and placed himself next to her body. As he moved, he whispered to her, "You know I was jealous, don't you?"

"Jealous of what?" she said in a slow whisper.

He brushed his hand over her hair. "I saw how he was looking at you."

"Who?"

"You know who. Don't play with me," he said with authority.

"I don't know what you're . . ."

"You don't want him anymore, do you? I'm your husband. No other man is going to put his hand on you."

Jermane didn't say a word.

"Did you miss me?"

"Yes," she said faintly.

"Please, don't you ever let any other man touch you. Do you hear me?"

"I won't," she said faintly.

"You are *my* wife," he said as he grabbed her tighter. "Am I the only man you want?"

"Yes!" Jermane said euphorically. The next thing she remembered, she woke up on the couch wrapped up in Rex. He was holding her so tightly she had to wake him up to go to the bathroom.

"I love you, Jermane."

"I love you, too," she said as she looked at the clock. It was 2 a.m.

CHAPTER FORTY-FOUR

The Preacher's Wife

*S*ometimes you need an outside party to sort things out.
I thought about the advice I'd given Jermane about seeing a marriage counselor and knew I was doing the right thing. I walked through the sanctuary toward the administration office. I'd finally gotten the nerve to make an appointment to talk to Carla, Pastor Graves's wife.

I didn't know exactly what I was going to say. I mean I barely knew her in that way, but she was friendly and kind and it seemed we had an unspoken connection. She'd been telling me to come see her if I ever needed to, so I just decided to push myself out of my comfort zone and meet with her. At this point, I didn't care about my pride. I needed to talk to someone who was somewhat impartial and who wouldn't judge me.

The space was unusually quiet, compared to the

crowded buzz during the worship service. I passed the
church bookstore, continued on the carpeted hallway,
and turned the corner toward the office. I didn't see
the receptionist, so I sat in a nearby chair. I fidgeted
and wrung my fingers out of anxiety. Finally, I heard a
voice. Still, no one came toward the front. Another two
minutes, I started to lose my nerve. I rose out of my
chair. Anxiety took over.

I gotta go.

"Lexi?"

Darn. I could've escaped.

"I apologize. I'm just running a few minutes behind." Carla turned to the woman next to her, obviously much older, and grabbed her hand. "Mrs.
Stevens, we'll be in prayer for your husband. We'll be
up to the hospital this evening." The woman nodded
her head and smiled faintly.

"I know. God is in control," she said with a strong
voice, and hugged her quickly. The silver-haired
woman smiled at me on the way out.

Carla hugged me. "How are you doing?" she said as
she smiled. Her hug was warm and reassuring.

"Good," I lied.

"Well, come on back."

As I followed her to her office, I noticed her attire
was an extreme departure from Sunday's worship service. She wore a terry cloth warm-up outfit and very little makeup. She was still naturally pretty, though. Her
smile just lit up her face.

"Have a seat," she said as she pointed to the wing-
back, fabric-covered chair in her office. She sat in the

one next to mine. "Oh, wait!" She jumped up to press the do-not-disturb button on her phone. "There, I'm ready for you now. What can I do for you today?" she said softly.

"Well, um, I don't know. It's silly. I just, well, Carla . . ."

"Lexi, girl, just say what's on your heart." She paused. "You know what, let's pray first, so the Holy Spirit can guide us." I reached out my hands, thankful that someone was taking the time to pray for me. After she said amen, words just started to pour out of my mouth.

"Carla, I feel so overwhelmed. I mean just drained. I just have so much hurt on the inside of me and I am extremely lonely. I mean, all I do sometimes is pray for my friends. I see God showing up so much, and then it's like my prayers go unanswered. All my friends seem so happy and well, I hate to say it, but I know my prayers have a lot to do with it. But I feel like there is no one there to pray for me. I don't want to appear desperate and weak to my friends, but . . ." I took a deep breath. Then I searched her eyes desperately for clarity.

"Hmmm. Well, Lexi, I think several things may be going on here. It seems like you have the gift of inter-cessory prayer. Do you like to pray for people often?"

"Yeah. I mean when I see God answer a prayer for someone else, it really makes me happy. I know my prayers are powerful."

"That's wonderful. What I think is happening is that you have discovered your spiritual gift, but you need to know how to use it more effectively. Sometimes, when you pray for others, you have to be careful that you don't burn yourself out, that you're not depleting your spiritual energy. You also need someone to pray for you. We call it a covering. Otherwise, you'll have nothing left for yourself, and you'll soon be walking in defeat. You'll be drained, and when you need energy for yourself, you won't have it. Lexi, it's wonderful that you like to pray for others, but you need to be balanced. You're not meant to fight every battle. After a while, you have to let people find their own way. Otherwise, this wonderful gift becomes a burden."

"I guess that's why I've been feeling so worn out." My eyes fell to the floor.

"Is there something else going on? I just sense you're frustrated about something else."

Should I say it? I just don't want to be another women whining about wanting a man. I guess I don't have anything to lose. Maybe she knows something I don't.

"Well, it's just that, I'm tired of doing all this by myself. I need help."

"Lexi, you're not doing it by yourself . . ."

"Carla, please, I don't want to be rude, but I just don't want a lecture about having God is enough and no man can take His place. Please. I've had enough of that. I mean, I don't want to be disrespectful, but I am painfully lonely. I'm trying to do things the right way, but it's not working. I know people living together, fornicating, all kinds of crap, and they have a relationship."

Carla took a deep breath. "Lexi, your feelings are valid. I felt that way right before I met my husband.

God may be taking longer to send you the right one for different reasons. Every situation is unique. Sometimes when God is calling you to do something special, He has to find a person who will add to and not take away from your purpose. His primary concern is that His will and purpose be fulfilled in your life. Believe me, I know this is one of the toughest waits you've ever had. But trust me, marriage is no joke. Even being a wife is a calling. You must be prepared."

"But I *am*. God has to know I'm mature. He has to know I have enough room in my heart for Him and a man."

"Perhaps He wants your commitment to Him to stay strong. That's why He'd have to get someone who'll share the same commitment to Christ that you have."

"Well, it's so tough. As a Christian, I feel so limited. The Bible said 'it's better to marry than to burn,' but Carla, I don't know how much more of this I can take!"

Carla chuckled a bit. "Well, you know what? Nothing you're saying is wrong. Everyone wants companionship. Everyone wants to feel supported and loved. I have to say . . . when you have the *right* man, it's a blessing. If that is a desire of your heart, God placed it there. So He is going to fulfill it."

I gave a sigh of relief. "That's the first time someone has validated my feelings on this. I just didn't want to hear another sermon."

"Lexi, I love the Lord, but I also have real feelings. I can relate. I will tell you this, though, marriage and partnership is no joke. I love my husband, but we are challenged all the time. It's tough sharing a man with a

whole congregation. You'd be surprised at the things—
and people—we deal with. I thank God he is so rooted
in the Word of God, or some of these women would
have broken up our marriage a long time ago. And despite what you see, we have our disagreements and challenges. I don't always feel like smiling or showing up
here every Sunday. I'd much rather be at home at times
listening to some music and reading a book. But most
of our life is dedicated toward serving others. It's a sacrifice, but this is a ministry God gave us."

"Wow, you just always look so calm, so happy."

"That's because I know regardless of what's going
on, God is with me. I also know that God sent me this
man," she said as she pointed to the photograph of
Pastor Graves on her desk. "So I can always go to God
when I need His help with my marriage or anything
else, and Lexi, that's worth waiting for. You don't want
a marriage that God has nothing to do with. I can smile
because of God's assurance. You also have to know
everything is not always about feelings. I don't feel like
studying the Word or praying for so many people at
times, but I have to remember it's God in me that en-
ables me to keep going."

I just sat there, wide-eyed, and nodded.

"But Lexi, even the strongest among us need to take
a break, which is what it sounds like you need. Why
don't you spend more time focusing on Lexi? Ask God
to lift your burdens. He says to cast our cares on Him.
You also need to just have some fun, even if it's just by
yourself. Rent a movie, go for a walk, do something
silly."

"I understand," I said slowly. "I'll try."

"Lexi, about the relationship thing. I have a feeling you won't be single much longer. God's getting ready to do something in that area of your life. Just hang in there a little longer. I know it's not easy. Keep a good attitude and stay focused. Enjoy these days, because your days of singlehood won't be much longer."

I wanted to believe her. I wanted to have hope. I looked at her and felt this strange calm come over me. I felt a release. I knew the words she spoke weren't merely hers. They came out of her spirit.

"Okay, let's pray before we go." We grabbed hands.

Dear Father, we are so thankful for the opportunity to come before You. I come to you on behalf of Lexi. Father, I ask that You refresh her spirit. Renew her strength. Lord, You know her heart. I ask that You grant her deepest desires in accordance with Your will. You know she has been faithful. Father, I ask that You help her reach her full potential, spiritually, mentally, emotionally, and financially. Father, I ask that she doesn't have to chase another blessing, but I pray that blessings chase her down. Father, we must bind the spirit of discouragement and failure, for it is contrary to what Your Word says about us. Father, I thank You that her husband will soon find her and he will love her as he should love the church. Father, lift every burden on her heart, honor her dedication to You and her friends. We give You the honor and the praise, in Jesus name. . . . Amen.

I felt refreshed and restored.

I was glad I'd been bold enough to talk to her. When I left the office, I felt renewed. I also was thankful God sent someone to pray for me . . . finally.

CHAPTER FORTY-FIVE

It's Official

Capri got off the plane and was almost relieved to be back in Houston. She felt a little better after spending time with her grandmother and Trina. Grandma was hanging in. She didn't tell her about her job because she didn't want her to worry.

She started looking around for Lexi and figured she was running a little late. She thought about Tony, too. She missed him and wanted to see him. She knew she had some explaining to do.

She went downstairs, gathered her bags, and continued to wait. Just as she was about to pull out her cellular phone to call Lexi, she saw her name on a sign being held by a limousine driver. Puzzled, she walked over to the man.

"Are you looking for me?"

"Are you Ms. Sterling?"

"Yes."

"Well, then, I'm looking for you," he said.

"Who sent you?" she asked.

"That's a surprise," he replied.

"You could be a maniac. I'm not going anywhere with you."

"Could you please just follow me. There's a police-man right there. You can have him walk out with us."

"I'll ask him to walk me out the door," Capri said.

"If you must. I'll take your bags."

After Capri spoke with the policeman, he escorted them to the limousine that was parked out front. The windows were tinted, but she knew who was in the car. The driver opened the door after loading the luggage. It was, of course, Tony.

"Hey, babe. Don't get mad. I made Lexi tell me where you went and when you were getting back. I have something for you," he said.

He reached under the seat and gave her a stuffed Minnie Mouse doll. Expecting a fight, he was surprised when Capri reached over and gave him a warm kiss.

"I really missed you," Capri confessed.

"I'm glad. I missed you, too," he said. "I fired Pear-son."

"What?"

"You were right about him. Only, he didn't tell on us. A firm associate saw us in San Antonio. Anyway, they're full of it. They knew we were seeing each other. It only became a problem when they realized it was starting to work against them."

"Well, I quit," Capri said.

"I know. Babe, I have a wonderful idea," he said after a slight pause. "Well, we've been seeing each other for a while. I like you. You like me. You're kinda cute and you smell good, too."

"Oh, now I'm just kinda cute. What happened to fine?"

"Hey, I didn't ask for commentary," he said as he opened the bottle. "Anyway, as I was saying, I think it's time for more of a commitment."

Capri froze. She hoped he wasn't about to ask her what she thought he was going to ask her. It felt too soon. "Anthony, now, I don't think I'm ready for . . ."

"I would like for you to be my attorney," he said as he clicked his glass against hers.

Capri felt a little disappointed. She had gotten ahead of herself.

"Oh, yeah, that would be great," she said.

"I think so. What's the matter? What did you think I was going to ask you?"

"It's stupid," she said with a half laugh. "For a minute, I thought you were asking me to . . ."

"To marry me? Well, if you would have given me a minute, I would have gotten to that next," he said as he pulled out a small, black-velvet box.

Capri was stunned and speechless.

Tony opened the box. It was a three-carat solitaire diamond ring.

"Ms. Sterling, would you do me the honor of being my wife *and* my attorney?"

Without hesitation, Capri felt her mouth take over.

"Oh, my God," she said. She sat there for what

seemed to Tony to be ten minutes. "Yes. Yes, I will," she said, not believing her own words. She grabbed his arms and pulled herself into his embrace.

He held her a little while before saying, "I know you want to call Lexi." He leaned back and handed her his phone.

"No. Right now, I don't want to share this moment with anyone but you," Capri said as she snuggled back next to him.

CHAPTER FORTY-SIX

"Bling"

I knew that Jewel was going to drive me crazy about this party. I had been recruited to help do the decorations the night before and she wanted me to be at the clubhouse as early as possible that day to help Kevin with other arrangements. Then she wanted to be able to make an entrance an hour after the party really started to get going. I had to admit Jewel had a talent for planning special events though she sometimes went overboard, which would normally be alright except she drove everyone else crazy along with her.

"Hey, girl," Jewel said as she came in with a baseball cap and jeans on.

"Hey, Jewel," I said.

"Put those table linens over there," she directed Kevin. "Didn't Capri say she was going to come help?" Jewel asked, turning to me.

"Yeah, she said she'd be here any minute."

"Well, she can't take all day. We have a lot of work to do."

"Jewel, I hate to break the news to you, but there is life outside of your birthday party."

"Hey, everybody, what's going on?" Capri said as she walked in with a huge smile.

"You're awfully enthusiastic. What's going on with you?" I said.

"Nothing, just happy to be alive."

Jewel and I just looked at each other.

"Well, get your 'happy behind' over here and start hanging these decorations," Jewel said.

Capri walked over and reached down in the box to grab some streamers.

"Is that an engagement ring?" Jewel asked as she looked at Capri's finger. I had noticed a quick flash as Capri reached her hand in the box as well.

"Yes, it is," Capri said.

"I can't believe you! When did you get it?" Jewel asked with excitement.

"Tony gave it to me when he came and picked me up from the airport."

"And you're just telling us? How did he propose? When are you getting married? Are you going to have a big wedding?"

"Jewel, calm the heck down," Capri said. "Well, he came and picked me up in a limousine. He asked me then. We're planning to have a long engagement and take matters slow."

"Oh, my God, look at that ring. Kevin, do you see

this? Now that's what I'm talking about. Tony is on his job!" Jewel said.

"Capri, I'm so happy for you," I said as I hugged her.

"Yeah, I feel so blessed to have Tony. He even talked about moving my grandmother down here so she can get treatment from a local medical center. Lexi, I owe you a lot. You gave me some good advice. Thank you so much."

"Don't mention it," I said as I smiled and walked toward the decoration box.

CHAPTER FORTY-SEVEN

It's the Law

Jewel stood in line and tapped her foot. She should have known that there was going to be a line regardless of what time she went to renew her license, even on the day of her birthday. She diverted her attention from her annoyance, thinking of all the great gifts she'd get later today.

She was excited about her outfit. She'd gotten a huge auburn Afro wig and fluorescent makeup. She'd also found a white miniskirt and a sky-blue top with sparkling, billowy sleeves that went perfectly with her white platform boots. Everything was just about ready. The event was going to be funky and fun.

"Jewel Whitaker," the man at the counter announced, "I need your current driver's license, your insurance card, and another form of identification. Fill out these two forms," he said in a dry tone.

After she filled out the paperwork, she handed the clerk all the necessary information and got back in line. She noticed a sheriff behind the counter checking her out. He was cute.

Too bad for him, I'm taken. Then she started singing happy birthday to herself.

"Ms. Whitaker?"

She looked up. It was the sheriff who'd been looking at her.

"Yes."

"Could you step back here please?"

Wow, she thought, *sometimes looks can get you places.*

"Ms. Whitaker, how are you doing today?" he said.

"I'm doing just fine," she said. "Today is my birthday."

"Well, Ms. Whitaker, are you aware that there's a warrant out for your arrest?"

"A warrant! That can't be true. I don't have any traffic tickets. I'm an excellent driver."

"Ms. Whitaker, do you know what theft by check is?"

"Theft by check? Yes."

"Well, you have two hot checks that have never been paid."

"What? I could have sworn I took care of those. Well, how much are they for?" Jewel asked.

"I can't get into all of that at this time. I have to take you down to the station."

"This can't be true. This can't be happening to me. Can't I just pay for them now?"

"Ma'am, I have to read you your rights."

"Now, Mr. Sheriff, you seem like a nice, rational

man. Do I look like the type of person who would steal on purpose?" she said. "You can't do this, you see, I have this party tonight, a seventies party. It's going to be fabulous and everyone's expecting me."

"I understand, but I'm only doing my job," he said. "You'll get to make a phone call."

Jewel just sat there. She wanted to bawl, but she held onto her composure. She couldn't believe this was happening. Wait until the Texas bar hears about this. How would she explain this to everybody?

The next thing she knew she was put in the back of a squad car and taken downtown. The whole thirty minutes she tried to count the times she said she was going to pay those checks. Had it been that long? On their way they passed The Galleria shopping mall and she slid down farther in her seat. *I have my own personal shopper, for God's sakes. This is so embarrassing. I've heard of this happening to other people. But how could this happen to me? My party! I just, I just* . . . She burst into tears. The policeman didn't even turn around.

Once they arrived at the precinct, she had to complete some paperwork. She was taken into another room with a bunch of other women. She sat at the end of a table, away from most of them.

"What's going to happen to me?" she screamed as her head fell on the table.

"Will you get a grip," a young woman said, sitting a few feet from her.

Jewel looked at her and turned up her nose.

"This is the wrong time to be uppity," the woman said as she rolled her eyes.

Jewel looked at her and got an attitude because she had on white after Labor Day.

"So what did you do, Miss Thing?" the woman asked.

"I didn't do anything. This is all a big misunderstanding."

"Yeah, right."

"No, really. I'm a lawyer, and I have four friends who are attorneys. I'll be out of here in no time."

Soon, another sheriff came and took them to another room with a phone in it. Jewel rushed to be the first one to use it. She tried to call everybody whose home number she could remember. No one picked up. They were either at work or preparing for the party, and the last thing Jewel wanted to do was leave a ton of messages saying she was locked up. She could only remember Lexi's and Kevin's cell numbers by heart, but their phones weren't allowing her calls to go through.

Jewel was about to break down again, but then she looked around. She was very out of place. Most of the people looked hard, tough. Some looked like they weren't even phased about being locked up.

"Girl, do you know Co-Co got locked up again?" one woman said. "Her dumb behind should have moved out of Frisco's old crack-house a long time ago."

Jewel cringed. She walked to the corner and found a seat to herself. She began to pray silently. *Lord, if you get me out of this one, I'll owe You big. I promise I'll get myself together.*

The reality of the situation had set in.

This is a nightmare. I don't belong here. These people might try to have sex with me.

What was worse, none of the officers were telling her anything about how long she'd have to stay locked up. They did give her some food, but she refused to eat it.

"So, Ms. Lawyer, why are you still here?" Jewel's new acquaintance questioned.

"Like I said, I'll be out soon. This is all a mistake," Jewel insisted.

"Well, you better hope you make bail," she said.

"I don't see why I shouldn't. I should be able to be released on my own recognizance."

"Well, I'm just sayin', you never know about these things. So, what kind of lawyer are you?" the woman asked.

"I don't actually practice."

"Well, what in the hell do you do?" the young woman said.

"I, well, I'm unemployed at the moment."

"Oh, hell," the woman said. "Well, have you ever worked?"

"Of course I have. I was a coordinator of special affairs."

"A what?"

"A party planner," Jewel said.

"Oh. I went to college, too."

"Oh, really. Where?" Jewel asked.

"I had two classes at Houston Community College. I was going to be a nurse's assistant."

"Why did you stop?" Jewel asked.

"I didn't have any help with my babies."

"Why are you in here now?" Jewel asked.

"Traffic tickets."

"Oh."

"You'll be alright, girlfriend. We'll get to see the judge soon. He'll set bail and maybe you can get out of here before tonight," the woman said.

"Maybe? You don't understand. I have planned this big party and, well . . . never mind," Jewel said.

After seeing the judge, Jewel's bail was set for five hundred dollars. She tried and tried, but still couldn't get in touch with anyone. She'd wondered if Lexi and Kevin were out looking for her. It was six o'clock.

"Toliver!" she said as she realized he was the only person she hadn't invited to the party.

She went over to the phone and waited for the woman in front of her to get off.

Please Toliver, please Lord, let him be there, Jewel prayed as she hoped she was remembering his number correctly.

"Hello."

"I have a collect call from Jewel Whitaker, at the Harris County Jail."

"What? Uh, I'll accept."

"Oh, Toliver. I'm so happy to hear your voice."

"Jewel, what are you doing calling me? I'm on the other line trying to put my love under new management. What do you want, and what are you doing calling me from the Harris County Jail? I don't want no trouble," he said.

"Toliver, listen to me. This is serious. I got arrested because I forgot to pay some hot checks."

"What were they for?"

"One for some lingerie, another was from a grocery store—wait a minute! Toliver, I can't talk about all that now. This is an emergency."

"You should be ashamed."

"Toliver, I know we've had our moments, but please, just this once, help me out. I need you to go over to Kevin's, find Lexi, Capri, or Jermane, and tell them I need to be bailed out for five hundred dollars and give them this pin number. I can be released by eight o'clock if you move right away."

"Jewel, I'll help you out. Give me directions to Kevin's. By the way, a package came for you today."

"Toliver, please hurry up. I can't take it in here."

"Lord, let me help this pitiful child. I'll go over there right now."

Jewel went back to her cell and silently prayed some more. She looked around and saw women she felt like she'd often passed on the streets with disregard. Right then, she realized that people were people, regardless of how rough they looked and acted.

The room got really loud. Women were laughing, and she heard the words, "ho," "crack," "powder," and "jail" so much, she thought she was on an episode of *NYPD Blue*. She resolved to sit there quietly, wait, and pray off and on. Finally, after about an hour and a half, she heard her name.

"Ms. Whitaker, Jewel Whitaker?"

"Yes, that's me."

"Your bail has been posted."

CHAPTER FORTY-EIGHT

I Love a Man in Uniform

I never thought I'd have to help post bail for one of my friends, but there I was, watching Jewel come through a door, running toward us. "Thank you all. Thank you, Jesus," she said as she hugged Kevin, Capri, and myself.

We were there in our seventies gear. Capri sported a blond wig to complement her gold lamé halter top and pants, while Kevin had on a frilled leather vest and a black Afro with a purple headband that matched his purple velvet bell-bottoms. I'd gone for something more out there and risqué—a black catsuit with a straight black wig and black platform boots, evoking the image of a seventies secret agent. We were a sight to see.

"Didn't I tell you that you needed to get your stuff together?"

"Lexi, don't start on her. You see the girl has had a long day," Capri said.

It had been a rough few hours for all of us. Something was up with cell phone transmission signals for most of the day, so taking care of last minute arrangements became a challenge. And we couldn't find hide nor hair of Jewel, that is until Toliver came speeding over to the clubhouse and grabbed Kevin and me.

"Do you know we've been trying to entertain these people at your party for the last hour or so?" Kevin informed her. "How in the world did you get yourself arrested?"

"I know, I know. Can we not talk about this now," Jewel said. "Who's hosting the party now?"

"Jermane, Rex, and Angel. Baby, we'll talk about this later. You need to get showered and come to the party. Nobody knows what actually happened," he said.

As we were walking out, I tripped over my platforms, stumbled, and almost fell. Luckily, I grabbed a banister and regained my balance.

"Are you all right?" I heard a voice say.

"Yes, I'm fine," I replied.

"That's an interesting outfit. Let me guess, seventies party?"

"Yes," I said as I reached for his extended hand. "And you are?"

"I'm sorry. I'm Sergeant Chris Reynolds," he said.

"Nice to meet you. You have to excuse the way I look."

"I think you look kind of cute," he said as he smiled and winked.

"Thanks," I said.

Mmmm. He's a little plain for my tastes, but he has a nice smile. He does have some long eyelashes to go with those puppy-dog eyes. I could see myself wrapped up in his muscular arms . . . plus immediate concern and warmth over a damsel in distress makes him even more appealing. Gosh, but his ears are just a bit big!

"Are you on your way out?"

"Yes."

"Well, I'll walk you to your car. Make sure you don't stumble again."

"Oh, sure, thanks. I'm riding with friends," I said.

"Lexi, come on!" Capri shouted.

"Well, what are you doing tonight?" I asked as I walked outside with Officer Reynolds, figuring I couldn't be humiliated any more than I already was.

"I don't have any plans."

"Wanna come to a party?"

CHAPTER FORTY-NINE

Good Things Come to Those Who

Wait . . . and Pray

Despite the day's events, the party turned out to be a fabulously funky success. The room was filled with peace signs, black light posters, and lava lamps. Everyone seemed to be enjoying themselves. And Jewel finally made her grand entrance—white platforms and all—without a hint of what had happened.

Rex, perhaps feeling loose and carefree because of the white pimp suit and wide-brimmed hat he was sporting, started a *Soul Train* line. Jermane was right behind him, getting down in a sweeping, flowing teal sheer dress that Diana Ross would've worn without hesitation in *Mahogany*. I managed to shake my thing without stumbling to the floor. Jewel and Toliver were doing the bump. We had a ball.

We were grooving to "She's a Brick House," by the Commodores, when the DJ stopped the music.

"Can I have your attention, please," Kevin said as he grabbed the microphone. "Everyone knows the reason we're here tonight. It's my baby's birthday."

Jewel was on the floor dancing with Octavio and Angel. She started blushing.

"Well, I'm going to put her on the spot. Baby, I know you weren't expecting this, and I know we've never talked about it. Well, what I'm trying to say is . . . you need somebody to take care of you . . . will you marry me?"

There was a collective gasp. Then the crowd started screaming and shouting. "Say yes!" some of us called out.

Jewel ran up to the stage and gave him a great big kiss before she even answered. "Is that yes?" the DJ asked.

Jewel grabbed the mike. "Yes, fool. The answer is *YES!*" Jewel said, straightening her Afro wig.

Everyone cheered. The DJ started spinning "To Be Real," by Cheryl Lynn. We started shaking our booties with renewed energy.

Five minutes later, Kevin got back on the microphone. "We have a second announcement. We have another couple in the house headed for the altar. Anthony Stanton and Capri Sterling!" The crowd cheered again.

"I'd like to make a request to the DJ. Could you put on some mood music, man?" Kevin asked. "I want to hear 'Turn Off the Lights' by Teddy Pendergrass."

People clapped. The music slowed down and couples became entwined.

I sat down after dancing. I was happy, yet feeling a little melancholy at the same time. Just then, I looked at the doorway and saw Chris. I walked toward the door. He was dressed in regular clothes, but he had managed to scrounge up an Afro wig. He looked cute.

"Hey, I didn't know if you were going to make it," I said.

"I changed my mind at the last minute. I don't know. I just felt like I wanted to be able to catch up with you tonight," he said.

"Do you mind if we go outside for a little while?" I asked.

"No, not at all. I'm not a big party person anyway," he said.

We walked to the pool area behind the clubhouse and reclined on the lounge chairs. We talked a little about our jobs and where we grew up. He was from Baltimore and had lived in Houston for several years now.

The conversation was flowing free and easy. Before we knew it, our discussion became a little more personal.

"So, do you have any children?" I asked.

"Nope, tryin' to wait until after I'm married," he said.

Good answer.

"How 'bout you?"

"Nope. I'm trying to do it the right way, too. Not that I have anything against men with children, but I'd prefer to give my husband his first child." *Am I saying too much too soon?*

"That's not such a bad thing. So, where do you go to church?" he asked.

Not if, but where! Do you hear that, Lord? Of course You do.

"I go to Living Truth Ministries . . . and you?"

"Lakewood. Pastor Joel Osteen."

"Wow, awesome. I heard that was a great church."

"You'll have to come visit with me one day," he said.

I smiled in response to his invitation. "So what do you like to do, Mr. Reynolds?"

"Umm, I'm sort of a homebody. I like old black-and-white movies, Black romantic comedies, and I like to listen to music. Actually, when I do go out, I'm usually attending some concert or another."

"What kind of music do you like?"

"Contemporary gospel, some old school r&b, all the jazz greats . . . even some of the modern stuff, like Jill Scott and Brian McKnight."

Wow.

We continued talking. I felt immediate chemistry with him. It wasn't sexual chemistry, since I had to admit that I wasn't particularly blown away by his looks or his line of work. I mean, me and a cop? Nonetheless, there was a spiritual connection, and he seemed genuinely interested in finding out more about me. I had his unabashed attention.

We talked about the Bible and discovered we'd read some of the same inspirational books. I took a deep breath and realized this definitely felt different. He didn't wear suits to work, he drove a squad car for a living, and he wasn't drop-dead fine. But he was genuine and overtly spiritual. I was leaving my comfort zone for real.

Before we knew it, an hour had gone by. We finally decided to join the party, but not before we made a date for church and brunch.

Then we danced a bit to, of all songs, "Love and Happiness." We were both a bit timid and shy, and I saw Capri smiling our way. Chris soon left to go home because he was beat. I walked him out and stayed outside a little longer, focusing on the moon. It was full and bright.

I felt abundant peace of mind. I was finally beginning to trust God with all areas of my life. My life was never, ever going to be the same again.

Amen.

CHAPTER FIFTY

Mo' Better Brunch

Our Sundays at Etienne's had changed. Antonio had to pull two tables together because our brunch party was so big. Everyone had a guest, including me.

Chris was sitting next to me. He was a little quiet because he didn't know everyone else very well. I kind of looked at him and smiled. He grabbed my hand under the table.

"So, where are you two going to get married?" Angel asked, looking at Capri.

"Well, I really don't want a big wedding, but Tony does. I wouldn't mind getting married in the islands somewhere. A nice intimate ceremony."

"Babe, you know I have a big family. They'd talk about me nasty if I didn't invite them," Tony said.

"Yeah, but I just don't want it to turn into a big media circus," Capri said.

"I can relate to that," Jermane said as she looked at Rex. "Planning a wedding is hard work. Our ceremony was beautiful and it wasn't nearly as big as it could've been. But it was still tiring to pull off."

"Well, we can hire a coordinator," Tony offered.

"I had a coordinator and it was still hard," Jermane said.

"Kevin and I are going to handle matters on our own," Jewel chimed in. "We're on a budget."

"Thank God," I said.

"Very funny. I've learned my lesson," Jewel said.

"It doesn't really matter, because I'm going to be in charge of the finances anyway," Kevin said as he stuffed a big forkful of pancakes in his mouth.

"Kevin, we discussed this the other night. There will be no more surprises in terms of my spending. Do you have to smack like that? Wait, I have a fabulous idea!"

"Yes, Jewel?" I asked.

"A double ceremony in the Bahamas!"

We all stopped eating.

"I don't know, Jewel," Capri said.

"Come on, it'll be fun. We can make it a year from now and we can all take a vacation. I'll do all the work," she urged.

Tony looked at Capri. They both smiled.

"Alright, let's do it," Capri said.

"Chris, you are going to come, right?" Jewel asked.

"Yes, hopefully we'll both be there," he said as he looked at me.

"Well, it's about time!" Jewel said as Angel and Octavio walked up to the table.

"Hey, we got stuck in traffic. We went to Octavio's church today, all the way on the other side of town."

"Well, you missed the latest announcement," Jewel said.

"Well, what is it?"

"We're having a double wedding in the Bahamas in a year!"

"Hey, well work it out! That sounds like just what I need. Will you be able to come?" Angel asked as she looked at Octavio.

"I don't see why not. Seems like plenty of notice to me," he said as he slid her chair out.

"I can't wait to start planning," Jewel said. "Kevin, we're getting married with Anthony Stanton!" Kevin gave a thumbs-up as he gobbled down some more pancakes.

"Oh, brother," Capri said, already regretting her decision. Tony just shook his head.

"Baby, remember when I mentioned what you're good at? Planning, talking, and spending money?"

"Kevin, are you trying to pick a fight in front of everyone?"

"Girl, just listen. What's wrong with becoming a freelance events coordinator. It just makes sense. Why are you fighting against what comes natural?" Kevin said as he mashed butter into his grits.

She took a deep breath. "I don't know. I guess this planning thing does come natural. I suppose I thought I needed to work in the legal field. I mean, Mama would kill me if I threw away all that money."

Then she paused.

"On second thought, I think she would be proud of me as long as I was doing something that made me happy . . . and spending other folks' money, shopping, and throwing parties would definitely make me ecstatic! See, this is why I'm marrying you, honey."

"Lexi, can you go to the restroom with me, please?" Angel asked.

I got up without hesitation.

"Hey, do you two need company?" Jewel asked.

"Girl, mind your business," I replied.

When we got into the restroom, Angel could barely wait to tell me her news. "I went to the doctor last week for more tests. I'm alright! I don't have to have the hysterectomy. God's healed me. My fibroids have shrunk dramatically. The doctor said the hormone treatments worked incredibly well, almost beyond belief. She said that I can think about having children." She started to get tears in her eyes.

I grabbed her and held her tight. I looked up and whispered a quiet *Thank You* to the Lord.

How Suite It Is

"Room service."

I looked through the peephole, then quickly opened the door.

"It's about time," Jewel said as she sprinted from the couch.

We all waited in anticipation as the hotel employee brought in the cart of entrees.

"I am completely famished," Jewel said as she pulled her satin robe closed and walked toward the food.

"Me, too," Capri said.

We tipped the young man, then resumed our festivities. We'd decided to have a pajama party before the upcoming wedding and had rented a hotel suite.

"This was a fabulous idea," Jewel said while dipping her shrimp in cocktail sauce.

"Yeah, it was," I said as I sat on the floor. It was a

welcome break since coordinating the weddings had become too intense. Jewel and Capri were barely speaking to one another.

Jewel stood up and climbed over Capri's legs. "Excuse me," she said, and went in the kitchen.

"This is ridiculous," Angel said. "Jewel, get your behind back here."

"What?" she yelled from the kitchen.

"You know what. Let's talk this out. What's your problem."

"I'll tell you what the problem is," Jewel said as she walked back into the living room, her robe flowing behind her. "Capri won't let me do anything. I mean, I have all these great ideas for the wedding and she won't agree to anything."

"Jewel, you're exaggerating."

"Well, wait a minute. Jewel honey, is there something specific that you wanted that Capri said you can't have?" Jermane said as she removed the silver lid from her plate.

"She wants a cage full of doves. Some freakin' live birds. I'm not feelin' that at all," Capri said as she buttered a hot roll.

"You see? She's said no to the fireworks, no to the photo gallery. She just wants some plain old, boring wedding."

Capri rolled her eyes and took a deep breath. "Why Jesus, why God?"

"Am I being unreasonable?"

"Jewel, is it that important?"

"Well, I don't ask for much . . ."

We all looked at her.

"Jewel, it's really not about the birds. Sometimes, you're just over the top," Capri said calmly. "You know this. A simple example: Tonight. This is a simple girl's get-together. Look at Lexi. She has on cotton pajamas. Angel has on one of Octavio's shirts, and Jermane has on a nightgown. But you, you have to be in a full-blown negligee and matching robe. I guess it's just you, but sometimes you can take it down a notch."

"I can't help who I am."

Capri took a deep breath, "Two doves, not 22. I can do two."

Jewel started to smile. "That sounds good. I prom-ise. That's the last thing I'm going to ask for."

"Right," Capri said.

After we'd finished eating, we stretched out on the sofas and floor and relaxed. There was a quiet, peace-ful silence, each one of us in our own little world. Capri broke the silence.

"Guys, I'm scared."

"Of getting married?" I said.

"Yeah. I mean, this is it. I only plan on doing this once. Gosh, can you imagine me being around some-one all the time? I need my space," Capri said.

"Please girl, as big as that house is, you can have space anytime you want it. Looks like Kevin and I will be stuck in his starter home for a while," Jewel said.

"Don't complain. You'd better praise God that that man knows how to manage money," I said.

"So, how are you and the cop doing?" Angel asked as she playfully slapped my leg.

"Good. No complaints so far."

"You better not blow this one, Lexi," Angel said as she picked up a magazine to flip through.

"Why does it have to be my fault? Maybe God was just waiting to send the right one."

"I guess so. He seems really nice."

"He is. I mean, honestly, I think I had some maturing to do before I could receive His blessings. I had to let go of my own material cravings and focus on the person."

"Are you two still going out on dates?" Capri asked.

"Yeah, we still go out pretty regularly, thank goodness. He likes low-key places, like cafés and quiet restaurants. And we're always attending this concert or that. I just saw Will Downing last week. And he's open to doing things I like. Except, well, there is one thing I can't stand."

"Here we go," Angel said as she sat up.

"He's always late. It's so frustrating, and sometimes he cuts me off when I'm talking. And he's not as tidy as I think he should be," I said.

"Please," Jermane said. "Rex is a slob and always leaves his drawers in the middle of the floor."

We all started laughing.

"What?" Jermane said.

"The way you said *drawers*," I said. "So high-class."

"Oh, forget you, Lexi."

"Speaking of drawers," Angel said, "have you heard back from old boy, Black Zorro? You never did give us the full scoop. I know there's a juicy story in there."

"A lady never discusses such things. Besides, there's nothing to tell."

"Please, girl, you are lying," Angel accused, "But I'm gonna let you slide. I'm just glad you and Rex came to your senses."

"Well, what about you?" Capri said. "Give us the details. What's it like Living La Vida Loca?"

"Very funny. Octavio and I are still taking things very slow. I met his mother recently. Octavio didn't tell her I was Black, and I almost gave the woman a heart attack. When we left, she was clinging to her rosary beads. I guess she'll get over it eventually. We've been battling a little over what church to go to, so we've been alternating every Sunday. I'm sure that'll all work out."

"I don't know. I guess you have to be very aware of what you ask for," Jewel said, flashing her newfound maturity. "I suppose Kevin is someone I needed. Thankfully, he's someone I want, too, with his greedy self. That boy can eat you out of house and home."

"Jewel, looks like you're finally thinking about someone besides yourself," Capri remarked. "Too bad you can't do the same for our wedding day."

After a few seconds, Jewel picked up a pillow and knocked Capri upside her head. The fighting commenced and we laughed and pillow fought to exhaustion. Eventually, we dozed off, one by one. I was too tired to get up, but as I lay in my bed, I prayed silently.

Father, You are forever faithful. Thank You for loving me, in spite of myself. In spite of my temper tantrums and struggles, You never gave up on me. I'm so blessed. I have good friends, a good church, and I am

surrounded by love. You didn't leave me out, nor did You pass me by.
I've come to know You in a personal way and am grateful I can call You
my friend. Don't ever let me go. I give You all the glory, the praise, and
the honor. In Jesus's name. Amen.

*I*t had been a long journey, but we'd finally made it.
Angel, Jermane, Capri's sister, Trina, and I were
bridesmaids. We wore fitted, salmon-pink gowns with
thin straps that criss-crossed in the back—simple, but
elegant. Aja was the flower girl.

Capri and Jewel fought almost until the ceremony.
At one point, I thought Tony was going to have to hold
Capri back from taking Jewel out.

There was a wide assortment of guests, including
our significant others, Jewel's parents, Aja's mother,
Toliver, and Capri's grandmother, who'd moved to
Texas and was in better health.

Jewel chose a traditional dress, with lots of lace, a
large skirt and train, while Capri's gown was straight,
streamlined, and contemporary. Tony wore all black,
while Kevin chose a black-and-white tux. The hotel was
right by the water, so the wedding was held outside in
the early evening, framed by a calm pink-and-golden
sky over a beautiful blue sea.

The sun set as the two couples exchanged their vows.
It was like something out of a novel. Throughout the
ceremony, Chris kept looking at me and smiling.

The reception was extra-festive. Finally, I got a
chance to spend time with *my* honey. He looked so

sharp in his suit. His hair was freshly cut, his skin was smooth, and he had trimmed his mustache.

They played "Could" you be the one for me, by Brian McKnight, and I couldn't resist grabbing Chris's hand to dance. I cared for him very much.

Just then, Chris grabbed my right hand and kissed the back of it lightly. He softly kissed the side of my neck and whispered, "Do you know how much I enjoy being with you, Lexi? I love everything about you."

I held him even closer. I felt safe. I felt like I could be vulnerable with him, because he was that way with me. Despite my initial reservations about him, I now thought that everything about him was perfect, including his big ears and officer's uniform. I believed that I had finally found my soulmate, or perhaps he'd found me, stumbling out of a police station in a crazy get-up.

The most beautiful part was that we hadn't slept together yet. I knew it was going to be difficult, waiting until marriage, but we both took a vow of abstinence and made God's word our first priority.

Finally, it was time to catch the bouquet. I refused to go out onto the floor for fear of making a fool of myself. But just after the brides made the toss, Trina pushed me out there. Jewel's flowers landed right on my head and then plopped into my fumbling hands. Chris looked at me, smiled, and blew me a kiss. I regained my composure, looked up again, and said a silent *Thank You* once again for all my answered prayers.

*S*unday Brunch is meant to serve readers with a fun, sassy storyline while also dishing out plenty of spiritual food for thought. Here are some questions designed to provoke discussion and gentle debate about the characters and the impact Norma Jarrett's debut novel has made on your life. (Be sure to also check out "The Sunday Brunch Experience," a list of fun activities for book clubs, which immediately follows the reading guide.)

1. What emotions did you experience while reading *Sunday Brunch*? What parts of the novel connect to your life?

2. In what ways are the characters alike? Different? Why do you think they remain so committed to each other and their Sunday brunch ritual?

3. What are some of the spiritual battles Lexi faces?

Why does she think it's her responsibility to support and pray for all of her friends? Why doesn't she feel more comfortable sharing her needs with them?

4. If you were Lexi, how would you have dealt with Reggie and Kyle?

5. Why do you think it took so long for Lexi to meet the police officer, Chris Reynolds?

6. Is Jermane being realistic about her needs? What advice would you give Jermane regarding her dilemma with Naegel? Do you see the kiss that they shared as adultery? Why or why not?

7. Why does Jewel struggle with finding her true purpose? How does God work in her life, compared to the other characters?

8. What is it about Kevin that made him give the spoiled Jewel a chance? Why is her ultimate response to him so positive?

9. Why does Capri have such a hard time opening up to Anthony? What do you mark as the true turning point in their relationship?

10. Many career-oriented women struggle with the same issues that Capri does—striving to maintain a healthy balance between work, family, personal goals, and romance. If you were Capri, would you risk your career for a man? Do you agree with her choices?

11. What motivates Angel to give her life to the Lord? What will be some of her obstacles in becoming a devoted Christian?

12. Based on the issues they bring to the table at the beginning of their relationships, what potential challenges do you think each couple will face in their future?

13. What do you think the primary struggles are for young single women and their faith walk? What situation in *Sunday Brunch* best represents a situation young singles must face?

14. Has *Sunday Brunch* influenced your prayer life in any way? Has it made you think differently about prayer? If so, how?

15. What was the significance of exploring the different levels of spirituality in each character?

16. What actors could you see playing each character in *Sunday Brunch—The Movie*? (Make a female and male wish list!)

17. Has *Sunday Brunch* made an impact on the relationships in your life (platonic, romantic, professional, and familial)? Describe how and discuss.

Sunday Brunch isn't just a novel. It's a celebration of friendship, love, and spirituality. In that spirit, here are some creative ways to indulge in the *Sunday Brunch* experience individually or as a book club:

1. Have your book club attend worship service together and then have your meeting over Sunday Brunch.

2. Have your very own Sunday brunch and cook the food mentioned in the book.

3. To make your brunch even more fun, dress up like a character from the book. Imagine what each character would wear and how they'd act.

4. Select a book-club member as an "accountability" partner for prayer, goals, and other commitments.

5. Keep a prayer journal. (Feel free to use some of Lexi's prayers as inspiration.)

6. Put your individual prayers on a piece of paper, fold them up, and place them in a box or jar. Release the tension and worry surrounding the request. Go back after some time and see what God has done!

7. Pool your talents for a community-service project once a year.

8. Commit to a walkathon as a book club. Read a book beforehand and discuss it along the way. You'll work your mind *and* your body.

9. As a book club, select one member to honor at each meeting as a "person of the month." Give them cards and a symbolic gesture of friendship and support. It'll give your members something to look forward to and make each member feel extra special.

10. Have an awards ceremony once a year for your reading group and hand out certificates for "Most Dedicated Reader," "Most Timely," "Most Technical Reader," "Most Dramatic," or any other humorous awards you can think of.

11. Plan a "girlfriend" retreat at a spa or have a grown-up slumber party at a hotel. Also, scout publications for literary retreats, which are popping up everywhere. (www.atlanticbookpost.com is one site to try.)

12. If you are like Lexi (a nonstop giver), you need to have a "me" day. Have an adult time-out and set aside a day or evening for yourself. Don't take any calls. Invest in one or two extravagant bath goodies and escape to a luxurious bath, eat a favorite dessert, and then read something that isn't related to work for *pure* entertainment.

13. If you're like Jewel, you may need to do a "financial house cleaning." Attend a seminar and take a realistic look at your spending and saving habits. Many churches offer free financial seminars. Start with the basics. Don't just admire that friend with financial savvy—ask for her help!

14. Sign up for a discount book-club rate at a local bookstore.

15. Sponsor an author to come visit your book club. It's easier than you think. Try getting in contact with the appropriate publisher's marketing department or contact an author via e-mail if they make their online address available.

16. For all of the all-female reading groups, invite the men in your lives to a special book-club meeting

and select a book they may be interested in, just so they can see what all the fuss is about. (Men play a prominent and positive role in *Sunday Brunch,* so the guys in your life might have a lot to say about it.)

17. Make up a recipe book with each book-club member submitting her favorite recipe.

18. Commit to reading at least one book dealing with another culture.

19. Have T-shirts, bookmarks, or other personalized items made with your book-club name or logo.

20. Use the main city mentioned in a book as a theme for your book-club meeting.

21. Have a mother-daughter book-club meeting one month. Have tea with games and goodies to keep it fun and interesting.

22. Send friends and family handwritten "love notes" on handpicked or personalized stationery. It's nice to be thought of and to get something in the mail besides bills.

ABOUT THE AUTHOR

Norma L. Jarrett is a native of Neptune, New Jersey, and currently resides in Houston, Texas. She is a graduate of North Carolina Agricultural and Technical State University and Thurgood Marshall School of Law. Ms. Jarrett is an active member of Lakewood Church, where Joel Osteen is the pastor. She is also a member of Alpha Kappa Alpha Sorority, Inc. She has written and self-published *Coffee Table Quotes for the Contemporary Christian*. She has also completed a second novel and continues working on other creative projects.